FOREWORD

I must confess that the success of the novel Robin Hood and the Caliph's Gold, produced by Angus Donald, a family friend, and published earlier this year through the Amazon website, took me completely by surprise.

I knew, of course, that Mr Donald's excellent series of historical novels about the notorious thief Robin Hood and his loyal lieutenant Alan Dale – collectively known as the Outlaw Chronicles – had been appreciated by a large number of readers over the past decade, but I had underestimated the continuing demand for adventures of this kind.

I'd thought there would be only a mild interest in more tales of Robin and Alan since Mr Donald wrote what appeared to be the final chapter of the series – *The Death of Robin Hood* – in 2016. I'd assumed, in fact, that *Robin Hood and the Caliph's Gold* would be a mere footnote to the Outlaw Chronicles, a curiosity rather than an event in its own right.

I was quite wrong.

Yet I find my miscalculation of the series' enduring appeal to be extremely gratifying for personal reasons. Family legend has long held that I am the many-times great-grandson of the Sir Alan Dale, the Knight of Westbury. I was told many gripping tales of Alan Dale and Robin Hood as a child but, for most of my adult life, I believed them to be no more than charming myths. However, I became persuaded last year that, not only are the stories based in historical truth, but also that I am, indeed, Sir

Alan's direct descendant. This came about though the discovery, after the death of my father, Professor Roderick Westbury-Browne, of a mass of dusty old papers in his neglected attic in Albert Street, Nottingham.

The papers, which are typed out on faded, yellowish A4 paper, seem to be a collection of ancient manuscripts transcribed into a modern format from their original decaying vellum by my father in his leisure hours, when he was not engaged in teaching Medieval History at the University of Nottingham. Of the crumbling calfskin that the long-dead author wrote on no trace remains, but the type-written copies produced by my late father appear to identify the work as nothing less than a series of fresh stories composed in the early 13th century by Sir Alan Dale himself in his final few years at his manor of Westbury, and concern his early life as a loyal follower of the Earl of Locksley. These stories were passed on by Sir Alan to his grandson and namesake, who passed them to his son, and so on, all the way down the generations to my own father.

The first tranche of this new batch of ancient adventures has been comprehensively edited and, in parts, lightly rewritten by Mr Donald and appeared as the novel *Robin Hood and the Caliph's Gold*. What you now hold in your hands is the second tranche, entitled *Robin Hood and the Castle of Bones,* which is a shorter tale concerning the affairs that took place in the Burgundy region, now in eastern France, in the spring and summer of 1192, when Robin Hood and his men were making the long journey home to England from the Holy Land after the Third Crusade.

The events described in these pages are quite shocking, to my mind, not only for their extremely sanguinary and brutal nature but also for the distinct lack of morality displayed by the Earl of Locksley in his dealings with the various members of the local nobility, and his indifference to the sufferings of anyone at all outside the small circle of his own loyal men.

Nevertheless, I hope a few readers may find them edifying in some small way, if only for their descriptions of ordinary 12th-

century life in the region, and perhaps for some they may even prove mildly enjoyable.

Furthermore, Mr Donald has said that if there is sufficient interest in *Robin Hood and the Castle of Bones*, he is willing to produce another two novels about the exploits of Alan Dale and his lord, the Earl of Locksley.

I admit I would find this rather satisfying, for the more I discover about my ancestor, the prouder I become of my connection with him. Alan Dale was a decent, honest and brave warrior; an extraordinary man for his age or any other; as I hope, after reading this tale, you will agree.

Michael Westbury-Browne
The Old Grange, Lichfield, Staffordshire
November 23, 2020

CHAPTER ONE

"Have you thought much about wine, Alan?" Robin asked me.

I turned in the saddle and squinted painfully at my lord, who was clopping along beside me on the dusty road. My head was aching more than a little, my stomach queasy from even the gentlest movements of my horse, and the bright spring sunlight seemed to spear my half-closed eyes.

My first thought was that Robin was mocking me in some inventive fashion for indulging too much the evening before at the large townhouse in Chalon-sur-Saone, in the region known as *Burgundia*, where we had spent the night. The wines of this area were, even to my rough, untutored tastes, quite simply delicious. And they were plentiful. And we were rich.

"Of course I have," I said. "It would be difficult not to think about the joys of drinking when we pass vineyard after vineyard on the road and sample a new vintage at every tavern. What are you saying, lord?"

"I know you think a great deal about drinking it," said Robin. "And from the unhealthy colour of your face this morning, and the vile, raucous bawling I heard from the hall last night after I went to my bed, I'd say you indulged the practice with enthusiasm. But that's not what I meant."

There had been a little joyful singing the night before. Not bawling by any means, nor was it vile or raucous. I was a serious musician in those days, a skilled player of the five-stringed vielle, and a honey-voiced singer praised by royalty, no less. But I had, in truth, stayed up late by the fire in the great hall of the house we had stayed in – a mansion owned by a Jewish merchant called Mordecai with whom Robin had some murky connection – with two companions, who were now riding behind Robin and me. Yes, we had enthusiastically sampled a few jugs of the local vintage – a sweet, strong, yellow brew – courtesy of the kindly old Jew and with a good deal of pleasure. Yes, we had engaged in some tuneful jollity; a rhyming verse or two, a mere *canso* or *salut d'amor*, perhaps, to amuse ourselves as we explored our generous host's excellent cellar. But our merrymaking could hardly be described as "vile, raucous bawling".

I heard the report of a prolonged belch from behind me and turned to look at its perpetrator. Hanno, a bald, much-scarred Bavarian man-at-arms, a friend of mine and mentor to me, scowled back as if he wished me to drop dead this instant, as if his discomfort today was all my fault.

His normally ruddy face was a greyish colour, and beaded with oily sweat, his body trembled like an old man suffering from a winter ague, and he gave the distinct impression of a fellow on the very edge of death – or perhaps just of bringing up his breakfast all over his horse's black mane. He scratched angrily his unshaven jaw, rubbed his round and stubbled pate and belched deafeningly once more. I caught the revolting sweet-sour waft of half-digested wine from two horses' lengths away.

Beside Hanno rode Ricky, a slight, dark fellow – an excellent sailor and blue-water navigator but a less impressive man-at-arms, who had chosen to take the role of Robin's servant while we were on dry land. He, too, looked extremely unwell – perhaps even in worse shape than Hanno.

It was just the four of us on that hot, dusty road in the heart of *Burgundia*, walking our horses along between sprouting rye fields and cow-cropped pastures, and seeing nobody but one sullen peasant with a wagon and pair of dusty mules to pull it, and once a muttering priest on a grey mare. We were a few miles west of Chalon-sur-Saone, the largest local town, on a straight road that would lead, or so we devoutly believed, after about a day's ride, to the more substantial settlement of Autun.

The rest of our company – more than a hundred souls under the command of Robin's gigantic lieutenant, amusingly nicknamed Little John – was some seventy miles to the south of us, between the towns of Lyon and Mâcon in the fecund valley of the River Saone. They were advancing north only at a snail's pace in a lumbering train containing three ox-drawn wagons. The Sherwood company, as we called it, was a mixed one, comprised more than three score English and Welsh bowmen, and a *conroi*, or mounted company, of thirty-seven men-at-arms, mostly Normans, recruited in Marseilles, as well as spare horses, weapons and kit, and a dozen women and their children, whom we'd collected over the past two years of hard travelling.

Hanno, Ricky and I were on a scouting mission – away from the village-like hubbub and chatter of the slow, ever-creaking ox wagons – with the self-appointed task of reconnoitering the best routes to get us safely back home to England. It was not an arduous task, to be honest, more a pleasant jaunt in the springtime. And the Earl of Locksley had decided, at the last moment, to accompany us, for reasons known best to himself. He *claimed* he was only seeking a break from the burdensome responsibilities of command and relief from the monotony of the journey. But, with Robin, who could say what was on his mind? Not I, for sure.

The weather had mostly been kind. The main roads in the Saone Valley, built by the Romans all those centuries ago, were still paved with big stone slabs and, for the most part, ran arrow straight. These ancient thoroughfares remained in a surprisingly good condition, despite the passage of so much time and the many generations of travellers, and allowed us to travel as a decent pace. Furthermore, the route was already familiar to us, since we had passed over this placid landscape only two years before. That spring we had come down from Normandy to Tours, then marched east, across to Chalon, and south down the valley to Lyon, with a mighty array of knights and noblemen of England and Normandy, part of King Richard's vast host, which was bound for the Holy Land.

How many of those bold Christian souls still walked the earth, I wondered? Certainly we had lost more than our fair share of noble men-at-arms to sickness, many more than to battle, over the past two eventful years. And what had we achieved? Very little fame or glory – that was for sure – although we *had* won one great victory over Saladin, the Saracen warlord, at a place called Arsuf, and sent him and his army reeling back.

But even that one victory had been sadly incomplete and the news we received from the Holy Land, in March, when we arrived by sea at the port of Marseilles, was all bad. Despite his best efforts, Richard had been unable to capture the holy city of Jerusalem and his exhausted knights now spoke only of making peace with Saladin and returning to England.

"I meant with your share of the Caliph's gold," said Robin, loudly and a little too cheerily for my frail constitution. "Have you thought much about investing all your hard-won money in the English wine trade?"

Well, yes, there was the Caliph's gold, of course. We might not have covered ourselves with everlasting glory on the long journey to the Holy Land and back, but we were, it could not be denied, indecently wealthy.

We had wrested, with much toil, sweat and pain, a large quantity of pure African gold ingots and several barrels of silver coin from one of the cruellest of the Almohad rulers of southern Spain and, although Robin had been forced to outlay a good deal of it since, I still had a fat purse full of silver coin hanging from my belt and in the iron-banded boxes in the three wagons, seventy miles on the road behind us, was my share of our glittering hoard, a sum to keep me in comfort for the rest of my days.

"I don't know very much about the wine business . . ." I began.

"Except how to drain three whole casks of Mordecai's finest in only a single night!" Robin said, chuckling away in a most irritating manner.

I didn't care to endorse Robin's jest, so I held my tongue.

We rode on for a furlong in silence then Robin said, in a more serious tone of voice, "You see, Alan, I know of a wealthy wine trader; a respected vintner of the City of London, a fellow called Ivo of Shoreham, who has a house on the river near Queen's Hithe. He makes a good living in the business and owes me a favour. I thought I might invest some of our gold with Ivo; and, with luck, make a good profit in a year or two. I wondered if you would like to come in with me on this arrangement."

"This Ivo buys his imported wine from here?" I asked, incredulous. "From the County of Burgundy? And he transports all those unwieldy great barrels back to England. It must be *five hundred* miles by land!"

"No, not from here, Alan; and, once again, we are not in the County of Burgundy, we're in the Duchy of Burgundy – they are two separate entities. Not by land either. The trade routes run by sea from Bordeaux in the Duchy of Aquitaine, west of here. The ships carry the wine across the Bay of Biscay, up the Narrow Sea then into London. Ricky knows the trade, don't you? You served on the wine cogs for years, no?"

Robin turned in the saddle to look at his whey-faced servant.

Ricky grinned feebly and, lifting a trembling index finger in the air, he said: "Drink wine. This is life eternal. This is all that youth will give you. It is the season for wine and roses, and drunken friends. Be happy for this moment. This moment is your life."

I dimly recognized it as a snatch of the reams of poetry that Ricky had spouted in the hall the night before. There had been a good deal more dense verbiage in this vein, I recalled. And we had applauded it heartily.

Robin grinned. "Yes, I've heard that silly bit of doggerel before. It's the old Persian *trouvère*, Omar Khayyam – a wretch who, like you three idiots, loved wine to an absurd degree. 'Drink! For you know not whence you came nor why; drink! For you know not why you go nor where.'

Robin swung around in the saddle to look at me. "It's people such as that old sot Khayyam, or boozy young Alan here, who'll make us rich!"

"Could we please not talk about this, my lord," I said, feeling my stomach lurch. "I become ill even thinking about taking wine today."

"Wine is the Devil's own foul, stinking piss," growled Hanno. "Ale is better for proper drinking. Fresh ale doesn't make your belly sour ... "

Hanno stopped abruptly and snapped his head round to look north. Beyond the thick hedgerow that lined the road was a patch of rough grassland, which rose gently to the summit of a knoll. There was a wide, spreading yew at the brow of the knoll and, at that moment, a small flock of pigeons had, all at once, risen from their perches and, wings clattering madly, they flapped upwards and wheeled away into the empty blue sky.

There was the sound of drumming hooves and over the crest of the hill, outlined clearly in the light, came a thick line of horsemen.

They were knights or men-at-arms with green surcoats, grey iron mail, chequered shields and full helms, and carrying long, lethal lances.

A score of hostile riders.

"Ware right!" shouted Robin. "Ware cavalry. Back everyone, back down the road. Back to Chalon! Alan, wake up, man – ply those spurs!"

The attack was so unexpected, and my brain was so dulled by last night's festivities, that I completely froze. I sat like a lump in the saddle staring stupidly at the oncoming horsemen. And they were oncoming fast, now in the centre of the field, barely fifty yards away from us now, on the far side of the thick hawthorn hedge.

But Robin's words did rouse me. I hauled my poor horse round, yanking on the reins. He was a well-schooled gelding called Ghost who was used to the alarms of battle and seldom panicked. Ghost wheeled and responding to the prick of spurs, he set off at a canter back down the road after the others, the same road we'd ridden up so carelessly that morning.

The four of us were spread out along the broad highway. Ricky was far in the lead, crouched up over the neck of his bay, urging her on with soft words. Then came Hanno, twisted in the saddle and looking back at the enemy horsemen thundering behind us. Then Robin and – last of all – me. I snatched a fast glance behind us, too, and saw the enemy were leaping the hedge, clearing the hawthorn like fallow deer, and gathering themselves and their mounts, before pounding up the road behind us.

I could clearly hear their excited cries – they were hallooing to each other like excited huntsmen in pursuit of some frightened hart – although the language they used between them was quite unintelligible to my ears.

That's odd, I thought. *They don't seem to speak in French. Is that not the tongue in these parts? Why is that? Who are these folk?* Then I dismissed these irrelevant notions and concentrated on riding for my life.

I was last in the line, with Robin two horses' lengths in front of me, and now we went up from the canter to full gallop, our horses at their longest stretch. Some three miles down this arrow-straight road was the walled town of Chalon, seat of a local bishop, with whom we had dined the day before, and to whom Robin had made a generous gift of Almohad silver. This was ostensibly alms for the poor but in reality a big fat bribe.

The bishop had plenty of his own men-at-arms on the high walls of that town, and mercenary crossbowmen up in the strong gatehouse, too. Chalon meant safety for us – if only we could reach it in time. I glanced back again. We were easily outpacing our pursuers; the gap between our galloping mounts and the madly yelling men in green surcoats was growing with every pounding stride. *A very sloppy ambush,* I thought. *Our horses are much faster. They have done no more than chase us away.*

I laid a hand on Ghost's straining neck, willing him to more speed. He was a fine, strong horse; he would never fail me, I knew that at least.

Robin was twisted in the saddle too, looking beyond me to our noisy pursuers, fifty yards away, the gap between us and the foe growing larger.

"Something's not right," he yelled. "Something is wrong."

In a moment, we discovered the nature of that wrongness.

I heard a man scream, high and desperate, and saw little Ricky was now flying right over the top of his horse's head; and the poor animal whinnying in terror and tumbling over its legs. Then the awful crack of equine bones. The horse was now sprawling in the dirt of the road, kicking a loosely flopping foreleg; Ricky lay in a heap a few yards further on, quite still. I simply could not understand what had happened.

Then Hanno, just a few paces behind, leapt his horse into the air, as if he were jumping an invisible hurdle, and came skittering to halt on the other side. There were now strange horsemen on the road ahead of us – five or six more of the green surcoated fellows, all with mail, helm and lances. I saw that a heavy rope had been stretched across the road at the height of a man's belly, a yard high, tied to two oak trees on either side.

Robin was shouting, "Halt, halt!" and I was desperately reining in Ghost, his four hooves locked and skidding in the dust of the road. My body was hurled against his silky neck, I found I was fighting just to keep my seat, and not to slip right forward over Ghost's grey head.

This was no sloppy, ill-conceived ambush. It was a well-laid trap.

On the far side of the rope, Hanno was already in a savage melee; sword out, laying about with his usual lethal skill. There were half a dozen horsemen milling around him and, as I watched, he cut down one fellow with two flicks of his sword. Then slashed another across the face.

But Hanno took a hard, clanging mace blow on the back of his steel helm and I saw him reel in the saddle, and suddenly spur onward, his big horse shouldering another out of his path. Hanno's sword jabbed out and skewered an enemy through the thigh – the fellow screaming in a strange tongue, and lashing out again with the mace, and Hanno yelling back at him in the same language, as he struck again, a pounding hack into his enemy's left shoulder, smashing his long blade into the man's grey mail.

It's German, I thought madly. *They're speaking a kind of German.*

Our first line of pursuers had caught up with us by now. I had my own sword out and was wrestling my left arm into the tight leather slings of my shield. A big blond fellow, lance couched, was coming straight for me. The deadly point of his spear aimed right at my heart. But I did the correct thing. I gave Ghost a tiny signal with my knees, and my brave animal waited for the exact perfect moment and made a little dancing step to the right. The charging knight's lance hit my leather-faced shield, but only a glancing blow and, rotating my body with the force of his lance strike, using his momentum, I lashed out with my sword and crunched the long blade into the back of his coif as he thundered past me.

I heard a sharp snap, like a twig underfoot, felt his iron mail give in under my powerful strike and reckoned I'd broken the bastard's neck.

Robin, too, was engaging a knight now, sword to sword, steel scraping against steel, sparks flying in fiery arcs. I saw that Hanno was past his mass of opponents, beyond the tight-stretched hempen rope, and that three of them already lay dead in the road. He was free and clear. Yet Hanno was circling his horse now, turning it, as if to return, brush aside his foes once more, and jump back over the rope and come to aid us.

I dodged a snake-fast lance-strike at directly my face. It came out of nowhere but I felt the horrible wind of it on my left cheek. I swung my sword into a passing horseman, and felt it thump uselessly on his shield.

Robin had killed his opponent – a straight hard thrust through the fellow's Adam's apple, gory point bursting out of the fellow's mail-clad neck. My lord was now yelling over at Hanno. "Ride away, man. Get back to Little John. Go! Go!" But

Hanno still hesitated.

I got my shield up in time to block a vicious sword swipe from a man with a steel helm and full lattice-like facemask, the curved steel face-plate punctured with little square breathing holes. A pair of curled goat's horns were affixed to the flat top of the helmet, giving him a unearthly, even a slightly demonic, air. I could not see the fellow's eyes behind the mask – an effect that meant he looked to me like a living monster, like some foul creature of a deep, disturbing netherworld.

Indeed, I was so shocked by his ghastly appearance, that my instinctive counter blow was badly mistimed. He easily batted off my sword blow with his own, and struck at me again, his sharp blade thwacking against the leather face of my shield, and slipping off the surface, sliding upwards to crash painfully into my mailed shoulder.

"Yield, sirs! Surrender or die," said the man in the hellish steel monster-mask, the words muffled but intelligible as a kind of French.

I glanced at Robin. Then looked at the road ahead, Hanno was two hundred yards down the road and galloping hard back towards Chalon. Ricky was still unconscious – or dead – lying in a heap in the dust. There were a dozen men in green all around us; some armed with lances, one man, a veteran sergeant, had a crossbow pointed right at Robin's chest.

There was no way though them, or none that I could imagine.

"Yield or die!" the masked man repeated, shouting more loudly this time, his menacing sword raised, ready to cut me down. "Yield to me!"

"Very well," said Robin, lowering his own blade. "We surrender."

CHAPTER TWO

The sword was ripped from my grasp by rough hands; and I was deprived of my misericorde, a long, black-iron, killing dagger, that I kept in my right riding boot. One greedy, green-clad bastard eagerly snatched away the heavy purse of silver from my belt. Then our hands were tightly bound together in front of us but we were otherwise unmolested.

I saw that Robin had been similarly stripped of his purse, sword and a fine jewelled dagger he had purchased in Marseilles and, shaking my head at this loss, I realized that the bout of action had completely rid me of my hangover. I felt intensely alive – and, more than that, angry. Who were these men to attack us like bandits? We had given no offence. We were not making war on them. The uniform green surcoats told us that these men were soldiers, men under military command, not mere bandits.

The man in the inhuman steel mask, untied the leather strap under his chin, took off his horned helmet and revealed his face.

His sweaty skin was pale; a dead white colour as if he lived his life in some dank subterranean cavern and never saw the light of the sun. His eyes were very deep green, and cold as whale's skin, his hair thick and black, so dark it was the colour of tar. He was bearded like a Templar, this green knight, but the beard was neatly trimmed against his angular jaw, and his long moustaches had been treated with oils, or perhaps wax, to make them stand out from his upper lip on either side in sharp spikes.

It was a striking face, intelligent, refined and almost pretty, despite the beard, but perhaps more than a little cruel as well. He spoke French with a slight Burgundian lilt, easily understandable, and introduced himself to us with all courtesy before asking the names of his captives.

"I am Raoul, Seigneur de Beaune-du-Bois, at your service," he said. "And you gentlemen are?"

"Robert Odo, Earl of Locksley, liegeman of Richard of England; this is my personal *trouvère* Alan Dale of Westbury."

"An earl, no less? What a fine catch for a morning's hunt! You are what we would call a count here in Burgundy. And I'm but a humble *chevalier* – I believe you far outrank me, my lord."

"So it would seem, and yet I'm your prisoner. May I ask whom you serve, Messire de Beaune-du-Bois? Who is your lord?"

"You'll meet him soon enough, my lord. My master is Otto, Count of Burgundy, and I shall bring you before him this day."

"You hunt far from your own lands, do you not, *chevalier*?"

"I might say the same to an English nobleman riding on a road in Burgundy. But these are times of great wanderings for all the chivalry of Christendom, are they not? But you subtly enquire, I believe, why my men and I are *this side* of the great river, no? Well, I shall answer you. My master the count claims lordship of *all* the ancient kingdom of *Burgundia*, even that which lies on this bank of the Saone, and which is at present under the thumb of that fellow Eudes, the French king's lapdog. So we hunt where we choose on both sides of the river. One day, perhaps soon, all Burgundy shall be Count Otto's domain but until that day we must hurry back to the Free County with our prize. You will kindly mount your horse, my lord. We must be away before our enemies converge on us. I trust you will give me no good cause to punish you."

Robin gave him one cold, hard glance, but replied only: "I am, of course, entirely at your service, my dear *chevalier*."

Ricky, praise God, was not dead but merely stunned by his fall from the horse. He gazed about owlishly as they bound his hands and removed his weapons and he was helped up behind me on to Ghost's strong back.

His own horse had snapped its right foreleg after the fall caused by that devilish rope, and one of the green-surcoats had sliced open its jugular, giving the animal a swift, merciful death. The men we had killed or badly wounded were tied to their horses, and the cavalcade made ready to depart. We three prisoners were soon mounted again, and were surrounded by the soldiers of the Chevalier Raoul. Then we all set off at a canter north-east, across open fields and down little-frequented tracks.

As we rode, I studied the pennants and shield devices of the men who had captured us, which all bore the same design: a cup shape in dark green arranged in lines with an upside down cup shape in white, to give a sort of checkered effect of green and white. I had seen the device before, and I knew it was called *vair*, the French word for fur, because the design was based on a kind of cloak or mantel made from two kinds of squirrel fur. Indeed, I saw that many of the riders wore squirrel-skin mantels over their surcoats or had these cloaks rolled and secured on the backs of their saddles. The men themselves rarely spoke but when they did it was in one of the brutal-sounding German dialects I had heard often in Outremer from the followers of the Emperor, Frederick Barbarossa, who had so tragically drowned in a river on the outward journey to the Holy Land.

Their native language made sense to me now.

Robin had delivered a long lecture on the region we were travelling through over supper a few days ago. However, I had been sampling a good deal of the local wine, as usual, and had retained only the bones of his rather boring sermon. There were two Burgundies, he had said. The Free County of Burgundy on the eastern side of the River Saone towards the Jura Mountains was part of the sprawling Holy Roman Empire. Count Otto, fourth son of Barbarossa, and brother of the current emperor Henry, ruled over the County. While the official language of the Holy Roman Empire was Latin, its nobles mostly spoke French to each other, while the lower orders more often used in their native German tongue.

I suddenly wished Hanno were with us. As a subject of the Empire, hailing as he did from the deep forests of Bavaria, he would have understood what these men-at-arms were saying. Then I chided myself for my selfishness: Hanno was free, while we were bound. He was no doubt safely back in Chalon by now with a big cup of his beloved ale, or perhaps he was on the road south the rejoin the wagons and Little John.

The French-speaking Duchy of Burgundy, Robin had said, where we now were, was located between the west bank of the Saone and the River Loire, a hundred and fifty miles further west of us, which roughly formed the border with the Angevin lands of our own King Richard.

That had been our intended destination – once across the Loire we would be more or less in safe territory. To the north of the Duchy was the kingdom of France, our sovereign's great rival. The dukes of Burgundy, in times past, had often been the allies of France. Yet Hugh, the current duke of Burgundy, had fought shoulder to shoulder with us in the Holy Land, and we had been offered safe passage through his realm on account of our shared struggle against the Saracens, our common foe.

Until the road attack this May morning, we'd been unmolested.

I remembered seeing Duke Hugh before the battle of Arsuf – a big, broad-shouldered French-speaking nobleman with a booming voice, and a roaring laugh that made me feel cheered by its echoes. As far as I knew, he was in the Holy Land, in command of the remaining French knights.

I also recalled Robin had said that, in Hugh's absence, his eldest son Eudes had been named regent and was ruling the Duchy of Burgundy.

We came across the River Saone after an hour of hard riding, mostly east through an almost empty countryside. The river was a formidable barrier across our path. I wondered if the Green Knight – as I had now dubbed our captor – expected us to swim our horses across this wide river. It would have been a risky endeavour, for the water was deep here, the current strong, and there were now two grown men on Ghost's back. But the Burgundian *chevalier* had evidently made this crossing many times.

Under a thick, yellow curtain of willow on the right bank, hidden from view, was a substantial raft, with rails around its square sides, large enough to carry a score of horses and men-at-arms. There was even a weed-draped rope well concealed under the water's surface for the men to haul the raft over to the far side.

As the Germans wrestled with the thick, dripping, water-logged rope, dragging the heavily laden raft across the surface of the Saone, I looked eagerly both up stream and down but could see no possible help to hand – a few fishing craft downstream towards Chalon, but these poor local fishermen resolutely minded their own business.

As we skimmed across the dark, soupy water, I heard Robin at the front of the raft engage the Green Knight in a little conversation.

"I collect you are fond of hunting, *chevalier*," said Robin.

The Green Knight smiled at him revealing small, sharp, pointed white teeth. "It is my passion, my lord. I believe that, short of war itself, it is the noblest pursuit of all. Do you hunt much in England?"

"I've been known to take a deer or two," said Robin, with a smile.

"Indeed? I confess that I live and breathe entirely for the chase," said the Green Knight. "The hart and the hind, the boar, the wolf and the bear – I have hunted them all in my own dear forests around Beaune-du-Bois, and across these foreign lands, as well."

"Do you and your men range freely over the Duchy, *chevalier*?" said Robin. "You do not fear the anger of Duke Hugh when he returns from the Holy Land – nor reprisals from his son Lord Eudes before then?"

"Eudes is a weakling – a mewling puppy unfit for the role of regent of a once-great fiefdom. And Hugh? He may never return. Many better men have embarked on a great pilgrimage never to be seen again. Many."

On the far side of the river, the green surcoats untied our hands and we ate a bite of cold, greasy pork and rye bread provided by the Green Knight. He offered us a cup of wine to drink with our noonday meal but I refused and asked for plain water instead. The German men-at-arms seemed to be relieved and almost in a celebratory mood, now that they were safely on the County side of the river, and I heard bursts of singing and soldierly jokes in their language, which of course I did not fully understand. My hangover had passed from me but I decided to eschew wine to keep my wits sharp in case there was an opportunity for escape.

"May I enquire where you are taking us?" I asked our captor.

"You may certainly ask me that, young fellow," said the Green Knight cheerily. I didn't care to be called that: this *chevalier* couldn't have been more than three years older than me; no more than twenty.

"We are going to the town of Dole, which my master the Count is greatly honouring by holding his court there this month."

"Never heard of it," I said churlishly. I was still irked this bandit-knight had captured us so easily. I was even more angry, in fact, at myself for my poor performance on the road. Had I not been so wine-sick that morning, we might still be free men riding west on the road to Autun.

"It is a beautiful market town on the River Doubs, with a fine old church and a powerful keep. They say that the young girls of the town of Dole are the most beautiful, the most obedient and the most loving in all of *Burgundia* – once they have been caught and tamed, that is!"

I grunted something meaningless. I was in no mood for talk of love. And "caught and tamed" seemed a rather odd phrase to use of a person; as if these pretty girls were creatures of the wild or just beasts of the hunt.

There was no opportunity to escape that long, unhappy afternoon. My horse, which still carried both Ricky and me, was lashed to one of the green-surcoats' saddles and the Green Knight's dozen or so men-at-arms constantly watched us. I was concerned too about the condition of poor Ricky, who had not uttered a word since he had fallen from his horse. He seemed to be sleeping, with his head slumped against my back, and on one occasion he almost slipped from the back of our mount. I had to ask one of the green men-at-arms to tie his arms securely around my waist.

We followed the winding course of the River Doubs, heading roughly north-east along its southern bank, wending slowly at first across flat meadows and pastures, but the farther we ranged from the rich valley of the Saone, the more rough-hewn the landscape became. This territory, I saw, was rather poor compared with the plump and fecund Duchy, and somehow meaner, even the grazing sheep and cows seemed smaller, more wizened; the crops were thinner, too, the patches of woodland thicker, more tangled. We began to see stretches of proper forest, dark, trackless wastes, no doubt haunted by evil witches, elves and wolves.

It was a menacing landscape, to my eye, fell and unnatural, perhaps because I was a bound prisoner and I had no idea what my fate would be when we finally arrived at our destination. Robin, in contrast, seemed completely at his ease on the long journey, chatting with the Green Knight on the road as if they were old and trusted friends, rather than recent enemies, and our pale captor, too, behaved with perfect chivalry.

Perhaps, all would be well, I thought, when we reached this place Dole – perhaps Robin would pay over a small ransom to the Count and we would be set free and allowed to continue on our merry way. Perhaps.

The town of Dole was perched on a ridge on the north side of the River Doubs with a very fine church, just as the Green Knight had said, by a wide square, overlooked by a powerful-looking stone castle with a long stone curtain wall, but not very much else besides. The townsfolk lived on a poor one-storey houses or even ramshackle shacks and hovels that huddled at the base of the castle walls or around the square by the church. There were many wattle pens in the market square, filled with small bleating sheep awaiting slaughter. I hoped this was not an omen.

The Count of Burgundy was holding court in his great hall, inside the precincts of the castle of Dole, and the Green Knight and a quartet of his men-at-arms showed us into the high-beamed, drafty wooden building. Our bonds had been cut when we dismounted in the courtyard of the castle – and I discovered with huge sorrow that Ricky was stone dead. His skin was cool to the touch and I realized he had been gathered unto God while he was tied to my back, some hours ago. My anger came flooding back again then – one of these men, or their master the Green Knight, had killed my poor friend. There must be a bloody reckoning.

But not now. Now was not the time.

Robin had helped me to lay out the body of our comrade in the castle's chapel for burial in the churchyard the next day.

"Keep your countenance, Alan," Robin hissed to me. "Hold your peace, I beg you, and let me do all the talking here. I need you to be calm. They shall be paid out for this gross insult in due course, I swear it, but not now, Alan, do you understand me?"

I said nothing. I was, in fact, trying to hold back tears. Ricky had been a good man – well, perhaps not exactly *good*; he had been, in truth, a ruthless pirate of the Mediterranean Sea and only God knew what terrible sins he had committed, but he'd been a good friend to me. He did not deserve to die by falling off a horse on a road so far from his home.

So only Robin and I were ushered into the great hall by

our captors and we entered the presence of Otto, Count of Burgundy.

The hall was thronged with men and women. Many of the men had long swords at their belts, and daggers too, others wore rich velvet and silk robes, yet others were dressed in plain woollen tunics, cloaks, robes and hose. The women wore fine gowns and furs and a few sported some exquisite jewellery, brooches, rings and necklaces. Others wore drab brown smocks, and had simple white headdresses that covered their hair. There was a background in the court noise like a swarm of bees, as scores of Burgundian folk moved around, conversed, gossiped and flirted with each other, and above the noise a distinct smell – an all-pervading and perpetual hall scent of damp dog, old wood smoke and ancient sweat.

It was a rustic place, chilly and dirty too, with damp, stone walls and slippery, weeks-old rotting rushes underfoot. A rather mean log fire smouldered in the big hearth in the centre of the room, with a bored page boy whacking it with an iron poker to make the sparks fly upwards.

At the end of the hall in front of a long, silver and blue hanging cloth, lolling on an X-shaped stool entirely at ease, was a young, slender nobleman with shoulder-length, flaming red hair held back by a thin gold circlet. He had sharp, glinting blue eyes and a big golden goblet of wine in his ring-covered right hand, and he was talking to an older man, a cleric in a grubby white robe – a burly fellow, sunburned on his tonsured head, who was wildly gesticulating with his hands and who appeared to be trying to convince the seated young nobleman of some urgent matter.

The redhead laughed and shook his shaggy locks, flipping his fingers twice to dismiss the old monk – the discourse, whatever it had been about, had failed to move him – and, as we prisoners approached, he caught sight of us, sat upright in his chair and regarded us with interest.

The Green Knight strode ahead of us, made an elegant bow before the count and said in good French: "My lord, I acquired a prisoner this day in the Duchy, a captive of my sword. I present to you Robert, Earl of Locksley, a rich English nobleman, who has yielded to my valour."

"An English earl, you say?" said Count Otto. "And wealthy, too?"

Robin was now making his own courtly bow, deeper and even more elegant than the *chevalier*'s. I ducked my own head, too.

"Not wealthy, sire," said Robin. "Just a humble pilgrim of God returning home, after having fought for Christ in the Holy Land."

"One of those, eh?" sneered Otto. He did not seem at all impressed with Robin's claim to be a pilgrim. "A fellow who cloaks himself in piety as an excuse to plunder the riches of Outremer to his heart's content."

This was so close to the mark in Robin's case that, without thinking, I involuntarily let out a tiny snort of amusement.

"Who's the simpering pretty boy?" Otto pointed at me.

"Nobody. Just the earl's servant," said the Green Knight. That killed my mirth. I glared, yet, ever mindful of Robin's words, I held my tongue.

"Yet I maintain, sire, that this Earl is indeed a wealthy man. Look at his fine clothes! We took a purse filled with gold bezants from his belt this morning. Even the servant-boy had a purse of silver on his person."

Robin's clothes, although covered with a fine layer of the dust of the roads of Burgundy, were made from the best cloth that Marseilles could provide; my own attire was not so shabby either.

"Well, well . . . a rich English earl has fallen into my lap like a ripe plum. That's improved my day considerably. You've done well, Raoul!"

"My dear count," said Robin in a calm, friendly voice, "I hesitate to be so rude as to correct a great nobleman in his own court, but I am by no means wealthy. Not rich at all, in truth. Since my purse of gold was taken, I own no more than the clothes – fine as they are – that I stand in. Furthermore, as a pilgrim returning from the Holy Land, Pope Celestine has decreed that I must not be molested on pain of excommunication."

The count laughed then. "Do you think, Englishman, that I give a single squeaky fart for that grasping old fool in Rome and all his threats of excommunication. I can buy my forgiveness from the good bishop at Besançon, if I require it, or from any other high churchman, for less than one hundredth of the sum that I shall receive from your fat ransom!"

The count looked over at the old, white-clad monk he had so recently dismissed: "What say you, Prior? How much would it be to absolve me from a Papal excommunication? A *livre* of silver? Less? What do you Cistercians charge for that service these days? You come here boldly seeking patronage for a new house for your order, the least you can do to gain my favour is help me circumvent the pope's decrees and wring some riches from this wandering Englishman!"

The big monk stepped forward again. His face was swollen and purple with anger. It occurred to me that were he not a man of God he might be a fellow you would do well to avoid in a street fight. He raised one gnarled old finger and aimed it like a spear directly at the Count.

"Do not mock His Holiness the pope, my lord. Nor Holy Mother Church, nor even excommunication – lest you mock God himself!"

"You mistake me, Prior Gui," said Otto, "I spoke only in jest."

Slightly mollified, the monk subsided a little. He let out a hot gust of angry breath and said: "There's one thing, my lord, that I would say to you to further my cause. This man claims to be Robert of Locksley, yes?"

"He does not deny it," said Otto.

This purple-faced prior – from his ecclesiastical title I knew him to be a powerful man in his monastery, deputy to the abbot himself – stepped forward and whispered for a long time in the count's ear. They were talking about Robin, that was clear, and

Otto did not take his bright blue eyes off my lord for the whole time that the old monk was speaking.

"Indeed," said Otto, when the Cistercian had fallen silent. "I must thank you, Prior Gui, you have been most helpful this day. I will certainly now consider the matter of a new house for your order afresh."

The monk bowed and retreated and Otto sprang to his feet.

"You're Robert, Earl of Locksley, also known as Robin Hood?"

He was approaching my lord, his young face alight with a burning excitement. Robin said nothing. He nodded, cocked his head on one side, and observed the approaching nobleman with an iron-hard eye. I knew what was coming next. So, it seemed, did my lord.

"You have been travelling across the Mediterranean Sea?"

"I am a humble pilgrim of Christ, protected by the pope's decree, travelling home from the Holy Land," said Robin coldly.

"But to came to this territory, to *Burgundia*, by sea, on a ship – after visiting Tunis in North Africa, and the city of Valencia in Spain, and the old Hospitaller castle of Ulldecona, did you not?"

Robin said no more; his eyes gleamed like a wet blade.

Otto stood a few feet from my master. They were both tall men, similar in height. He was staring right into Robin's face.

"Then I *shall* hold you for ransom, Robert, Earl of Locksley – or Robin Hood, or whatever name you travel by," said Count Otto.

He was smiling unpleasantly like a ginger tomcat with a mouse trapped under one paw. "And the price for your release shall be a princely one; it shall be a sum worthy of your great dignity. Can you guess what amount I shall demand for your freedom?"

Robin remained silent. But he met and matched Otto's blue gaze.

"Nothing to say, my lord? You do not wish to estimate your life's value? Well then, I shall tell you. I will demand that your people hand over no less than a hundred and fifty pounds in gold for your freedom. In ingots, if you please. And until this great treasure is delivered to me, and I shall insist on the full amount, you will rot in my deepest dungeon at my castle of Besançon. What say you to that, my fine, gold-stealing friend?"

CHAPTER THREE

Robin laughed. He guffawed directly into Count Otto's flushed face.

"You cannot be serious, my lord," he said. "For a moment I was a little confused by your words and then I realized that you must have spoken in only as a kind of jest – just as you did a moment ago when you made mock of the His Holiness the pope."

Otto stopped smiling. "You may ponder my 'jest' at your leisure for a month or two in chains at Besançon – then we shall see if you still find it so amusing. Chevalier Raoul! Bind them both and take them away."

"One moment, my dear count," said Robin. "Let me speak my piece before you cast me into your prison. The weight of gold that I took from Christ's enemies *was* – I admit – a hundred and fifty pounds. But I don't have anywhere near that amount left. I swear this on my immortal soul."

Robin's soul was already forfeit, and many times over, but he was, most unusually for him, telling the truth in this instance. We'd taken a hundred and fifty ingots of African gold, each weighing one pound, and some barrels of silver coin from the cruel Almohad ruler of Valencia. But in truth we no longer possessed that fabulously vast amount of treasure.

"I have dispersed a goodly amount of the gold already," continued my lord and he made a gesture that encompassed his fine clothes under the layer of road dust. This was also true. He had freely spent a fortune in Marseilles. "I have also outlaid a great deal on equipping my men, and I have paid out generous stipends to all my followers." Otto was listening intently to Robin; you might even say he was hanging on his every word.

"But now, right *now*," he said hammering his point, "I have only a meagre ten pounds of gold left to my name. I swear that is all I possess."

That *was* a barefaced lie. But I was not going to betray it.

"And do you think I am foolish enough to carry even that small amount of treasure with me on a dangerous journey across unfriendly territory. I have of course deposited what is left of my gold with some friends, and cannot retrieve it unless you allow me to go to them myself."

It was Otto's turn to laugh. "What sort of fool do you take me for, Englishman? Do you think I would release you on your word of honour?"

"No? Then consider this. If you free me, I shall render you a service that will, in the long run, bring you a far greater fortune."

Otto seemed amused. "And what would this service be?"

"I will tell you privily," said Robin. "It is not for all the ears here."

"You shall whisper it then in *my* ear," said the count.

He leaned his head forward, presenting his ear. I felt rather than saw the *chevalier* behind me stiffening and taking a step closer. A man-at-arms behind the count put his hand on his hilt.

Robin spoke very quietly, yet I heard him clearly.

"I shall remove the regent of the Duchy of Burgundy, Lord Eudes, from this mortal world for you. That shall be the price of my freedom."

Otto jerked his head back. He stared at Robin, shocked.

"You would do this for me? You *could* do this black deed?"

"You don't believe me?" said Robin. He shook his right wrist, dropped it to his thigh and a winking steel blade dropped into his palm. In one smooth movement, my lord turned and hurled the knife at the far side of the hall where it thwacked into a beam and shuddered for a moment.

"How about now, my friend?" said my lord. "You believe me now?"

The count staggered back a step or two, gaping, obviously realizing that he had just offered his throat to a prisoner with a blade up his sleeve.

"I ... I should like to hear a little more of your ... your intriguing proposal," Otto stammered. He clapped his hands. "Leave us – all of you," he said. "Leave our presence now." As the hall began to empty, he thought better of his order: "Remain with the captives, *chevalier*; and you'd better keep a couple of reliable men to hand, too, if you please."

The accommodation they allocated us was hardly sumptuous, a single, large, damp-smelling bed in a small, round, stone-walled, windowless room, with a pair of rickety stools and a rough wooden table holding a jug of wine, a heel of day-old bread and some cheese; and there was a pair of men-at-arms standing outside the bolted, iron-bound door. But it was a much better than being slung into some dank, lightless dungeon.

"You can't be serious, Robin," I said. "Surely you would not cut down a good man – a Christian lord – in cold blood. It was a clever ruse, yes? A cunning trick of some kind?"

"Sometimes, Alan, despite all our years together, I feel you do not know me at all," said Robin.

I noted that he had not actually answered my question.

"I will tell you this," my lord continued. "I shall not give over all our hard-won gold to this greedy stripling without a good reason. We shed blood for that gold; we all suffered for it. I shall not easily part with it."

We were still in Dole, inside the keep of the castle, in a room on the third floor. It was the hour of Vespers on the day of our capture and full dark. Count Otto had said he would speak with us again in the morning after the burial of poor Ricky and give us his decision.

When we had been in the emptied hall with Otto a few

hours before – under the watchful eye of the Chevalier Raoul and four of his men-at-arms, all with drawn swords – Robin had outlined his plan to murder the Regent Eudes. At first, I could scarcely believe my ears, nor credit his words but, as Robin explained it, it became more and more plausible.

"You have seen, my dear count, how I might bring a killing blade discreetly into the regent's presence," Robin said. "But that's not the method I would choose to dispatch the eldest son of Duke Hugh."

Robin shook his head at such obviousness. "No. I could quite easily end his life in this manner. Easily. But I would not survive the dark deed. His guards would seize me a split instant after I struck him down."

"So how then would you do it?" said Otto, who seemed appalled and intrigued in equal measure by Robin's suggestion. The emotions surging through my own heart were similarly confused.

"Oh, with poison, of course," said Robin calmly. "It would be simpler, cleaner, and, of paramount importance to me, I would be able to preserve my own existence with this more subtle method. By chance, I happened to purchase a very fine gold ring from an Italian gentleman in Marseilles earlier this month. The ring has a small hidden cavity beneath the sapphire stone that holds a single dose of a lethal poison. A hinged lid opens under the stone at the press of a tiny stud and this allows the wearer to discreetly add a measure of deadly powder to a goblet of wine or ale."

Otto, who had been in the act of drinking from his wine goblet, suddenly lost his thirst and put down the heavy cup without taking a sip. I could see him looking closely at Robin's hands.

"Where is this poison ring?" Otto asked.

"It is well secreted among my personal belongings on my horse."

"And the poison, what poison would you employ?"

"I usually find a distilled extract of the root of wolfsbane to be the most effective," said Robin nonchalantly. "Combined, of course, with a dash of henbane and just a suggestion of foxglove. Wolfsbane alone, I have found, makes the lips tingle when it is tasted. My ring contains a whole drachm of a fine, greyish powder, which dissolves completely in wine or ale, and does not affect the taste of the drink beyond a very faint bitterness, which usually goes unremarked by the victim. But the best feature of this particular poison is that the victim does not feel a thing for at least a half hour to an hour after drinking it. It needs to work its way deep into the stomach lining to be truly effective. This would allow me to make my escape. Then, within the hour, the victim is as dead as a stone. And no physician can explain why."

I'd never heard Robin speak of poisoning before, yet here he was, discussing its finer points as if he were a murderous apothecary.

"How can I know you will do this, if I were to release you?"

Robin dropped his voice to a whisper. "Because this was ever my design, my dear count, even before I had the pleasure of meeting you. This was always my mission. I was sent here, to *Burgundia*, in secret, to remove Lord Eudes by the Lionheart himself. Why else would Richard allow me to leave his side in the midst of a war and return to Europe?"

I could see a hole in this argument but Robin did not allow Otto to think too hard on this. "The king wishes to expand his Angevin territory and take the western part Duchy of Burgundy for himself – he desires the counties of Nevers and Auxerre, and the county of Autun, if he can take it. That's why I'm in Burgundy. I'm here to take possession for Richard."

Otto was gaping like a straw-chewing yokel at Robin by this point.

"War between England and France is on the horizon, as I am sure you already know, my lord," Robin continued. "There can be no avoiding a conflict between these two rivals. The Duchy of Burgundy will stand with their ally King Philip of France. But if King Richard can remove the regent here with a little poison – and have the duke himself assassinated in the Holy Land – the

Duchy will be rendered leaderless, and utterly at the mercy of a swift invasion from Berry, Touraine, Anjou and Maine, the king's powerful patrimonies in the west."

Robin paused, gauging the reaction in his audience.

Otto said, "I follow you. Go on, man."

"With Richard's men controlling the western part of the Duchy of Burgundy," Robin said, "France would be weakened, wide open to an attack from the south. This is as my lord desires. This is why I'm here."

"What of the eastern part of the Duchy?" asked Otto, his eyes were now gleaming with greed. "You speak of annexing the west. But what of the east? What of the counties of Langres, Chalon and Mâcon? Who should rule them, I wonder, if Richard possessed the rest of the Duchy?"

"My noble sovereign was ever an admirer and also a stout supporter of your late father, the Emperor Frederick. I know for sure that my king would gladly welcome a strong partnership with his equally illustrious son. Between you, two great and puissant Christian warriors, Otto and Richard, you would tear into the King of France's vulnerable southern flanks like ravening lions. And who knows what further benefits that conquest might bring – an expansion of your both territories far into the north, perhaps, when the conflict against perfidious King Philip is won?"

I could see Otto was excited by this idea. "But do you, Locksley, have the authority to act in King Richard's name?" he said.

"I do," said Robin. "But it must remain a close secret between us. I have trusted you, my dear count, with sensitive information – knowledge that if it came to light would wreck all Richard's plans – and I am trusting you to keep silent, my friend, and not to obstruct me *at all* in my actions."

I slept very poorly that night – Robin's intricate plans for the takeover of the Duchy of Burgundy, and the carve up of the region between King Richard and Count Otto, were whizzing through my mind long after the castle watch called the hour of midnight. I could still not get used to the idea that Robin was going to do cold-blooded murder to achieve his aim.

The morning was grey and sombre, and we buried poor Ricky in the dreary churchyard at Dole with very little ceremony. An elderly chaplain mumbled over the hastily dug grave and Robin said a few words about his servant and friend. I felt that I ought to say something, too, and that snatch of poetry that Ricky had quoted the day before had stayed in my head. I stepped forward and said: "Drink wine. This is life eternal. This is all that youth will give you. It is the season for wine and roses, and drunken friends. Be happy for this moment. This moment is your life."

Robin gave me one look of chilly steel from under his gathered brows, then the earth was pattering down on the shroud-wrapped body.

Goodbye, my friend, I thought. *Farewell, Ricky.* I shall see you in Heaven, through God's infinite mercy. If that is His will.

Then we went to look to our horses. Otto had spoken at length to Robin that very morning and he was now setting us free.

"I have my agents in Dijon," said the count, as we climbed into our saddles. He shook a warning finger at Robin. "Ruthless and capable men. They will be watching over you day and night."

Count Otto was not a complete fool, then.

"You will hear soon enough when the deed is done," said Robin. "But I shall not strike for at least a week, perhaps two, and do not seek to rush me. I must choose the moment with care. And remember, my dear count, not a word of this to anyone. It must remain secret. If word were to reach Eudes, I'd be dead within the day, after they had tortured me and forced me to reveal that *you* were complicit in the plot. The regent would move against you immediately. You'd be wise keep this matter private."

"Yes, yes," said Otto. "I'll keep quiet. But do not wait too long, and do not play me false. You would find me a bad enemy."

With those parting words we were off – alone, Robin and I – back on the road beside the River Doubs towards the border.

When we were a mile or two from Dole, I said to Robin, "When did you buy the gold ring? I don't remember you doing any business with an Italian gentleman in Marseilles."

"What ring?" said Robin.

"Your special sapphire poisoner's ring."

Robin turned in the saddle to stare at me. "You're a very good man, Alan," he said, "and one of my bravest and most loyal and followers. You have fine skills with a sword and a vielle. But you need to work much, much harder with the few brains that God gave you."

"There's no ring," I said. And with this realisation my spirits lifted. "You do *not* plan to murder Eudes. There is no plot to seize Burgundy."

"I knew you'd get there sooner or later," said my lord.

We grinned at each other: happy in that moment. Two free men riding out in the countryside on a bright spring day. Our horses, weapons and belongings had all been returned – even our purses, a little lighter, had been given back to us. We crossed the Saone by an old Roman bridge a few miles east of the abbey of Cîteaux – the home of that meddling old monk, Prior Gui – and entered into the Duchy of Burgundy.

There we came to a fork in the road and had to make a choice.

So far as we knew, we had not been followed into the Duchy by Otto's henchmen, although there was no way to be sure. The count had spoken menacingly of his spies watching over us. I suggested to Robin that we should turn south and ride to Chalon and beyond to rejoin Little John and all our friends. There must surely be safety in numbers, I said.

Robin shook his head.

"If we turn south, we will obviously be breaking our agreement with Otto. He will know that I lied to his face and may well try to take revenge on us. The County of Burgundy is not weak. It has a many well-trained knights – and remember that Otto is the younger brother of the mighty Emperor Henry. The count is a powerful man – don't ever forget that. He could raise five hundred men-at-arms and attack the wagon train, if he chose. We'd be overwhelmed in a few moments – all be killed and the gold lost. No, Alan, the best thing we can do is to head for Dijon, as Otto expects. It will also give us time to decide on our next move."

So we turned our horses northwest took the wide and well-travelled road to Dijon, seat of the ancient dukes of Burgundy.

The guards at the gatehouse on the southeastern side of the walls of Dijon stopped us at spear point. Two horsemen, two well-armed, warlike strangers who spoke French but with an odd Norman accent, and who were seeking entry into their peaceful town as the shadows lengthened – I could see why they found us a suspicious. The guards brusquely asked us our business and when Robin declared himself to be Earl of Locksley and demanded an audience with Eudes, the regent, they looked askance.

"You claim to be an English earl and yet you travel with only one solitary attendant. How so?" said the middle-aged sergeant-at-arms.

I wondered if Robin would explain that we had been four until the day before, the advance party of a large armed company of men returning from the Holy Land. Instead, he took a high hand.

"How dare you question me? Stand aside, immediately – or better yet, man, take me directly to the regent. Now!"

The guard, to his credit, bravely stood his ground. "I am tasked with protecting the town of Dijon from all enemies. I only ask in, all proper courtesy, for you to give an account of yourself, which is my right..."

"I have a message from Duke Hugh in the Holy Land," said Robin, "for his son Lord Eudes of Burgundy. I have travelled many months to bring it here – will you now delay me further?

We shall see what your master has to say about that!"

That was enough for the sergeant-at-arms, he swung open the gate and allowed our two horses to come through, and I noticed that Robin flipped the man a golden coin as he passed. The guard snatched it out of the air, bit into the soft metal to check its authenticity, and then tucked it away inside his tunic and grinned cheekily at Robin as he clattered past.

"Welcome to Dijon, my lord. If there is anything I can do to aid you, any service you require, while you remain within our excellent walls, do not hesitate to summon me, I beg you. Name's Etienne, Sergeant Etienne of the town guard, everyone in Dijon knows me."

"You can tell me where to find Lord Eudes at this time of day."

"Why, my lord, it is near the hour of Vespers, see, the sun is just beginning to set, and so my lord will be at the church of the old abbey. He attends the holy service at Saint Benignus every evening without fail. They have some very fine-voiced monks who sing in the choir. Truly beautiful to listen to, they are! You follow this street to the castle and the big square then take the lane west – you will hear the pealing of the bells before long, my lord, and they shall guide you to Saint Benignus. I would come with you but I must now bar this gate for the curfew. God speed!"

We made our way through the town – it was a spacious place of wide muddy streets lined with substantial, two-storey, wood-framed, red-tiled houses and little plots of land dug over for kitchen vegetables. I even spied an orchard or two, the fruit trees laid out in neat lines. We came after a few hundred yards to the palace of the dukes of Burgundy in the very centre of Dijon – a strong, square-built stone tower three stories high with arrow-slit windows and flanked by a pair of long, low, fortified halls built of brick and stone and some lesser wooden buildings, kitchens, store houses, brew houses, barracks and stables, and the like. But the ducal palace itself had no outer curtain wall – which surprised me a little – and instead obviously depended on Sergeant Etienne and his brave comrades to defend the ramparts of the town against their enemies. The castle of Dijon was, then, beguilingly open to the town with the door of the big keep leading out directly on to a market square, which, as we passed through it, was filled with hundreds of townsfolk packing up their stalls and loading their handcarts and wagons at the end of a long day's trading.

We turned left at the market square, dived down a narrow lane and came, after a short while, to the abbey church in the western part of the town. The sweetly tolling bells that had guided us in had ceased by then but I could hear fine many-voiced singing coming from inside the large stone church. I would have liked to enter the House of God immediately but my lord had no interest in church music. Instead of joining the crowd at the evening service, Robin took us in search of the abbey's *hospitarius* – the monk who was responsible for providing hospitality to all travellers. Robin had decided it would be better for us to wash and clean ourselves of the dirt of the road and spend a night in the abbey before paying our formal respects to the regent in the morning.

The *hospitarius* was a harried little man, tonsured and dressed all in sombre black, for the abbey was a house of the Benedictine order, but he made us most welcome. After Robin had made a generous donation in silver to the upkeep of the old stones of the abbey and its monks, we were invited most cordially to make ourselves at home within its walls.

There was no hurry now since we had decided to present ourselves to the regent the next day, for which I was grateful. An hour later, after a long, very pleasant, hot-water sluice in the abbey's wash-house, and a welcome change of linen, Robin and I found ourselves were sitting alone at a long communal table in the refectory with a steaming bowl of bean soup apiece, several thick slices of bread and a jug of excellent local red.

When we had finished eating and were sitting contentedly with our wine, Robin leaned in and said quietly: "There is something that I must tell you, Alan, although I do require you to keep this to yourself. Little John knows all about this matter but no one else of our company..."

He checked that there was no one in earshot and continued. "As you know, I have no orders to harm, by poison or any other means, the Regent of Burgundy. But that does not mean that I plan to remain aloof from the power plays of this important region. I spoke with the king before our departure from Outremer about the situation here, and how it might affect the balance of power in his own Angevin lands and in Normandy, too, and what I said to that greedy fool Otto was, in fact, substantially true."

He took a small sip of wine.

"War is coming between King Philip and King Richard – there was too much bad blood between them on the Great Pilgrimage, too much mistrust and hatred – and the conflict between them will be played out on this side of the Channel – in Normandy, and Anjou, Maine and Touraine.

"The Duchy of Burgundy will almost certainly side with France, solemn undertakings have already been made between the two rulers, and this will give Philip a huge advantage in the south in the war. We also know Richard's treacherous brother Prince John is already intriguing with Philip in the north, and in Normandy, so Richard has asked me to do whatever I can while in Burgundy to weaken the power of the Duchy."

"What will you do?" I asked. "Not black murder, I beg you."

"I'm not going assassinate anyone," said Robin. "I'm just going do what I've done my whole life. I shall make some trouble."

He grinned at me like a pirate. And I felt relieved. But only partially relieved. Robin's troublemaking, I knew from experience, could involve a great deal of unpleasantness, pain and the shedding of innocent blood.

My lord continued, still speaking quietly. "I'm going to speak with someone here, in this hall, in a little while, and I need you to keep watch over us both; but more importantly to keep your mouth shut about the matter. The meeting I'm about to have never took place, understand?"

I said I did but, in truth, I was more than a little confused. How had Robin arranged to have a meeting here? We had spoken to nobody except the abbey's *hospitarius* and Sergeant Etienne since we'd been in Dijon.

As he so often did, Robin read my thoughts. "I knew I'd be in Dijon at around this time. I'll admit it now," he said. "I always planned to be here in this week and I arranged the meeting at this time and in this place by a local messenger from Lyon. But ask no questions now, Alan, take yourself off, but keep a close guard over us both. Here he comes!"

I got up and left Robin at the long table amid the remains of our humble meal, going over to stand by a pillar by the far side of the refectory, and leaning against it casually, with one hand on my sword hilt. As I watched, a young nobleman stepped into the low, dimly lit stone room, and peered about, clearly seeking Robin. Since we had been the only folk eating at the time, apart from a table of two young monks at the far side of the space, it did not take long to spot my lord. I observed the newcomer as he came to our table and Robin rose politely to greet him.

He was a slim man of about nineteen years, clearly nobly born judging by the rich furs on the collar of his mantel and the gold-chased handles of his arming sword and belt dagger. But he was also curiously diffident, shy and almost cowering in his stance, as if unsure if he would receive praise or a curse; a blow or a caress. He reminded me of a stray cat I had befriended in the Holy Land while recuperating from a wound in Acre; the animal had been preternaturally timid, starting at the slightest sound and fleeing when approached even by the kindest souls, as if at any moment one of them might boot it in the ribs or swipe it with a broom.

But the most distinguishing feature of this nervous young lordling was his complete absence of a chin. His face below his plump lower lip dropped away and merged in a smooth swoop directly into his skinny neck and prominent Adam's apple. It gave him an odd, feeble-minded look, as if the absence of prominent facial bones made him somehow more stupid.

Robin spoke to the chinless young nobleman for a good hour and a half. And, at one point, I saw my lord remove a parchment document from inside his jerkin, spread it out on the table and indicate something on it to the young man. From the brief glimpse I caught, it looked like a family tree, a patent of nobility of the kind used by lawyers to prove a tricky inheritance. Then Robin took the parchment back and tucked it away again. After a long conversation, none of which I could hear, and which was quite undisturbed, this youngster got to his feet, clasped hands with Robin, evidently having agreed the matter, and left the refectory.

When he had gone, I returned to my lord.

"Who was that fellow?" I said. "And where has he left his chin?"

Robin laughed and poured wine. "Don't be disrespectful, Alan. That young man may one day be a great prince in these parts."

"So who is he?" I persisted.

"This is to be kept a secret, yes?"

I nodded.

"His name is Stephen of Auxonne and he maintains that he, and not our fine new friend Otto, is the rightful Count of Burgundy."

CHAPTER FOUR

We sent word the next morning to the court of the regent that we desired a private audience with Eudes as soon as possible, and while we waited in the abbey for an answer, Robin disappeared on some mysterious business of his own and I was left to kick my heels in the empty cloister.

So after an hour or so of mind-numbing boredom, I decided to stretch my legs and go for a walk about the town. I headed east through the narrow lanes and found the market square and, after wandering around examining the range of fruits and vegetables on offer, after inspecting several stalls of pots and pans, and feeling the quality of the fine cloths laid out for sale to passing townspeople, I felt a growing void in my belly, so I began looking for something to eat for dinner.

I soon found a tavern next to a row of buildings west of the castle on the edge of the main square. I sat down on a bench at a long table on the stone terrace outside the entrance, my seat partly shaded from the sun by a large curling vine on a trellis above, and I was pleased to see that, as well as selling local wine and ale, the tavern also boasted a cook-shop.

I made myself comfortable and gave my order, and I was very soon sipping a large cup of excellent red, and munching a mutton pasty, with a dollop of a sharp local mustard on the side of my platter to give it some extra zest. I let out a long breath and felt my shoulders finally droop.

It was good to be alone and at my ease, just for an hour or two, for we had been riding hard almost every day for the past few weeks and, although the wounds I had taken in battle in Spain some months past were healed, I felt a deep sense of soul-tiredness, a bone-deep ache, which would not be assuaged until I was home in my manor at Westbury.

I was musing on the many charms of my part of Nottinghamshire in the springtime, my eyes half-closed, my long legs stretched out in front of me, when I became aware of a shadow across my face and realized that someone was now standing in front of me blocking out all the sunlight.

"Do you sleep well in our tavern, messire?" said a voice. "Shall I fetch you a warm blanket or two and perhaps a soft feather pillow?"

I pulled in my legs and sat up straight on the bench, and found myself gazing up at a pretty girl with a jug in her hand.

"Whu-ha?" I said, wiping a trickle of drool from the corner of my mouth with the back of my hand. I realized I had indeed been asleep – and blamed my tiredness, the food, the wine and the warm May sunshine.

"I thought you might enjoy another cup of our local red," she said. "It comes from the patron's own vineyard down on the Côte."

I sat up and tried to gather a tiny shred of dignity. "That would be all right," I said. "I mean, thank you, yes, I *would* like some more wine."

She refilled my cup and I watched her discreetly. I had been wrong in my first impression – the girl was not pretty. She was, in truth, quite lovely. Simply wondrous to look at. Her straight auburn hair, shot-through with strands of gold, was parted in the middle and two plaits hung down on either side of her long face. It was a beautiful face, if rather melancholy; with fine cheekbones, eyes dark and liquid as rock oil but shining with mischief. Her skin glowed in the sunlight; she bore an intriguing dimple on her right cheek that winked at me when she smiled.

She was smiling now.

"You must be a visitor to our town," she said. "I would surely remember seeing such a handsome young man, had we met before."

Could she actually be flirting with me?

"It is true. I am a traveller far from my home," I said, aiming to sound mysterious and deeply exotic. "Newly come to beautiful Dijon."

"You are a Norman, if I may ask?"

"I'm an Englishman," I said, "returning to my country from the Holy Land where I battled the fierce Saracens on behalf of my lord Richard of England." I thought that struck a properly impressive note.

"We are honoured to have you in Dijon, my lord."

She smiled again, took my empty plate and went back inside the tavern before I could correct her misunderstanding that I was a nobleman.

She came back a moment later with a dish of apple pie.

"These apples are from my own family's orchard," she said. "They are the best in all Burgundy." She put the laden platter down in front of me, and adding a huge spoonful of thick yellow cream from a small tub.

I made a show of tasting the pie while she watched me, and found that was perfectly all right – but no better than some I'd had in England. Nevertheless, I praised the dish inordinately and asked the whereabouts of the much-blessed orchard was that produced such wondrous fruit.

"I live with my mother outside the village of Fontaine, a few miles north of Dijon," she said, smiling even more beguilingly at me. "We are free folk – not serfs – and have a little land that we rent from our lord, and an orchard, a dozen pigs, too, but it is not enough for us both to live on. So I come in to Dijon and serve the tavern customers for Gregoire."

"Who's this Gregoire who cruelly forces you to serve him?" I asked. "Your husband? Your betrothed? Your lover, perhaps?"

She laughed then. "No, my lord. Alas, I have none of those. He is my uncle, my mother's brother, who owns this very establishment. This place is Gregoire's tavern. You spoke with him earlier, no?"

I vaguely remembered giving my order to a small, ogreish fellow of middle years. That moment, I heard an angry roar from inside the tavern: "Jacqueline! Stop bothering the fine gentlemen; let him eat his pie. Come tend to the spit – the capon is burning!"

"I must go," said the girl.

Jacqueline, I thought, *a lovely name for a lovely girl!*

"If I were to take a ride out to this place, this Fontaine, say tomorrow morning, perhaps I might set eyes on this amazing orchard. And perhaps you might be kind enough to show me the marvelous trees that bring forth such sweet and tender apples."

"If you were to do that, my lord, you should have some of your stout men-at-arms accompany you there," said Jacqueline. "Or your priest. For your soul as well as your body would be at risk on the journey. They say all the deep woods north of Dijon are infested with wicked faeries. The grey riders, we call them in these parts, and they come from the otherworld to claim our souls. Many a girl has been snatched away by the grey riders, never to be seen again, taken, they say, to a mysterious land below the surface of the world. Boys, too. Those faeries are not fussy!"

"I'm not afraid of faeries," I said, lifting my chin. "Or these grey riders or any kind of fell inhuman creature – grey, pink or green."

I was, in fact, not being entirely truthful. But she was so beautiful that I hope I may be forgiven. Every Christian soul knows the danger of faeries. They are said to be child-stealers and players of cruel tricks on unwary travellers, who often lead honest pilgrims astray, sometimes to their doom. I had taken in the tales of these otherworldly lords and ladies – or, as they were sometimes called, or the hidden folk – with my mother's breast milk. Some people say that the hidden folk did not truly exist; that they were no more that silly stories made up to frighten naughty children and village simpletons – Robin was one such, and my lord has expounded at length on the subject to me several times before – but any man or woman who has ever been alone in a deep wood at midnight, or at a crossroads at twilight, the witching hour, will have sensed them. You can feel that something is out there, watching you, just beyond sight. You feel the hairs on the back of your neck rise in warning.

"Yet you travel there to your home in Fontaine, quite regularly I would imagine, unmolested by these mischievous creatures," I said. "Do you have some kind of magic charm to protect you against their malice?"

"Indeed, I do," she said. She reached into the top of her dress and pulled out a small bronze disc that hung from a thread around her neck.

"This is an image of Saint Christopher," she said, holding it under my nose. "He is the saint who protects all travellers and this very medal has also been blessed by the bishop of Dijon himself. The saint always guards me on the roads. But even if that were not enough, I know all the secret ways and paths around town, too. The faeries will never catch me!"

I tried to look only at the holy medal but found myself a distracted when she tucked it away again between her perfect milk-white breasts.

"Jacqueline – the capon, it burns!" The ogre was still yelling.

"Well, turn the spit then, *imbécile*," shouted my new friend.

To me, she said: "However, I shall *not* be at Fontaine tomorrow. I shall be here, worst luck, all day tomorrow and the next day. I shall not return to my village and my mother until Sunday Mass at the earliest."

"Perhaps I shall come *here* to see you tomorrow," I said.

"Just as you desire, my lord," said Jacqueline, with another of her lovely smiles. "We serve a very nice fresh fish stew tomorrow – since it is Friday." Then she turned and disappeared inside the tavern.

As I rummaged in my purse to leave her a coin or two, it occurred to me that, for the second time, I had not told her that

I was no lord. My clothes, even after the rigours of several weeks' hard travel were still obviously of very fine quality, even lordly quality. And, if I was honest, I did not hate being mistaken for a powerful man by a lovely girl. There would be plenty of time to tell her the truth the next time we spoke.

"There you are, Alan!" said Robin. "This is where you've been lurking. You've been swilling wine all day in this shady spot, have you?"

I looked up and saw that my lord had found me.

"I have been eating, too," I said. "It has a cook-shop at the back."

"And is the food as delightful as the one who serves it?" he asked.

"It is adequate," I said grumpily, "no more than that."

The court of Lord Eudes, Regent of Burgundy, was far more lavish than the corresponding set-up of Count Otto, on the far side of the great river.

Robin and I, after a hasty wash and brush up in the abbey were standing now in the hall of Lord Eudes not fifty yards from Gregoire's tavern and cook-shop as the crow flies but a world away in terms of wealth and splendour. The stone walls were hung with brightly coloured hangings, beautifully woven and embroidered with gold and silver threads and depicting familiar scenes from the Bible – here was King Solomon delivering justice over a naked baby; there was Jacob wrestling with the Angel of the Lord. I noted idly that Jacob's grip was quite wrong – my friend Hanno would not approve at all – no wonder the Patriarch had dislocated his own hip during that famous match.

The whole vast space was lit by a dozen free-standing golden candelabras, each highly polished and set with a score of sweet-smelling beeswax candles, even though it was only the middle of the afternoon, several hours before sunset – this was, as far as I was concerned, the very height of extravagance. One thing was clear; the Duchy was rich.

The regent himself, the lean, elegant young man who took

the place of his absent father, sat in a gilt-covered throne at the far end of the hall, an enormous, high-backed chair, flanked by two smaller empty ones, which make his figure seem somehow more imposing, almost regal.

We made our bows and a silk-clad herald announced my lord by name and title. Then Robin stepped forward, saying: "I bring greetings, your grace, and blessings from your honoured father, and a letter which he personally entrusted to me in the port of Jaffa..."

This was the very first I had heard about a letter, but Robin was full of surprises that spring. It crossed my mind that Robin might easily have confected this missive himself; the duke would ordinarily use a number of scribes and clerics for his everyday letter writing – even if he could actually make out the ABCs by himself – and so the hand need not be recognisably the duke's own. And Robin had spent much of the year before in or around the great man's company and would be able to throw in some of the man's typical habits of speech without too much difficulty.

Then I saw a man standing in the shadows of the hall, to one side, and a cold shiver ran down my spine. All my instincts warned of danger. It was the white-clad old monk, the same fellow who had been at Dole when we met the Count of Burgundy as prisoners of the Green Knight.

Robin was cheerfully making his report of the conduct of the war in the Holy Land, although I knew that his news must be sorely out of date, since we had spent much of the past six months in various locations around the Mediterranean, far from the more recent battlegrounds in Outremer. However, the regent did not seem to mind that our news was so stale. He listened attentively to Robin, then said: "You are welcome in my realm, Lord Locksley, for as long as you care to remain. Do you require my steward to provide your men with accommodation and food?"

"I do not, your grace," said Robin. "I am unaccompanied at present but for a single man-at-arms. However, I do seek a great boon from your grace: an audience with you, alone, and at your very first convenience."

With a deep sense of foreboding, I saw the white monk gliding smoothly forward towards the regent. I watched him stop short of the throne, lean in and whisper in the ear of a richly dressed older man, a courtier who was, perhaps, the steward the regent had just mentioned. The middle-aged courtier then approached the regent and spoke quietly to him. Lord Eudes nodded. And his expression completely changed.

"You wish to meet with me alone, yes? You have perhaps some more of this sad, out-of-date news from Outremer to impart to me?" said the regent. He was a young man, no more than a few years senior me, yet he already had a dignity about him that belied his lack of grey hairs.

"What could you wish to tell me in private, my lord, I wonder? Perhaps you have nothing to *say* to me but rather something to *do*."

The regent rose swiftly to his feet: "Guards, seize hold of that Englishman! Now! And his man-at-arms, too. Hold them both fast!"

Hands grabbed my arms and shoulders; I saw that Robin too had been seized. I twisted madly in their grip but a guard dropped a thick, muscled arm over my throat and began to squeeze. I stopped struggling.

"I have just been informed that you, Robert of Locksley, are in truth no more than a cowardly assassin," said the regent. "Sent here by the Count of Burgundy to murder me. What say you to this grave charge?"

"I say this – it is a God-damned fucking lie!" said Robin. Despite his loud and most intemperate language, I knew my lord was as icily in control as always when in danger. "And I challenge the God-damned liar, if he has enough courage, to speak this outrageous falsehood to my face."

The regent looked at the courtier, who looked at the monk.

"Speak up, Prior Gui," said Eudes. "Let us hear you clearly."

The monk shrugged and stepped out from the crush of

courtiers. His step was firm, full of resolve and the people moved apart as he advanced.

The monk bowed low to the regent: "Your grace, I cannot swear before Almighty God that this Englishman is an assassin – but I strongly suspect he is one of that accursed breed. All I can say is that I saw him, two days ago, in Dole, at the court of the Count of Burgundy, where I was myself petitioning for a grant of lands on that side of the Saone for the use of my order. This man was the prisoner of Raoul, Seigneur de Beaune-du-Bois, and he miraculously revealed, in a most flamboyant fashion, that he carried an assassin's blade hidden inside his right sleeve.

"Now I see him here this day, mysteriously set at liberty by his captors, in the court of the Count of Burgundy's most bitter rival. I refer to your court, sire, here in Dijon. I am only a humble servant of God – but I am no man's fool. He has clearly made a compact with Count Otto to secure his freedom. And what could he have traded for his freedom, I ask myself? He is very rich in gold, or so I have been informed, and yet there has not been enough time for him to arrange a suitable ransom to be paid. Nevertheless, he now stands in your realm, a free man. How could that be, I ask myself? And my best answer, the simplest answer is that he promised Count Otto that he would murder you – and that was the price of his freedom. It is mere conjecture, your grace, of course, but proving here and now whether he means you harm, should be simple enough."

The regent frowned.

"It would be easy to prove he means me harm? How so?"

"Why, sire, simplicity itself," said the monk, "If he intends murder, he'll have the same assassin's blade hidden in his right sleeve."

We are doomed, I thought. *Robin and I are both dead men.*

"Strip his sleeve," said the regent. "The right one."

The knot of men-at-arms around Robin wrestled with his fine silk jerkin for a moment and revealed Robin's bare, sun-bronzed forearm. There was no knife, no leather sheath; no sign of a weapon at all on my lord – save, of course, for the long sword handing openly by his side.

"Let me see the other arm." The regent was now craning forward. Robin's left limb, too, was entirely without a blade.

Oh, dear God, I prayed, *let them not search in my right boot.* For, out of habit, I carried in there that day my own *misericorde*, a long, slim, needle-pointed iron blade designed precisely for the art of silent murder.

They did not think to search me, thank God.

"Release them both," said Eudes, sitting back down heavily on his throne. "Apologies, my lord, for the rough handling by my men. But it is hardly unknown in Burgundy for an assassin to be sent to remove a rival. One can sometimes be too cautious."

Robin said nothing. He merely adjusted his clothing but I could tell he was extremely angry. His intense grey eyes were shining like wet steel. "The welcome in your court is not what I would have expected of a prince of your stature," he said coldly.

"I have apologised to you, have I not," cried Lord Eudes. "You there, you, the monk. I believe you now owe my lord of Locksley a sincere and handsome apology for accusing him wrongly of plotting my murder. You will beg his pardon now."

Prior Gui shrugged. "I spoke only what I knew to be true," he said. "Perhaps he meant to poison you instead, your grace, or strangle you: a bare arm does not guarantee a blameless soul."

Robin gave the monk a chilling glance. I thought: *That man is now marked for death. My lord will not forgive today's indignities.*

"The prior of Cîteaux is too churlish to apologise, I see," said Eudes coldly. "Nevertheless I am minded to refuse you a private audience at this time. Is there anything further you require from me, Lord Locksley?"

"No, your grace," said Robin, recovering his smile at last. "Only your permission to remain here in Dijon until my followers and baggage catch up with me; then we shall leave your realm and return to England."

"Do you expect them here soon?" asked Eudes, frowning. I got the distinct impression he hoped Robin would be quitting his realm without delay. He was deeply embarrassed, it was clear, by the false accusation.

"A week or two, probably no more than that," said Robin.

Lord Eudes grunted and flapped a hand to indicate our dismissal.

An hour or so later, Robin and I were back in the refectory, supping the monks' excellent bean soup and sitting in gloomy silence.

"Will his refusal to see you alone affect your plans, lord?"

"Perhaps," replied Robin. "It is something of a setback, certainly. Yet I still mean to act. I promised Richard I'd do what I could here."

"Do you wish me to take a message to Little John?"

"He knows where I am. And he'll join us soon enough."

In my cot later that night in the abbey dormitory, I pondered Robin's words: that Little John knew where he was. My lord had obviously made intricate plans for his operations in Burgundy. I only wished that he would share them with me. Then I thought longingly of Jacqueline for a while and, with her lovely face in my mind, fell asleep.

CHAPTER FIVE

Robin disappeared once again on his own business the next morning and, feeling the need to tend to my soul, I attended a Mass for a dead man I did not know in the little church of Saint Philibert's just a dozen yards from the abbey precincts. I sent up a tearful prayer for the soul of Ricky, and then, feeling refreshed and at peace with God, I bathed in the abbey wash-house, sponged my clothes, combed my hair and went off with a lighter heart to dine in Dijon town.

The fish was obviously very popular at Gregoire's and the dozen or so shaded tables outside the cook-shop were all full this Friday noon with exuberant diners, all except for one small round table at the edge of the terrace, which I gratefully occupied.

Jacqueline gave me a quick, heartbreaking smile when she saw me – and mouthed a greeting – and when I had sat down, without asking my preference, she brought me a jug of red wine and a basket of fresh bread and butter and, a little later, the famous house stew made from river fish.

She was busy that day, running in and out of the tavern to the cries from her ogre-uncle within, and bearing bowls of steaming fish to the large clientele. And, although I ate up my meal as slowly as possible – it went down well enough but there were too many little bones for my taste – and lingered over my wine, she simply didn't have time to speak to me.

Our only communication was when she said, breathlessly,

"You're here again, my lord, you must really enjoy our plain Dijonnais fare," before rushing off to accommodate an impatient customer who was loudly banging the table with his bone knife handle.

I managed to shout out, "I come for the view, not for the food," to her departing back, but I don't believe she fully appreciated my wit.

It was no good. I had long finished my fish stew, and there was a knot of hungry townsmen and women standing beside the terrace waiting to eat, and who were glaring at me sitting at the table with increasing impatience. I left a pile of silver deniers by my dirty plates and stood up. Jacqueline swept in, scooped up the coins, gave me a soul-melting smile of thanks, her dimple all but blowing me a kiss, and whisked away to deal with some emergency of Gregoire's in the dark depths of the kitchen.

On my slow, disappointed walk back to the abbey, I realised it would be far better to come back to the tavern at a quieter time, in the evening, perhaps, when we might be able to talk quietly and without constant interruptions. Then I might be able to tell her how she made me feel. I realised that to progress in the relationship, I needed her to see me as more than a customer, more than a man who looked to her for his food.

So when I returned to the abbey precincts, I dug out my new vielle from my few belongings, and spent a little while tuning its strings in the cloister. It was a fine instrument, which had cost me a good deal of silver to purchase in Marseilles. Then I set out to compose, just for her, a new love song or *canso*. I plucked a simple chord on the vielle and sang:

> "She wakes delight in me once more
> That's too long lain asleep,"

I strummed a few more idle notes, thinking furiously...

> "Unearthing stirrings buried deep
> She does my heart restore."

It's working, I thought with a sense of relief. *I still have the power to summon the muse.* I was very pleased with that last line. So I went on...

"A love that grows with each new breath
Fresh hope that blossoms sweet

I'll find my Heaven when we meet
My hell her frown, her scorn my death."

I wondered whether "death" was perhaps a bit too strong – would her scorn really mean my death? Hmm. No. But it *was* only a love song. Then I heard the sound of slow, regular hand-clapping and turned to see my lord, leaning casually against a pillar in the corner of the cloister.

"That's very pretty, Alan," he said. "It sounds as if you are in love once again. May I enquire who the object of your affections is?"

"Oh, nobody in particular," I lied. "Just some imaginary lady." For some reason I didn't wish to speak to my lord about my true feelings.

"Is that so?" said Robin. "Well, I suppose we are all entitled to our secrets. But tomorrow morning, if you are not too busy consorting with your new imaginary lover, I should like you to run an errand for me."

"As you command, my lord," I said.

He nodded, walked out of the cloister and left me with my muse.

After breakfast the next day, Robin took my arm and drew me aside, into a quiet corner: "I want you to go to a big house in the north of the town." He then described exactly where this grand building was located.

"Go discreetly. Ensure that you are not followed. I know you can do this, Alan. When you get to the door of the house ask to speak only to its master – he is named Amadeus of Montfaucon, Lord Montbéliard – and you are to give him this message from me. Say to him these exact words: 'Jerusalem is agreed, and the Jaffa fief shall be granted. The time to strike is two days after the Kalends of June.' Now, Alan, repeat all that to me."

I did so.

Half an hour later, I found myself knocking at the door of a large dwelling with an iron-studded door, clearly the residence of someone of consequence. After a moment or two, an elderly servant was showing me into a parlour where an man of, perhaps, sixty years was seated by a window in a shaft of sunlight, reading from a leather-bound prayer book. He looked very familiar to me, although at the same time I was certain I had not met him before. I delivered my message. He listened in silence.

"Two days after the Kalends?" he said. "That is much earlier than I had expected. That does not give me much time to prepare all my people. Are you sure your master insisted on that date?"

I said that I was, wondering who he needed to prepare and for what.

"I suppose it must be done then. Even in half the time I require to ready the men. The things we do for our family, eh?"

I had no idea what he was talking about. But with the bright sunlight catching his lined, old face, I suddenly realized why his features were so oddly familiar. He looked just like the old monk who had denounced Robin as an assassin in the regent's court the day before – Prior Gui.

That was very strange. Could they be closely related in some manner? Siblings perhaps? They were a similar age. Cousins?

"Tell me, young fellow, what do your generation say about a man's loyalty to his lord? Do they esteem it? Is it considered a virtue?"

It seemed rather an odd question to ask a stranger, a lowly servant who was merely delivering a message yet I still attempted to answer it.

"I cannot speak for all younger folk," I said, "but for me it is the paramount virtue. I esteem it greatly. I made an oath of loyalty to my lord and I shall never break it. I see it as a binding promise for a man's life."

"Thank you, young man," said Amadeus of Montbéliard, "that is most illuminating. You may tell my lord of Locksley that I agree to all his terms and to the date when action will commence." The old man made a little gesture of farewell and a servant ushered me towards the door.

As I walked back towards the abbey, I thought about the unusual meeting. I had done my part and delivered Robin's message but I was none the wiser about what it meant. What was my lord planning with this man? Was it significant that Lord Montbéliard resembled the monk who had twice disrupted our audiences with the lords of the two Burgundies?

I had no idea.

I did not go straight to the abbey to deliver my message. It did not seem to me to be a very urgent one, only confirming that the old man acceded to Robin's secret plans. Instead, since it was about the hour of noon, I stopped to take my dinner once more at my now regular venue in Dijon – Gregoire's cook-shop and tavern.

Once again the place was busy and Jacqueline was bustling around serving her many hungry customers, but she smiled warmly at me and exchanged a few pleasantries, asking after my health, and showing me to an empty place at one of the long communal tables. She looked lovelier than ever that sunny May day, the light catching the golden strands of her hair, her dress hitched up with a belt above her knees show her slim white legs as she dashed here and there. I watched in admiration for a while then I saw something that extinguished my joy like a pinched-out candle.

She was passing a series of plates to a fat merchant on the far side of the other big common table, bending over the board, when one of the other diners, a big hairy brute of an apprentice, reached a hand up under her dress and squeezed her naked bottom, evidently quite hard. She gave a little squeal of surprise and jumped away, and he said something stupid, a jest or crude comment of some kind, to his friend, another apprentice who was sitting opposite him at the table. They both cackled like geese.

I expected Jacqueline to remonstrate with the first apprentice, a dark oaf in a blue cap, for man-handling her in that fashion, at the very least a sharp word or two about minding their manners. But to my surprise she did no more than give them an angry look and carried on doing her work.

When Jacqueline returned a few moments later with a jug of red for the table, the second apprentice, a toad-faced young man with hair the colour of a Spanish orange, reached out and grabbed her right breast, saying something loudly about the enjoying the best "apples" in Dijon. Once again Jacqueline did nothing but brush the rude brute's hand away and scowl, before disappearing once again into the darkness of the tavern.

I got to my feet.

I sauntered over to where the two apprentices were sitting. They were at the end of the long table of about seven diners, on either side of the cluttered board. I smiled blandly as I approached but they paid no attention to me, talking quietly together across the table like a couple of conspiring cut-purses, their bent heads only a few inches apart.

I reached out both my arms and grasped them both around the backs of their heads; then with a hard surge, I smashed their foreheads together as forcefully as I could. Their two crowns met with a meaty thud. They reeled back, snarling and spitting and the fellow on the left started to get to his feet. I shoved him back down on to the bench, and said: "Let that teach you a lesson, boy. Let it be a lesson to both of you. You do *not* behave in that manner to a young maid. Keep your filthy paws to yourselves. Am I understood?"

Further down the table the merchant sniggered and pointed.

I jerked my head to the left, towards sweet Jacqueline, who

was now staring at me open mouthed. "She's under my personal protection, so treat her with all proper respect – or I shall make you pay for it."

Then I stepped back and let the two apprentices get a good, long look at me. I am a tall fellow and well-built, and solid in the chest and shoulder from many, many hours of sword practice and while I was of a similar age to these two boys, the scars of many a melee were visible on my scowling face and bare brown forearms. I projected an air of danger that was, in truth, entirely warranted. Yet I saw no reason to harm them further, so long as they accepted their punishment. I had made my point.

"If you wish to pursue this matter," I said, "I am staying at the abbey of Saint Benignus. Alternatively, I shall be dining over there for the next hour or so," I said indicating the other communal table.

"If you believe you require satisfaction from me, when I have eaten, I shall be happy to accommodate you – singly or both at once, I care not."

I was not wearing my long sword that day, but I had the *misericorde* in my boot – not that I wanted to spill Dijonnais blood. Robin and I were strangers in that town, and the law in a place always favours a local man.

They said nothing at all. They only glared at me – two angry faces, red as setting suns, but with their bodies still firmly seated at the table.

Jacqueline brought me my meal a few moments later, a big steaming pie made from rabbit, leek and fatty pork belly, and I thought I detected an air of genuine admiration, even of gratitude, in the way she neatly arranged the plate and a jug of wine and cup on the table in front of me.

"You are a good man, my lord," she whispered, her warm breath on my ear making me shiver from shoulder to shin, "and gallant for taking my part – but they are only big babies, Henrik the Tanner's lads – rough fellows but good-hearted. Do not trouble yourself with them, I beg you."

"I shall not trouble myself with them, so long as they do not trouble you – and so long as they respect your person!" I said this loudly. Every eye on the wide terrace was now on me, to see what foreign folly I might commit next. For an instant, I wished Hanno were with me or Little John or Robin. I dismissed the idea as cowardly. The apprentices looked across the space between us as if they wished to murder me with their eyes.

"Maybe I shall ride out to Fontaine tomorrow," I said, but with my eyes fixed on the furious pair at the other table, "and attend Holy Mass with you and your mother. Would you permit me that great pleasure?"

"Maybe," said Jacqueline. "Now eat up the pie while it's hot."

I did as she had instructed. While eating, out of the corner of my eye, I saw the two red-faced apprentices get slowly to their feet and slink away from the communal table, retreating like whipped dogs, going out into the busy square where they disappeared quickly from my view.

I relaxed, I admit. The rabbit pie was hot, and good, better than other dishes I'd had at Gregoire's, maybe because it was seasoned with victory.

I had another jug of wine, possibly unwisely, and sat for hours in the warm afternoon drinking and occasionally passing idle comments with Jacqueline, when her duties allowed her to speak to me.

I told her that I was a musician, a *trouvère* – one who composed or "found" his own love songs. I told her that I had written one especially for her, in her honour. She seemed utterly charmed by this.

"You must perform the song for me one day, my lord," she said.

"I shall," I promised, and asked her for yet another jug of her delicious wine, intending that she should sit with me while I sang it to her. It was too late now, I reflected, to tell her that I was no lord, nor even a landed knight. The moment had passed and surely it was just a harmless piece of nonsense, a little joke between us that we'd laugh about one day.

The new jug was brought out by Gregoire himself, which I found mildly irritating, for I was obliged to pass time with him from politeness.

When he finally let me be, I sat a little longer and drank, humming to myself, as the afternoon rolled on and the shadows began to lengthen. Where was my sweet girl? I wondered. Were they working her too hard? Perhaps I should have a quiet word with Gregoire. Jacqueline surely deserved a little rest from time to time from her labours. Eventually, I got unsteadily to my feet, and realised that it was now full dusk and the wine had taken its inevitable toll on my wits. I half-staggered into the candle-lit interior of the dim tavern looking for the girl – for it seemed a grand idea to me, in that rosy moment, for me to admit to Jacqueline that I loved her.

Women enjoy this sort of bold candour, I told myself – they like openness and honesty in affairs of the heart; besides, I truly *did* love her.

Instead of Jacqueline, I found Gregoire playing at dice with a stout old woman, a cook by the look of her scarlet cheeks and ample waistline.

"Where is Jacqu-, Jacqueline?" I mumbled. "The girl. The sweet young girl. My girl. I wish to have a speak with her ... I wish to speak with her about a matter of the im-most ut-port-ance. Or even, the utmost importance. Yes, it is an importance of the utmost."

"She's gone home," said Gregoire. "Long ago. Perhaps I could bring you something – a jug of cool spring water perhaps?"

"Gone ... home? Why? But ... I wish to speak with her."

"She has gone back to her village. It is Sunday tomorrow, the Lord's Day, and the tavern will be closed. Is there nothing *I* can fetch you?"

"It is no great matter," I said. "No matter at all." Just managing to keep my dignity intact, I turned in a wide, loose-limbed circle and strode out of the darkened tavern – and almost immediately tripped over a small stool unseen in the dark and crashed to the stone floor of the terrace.

Gregoire and the red-faced cook hauled me more or less upright and with many soothing words, they pointed me in the direction of the abbey of Saint Benignus, and I stumbled off calling out my thanks in the most effusive terms, telling them I would tell everyone in Nottinghamshire, all my many, many, many friends, to visit their cook-shop, if ever they found themselves in Dijon. Then it occurred to me – a brilliant notion – that I should practice singing the *canso* I had written for my Jacqueline, and very soon I was bowling along at a goodly speed, bawling aloud my finely crafted words of love, and occasionally bouncing hilariously off all the white plastered walls of the houses in the narrow streets of Dijon.

" . . . I'll find my Heaven when we meet . . ." I warbled, the tune echoing round me. A dog began barking further up the empty street.

"My hell her frown . . ." I told the dog, as I approached the chained animal, wagging an admonitory index finger.

"Her sco . . . orn . . . my . . . deeee . . . eath!"

I stopped. Suddenly. My blood running cold. Some atavistic fear had sharpened my senses. I became instantly almost sober – chilled and fearful. The dark street, less than fifty paces from the abbey, appeared to be empty of folk. The town had a curfew, Robin had told me, which meant that no honest man was supposed to be on the streets after nightfall, and there were watchmen to enforce the rule. Yet ahead of me in the blackness was a lump darker that the wall to which it was attached.

The lump detached itself from the wall and resolved into three human forms. They passed through a patch of moonlight, and I half-recognised the two brutish apprentices from the afternoon, and a third fellow, older, much tougher looking. All three of them were carrying heavy wooden clubs, the kind of weapon that could crack a man's skull with a single blow.

I pulled the *misericorde* from my boot and stood quite still.

The three forms came towards me, splitting up to fill the street.

"Time to teach *you* a lesson, you foreign dog," said one of the lads.

"Yes," said the other. "Dijon is *our* town; we do as we please here."

The older man said nothing at all – and to my fast sobering mind that made him the most dangerous of the three.

"You come at me with those nasty old clubs and at least some of you are going to die," I said. "Who will be first to taste my dagger?"

That stopped them.

There stood a few paces from me in the street, uncertain.

"It does not have go like this," I said, trying to sound as if I were in command of the situation. In truth, I felt sluggish and scared, and a little sick in my belly. Three against one: bad odds.

"If you stand aside and let me pass, nobody has to get hurt tonight," I said. "We go home, forget all about this, sleep safe in our beds. No one need bleed to death in the gutter. We can all continue to breathe."

I could sense the two apprentices wavering; in the faint glimmer of the moonlight I could see them glance uneasily at each other. One of them shrugged. The other shrugged back. They had agreement.

Then, without a single word, the older man attacked.

CHAPTER SIX

The man leapt in from my right, his club swinging fast at my head. I ducked under his arm and put my left fist into his side as his momentum carried him past me. He let out a cough of pain. The nearest apprentice swatted at me with his club and I felt its heavy wood graze my sleeve.

I stepped in close and thwacked him laterally very hard right across the mouth with the black iron shaft of my *misericorde*.

It was a thrusting weapon, a foot-long needle, essentially, which was triangular in cross section, used to stab through the iron links of a man's mail and into his soft body beneath; a weapon without a cutting edge normally used to dispatch the badly wounded on the battlefield or quietly murder the unsuspecting. But it was still a solid metal bar; and I smashed it full strength into his teeth and heard them crunch and splinter.

The apprentice dropped to his knees, mewling, spitting; but the older man was on me, swinging at me again, and his club whacked into my back and drove all the breath from my body in one painful whoosh.

I stumbled forward, staggering, keeping my feet but only with the greatest difficulty. I had been determined not to stab any of them with the *misericorde*, if I could help it. I truly did not want to kill this night, so long as I could preserve my own precious life.

The third man lifted his club over his head, double handed,

like an axe, and brought it down on me. I dropped just in time; half-collapsing under the blow, which caught my shoulder and mashed me further down. I lashed out with my right boot. The sideways kick chopped the legs from under the second apprentice just as he was about to swing at me again and he sat down hard on the cobbles, his weight half falling against me.

I caught a foul whiff of the tannery on his clothes, stale piss and rotting meat, and shoved him away with my left hand. His friend swung his club awkwardly, missed me and thumped into his companion across the meat of his right arm. I tried to rise but the heavy youth was now lying over my legs, groaning loudly like a pregnant sow about to farrow.

The second apprentice swung again, and I just got my head beneath the arc of the club's swing and, lunging desperately, I pinked him with the *misericorde* in the left calf muscle. He screamed in pain, and I struck out again and missed – I had drawn blood, my right hand was wet with it, but I was still on the ground, struggling to get up from my knees.

I booted the other fellow off my legs, started to rise and something hard crashed into my left shoulder, a club blow like a kick from a maddened horse, which knocked me back down to the cobbles again. I thought: *This is it. I'm a dead man. This will teach me to drink all day and dull my senses.* Another club thumped into my left side but this blow weaker than before.

I could hear other voices by now, someone shouting angrily in the Dijonnais accent, the round yellow glow of several approaching lanterns. The three club-wielding bastards around and above me instantly disappeared in a clatter of heavy boots. I was left lying, gasping for each painful breath, my back, my shoulder and my side throbbing in agony.

I found myself in a pool of dazzling candlelight, surrounded my half a dozen mail-clad legs, and a rough man's voice saying, "What's all this? Brawling in the streets after curfew, is it?" Even groggy and crippled as I was with pain, I immediately recognized it as a voice I had heard before.

The Dijon town watch saved my life, most probably. Three of them, grim men mailed and armed with swords, spears and lanterns, had chased off my three attackers into the deep night. And the man in charge of the night patrol was none other than Sergeant Etienne, the man we had met on our arrival. He remembered me, it seemed, and quizzed me about the attack.

"Footpads," I mumbled. "Ruffians after my purse, I'd guess."

"But why are *you* abroad after curfew," he said. "Did you not know about our night-time rule? Did the abbey monks not inform you?"

"I mistook the hour. I was running an errand for my lord, the earl," I said, stressing Robin's rank just a little, "and I set off home too late."

The sergeant sniffed: "This errand was to a tavern, was it?"

I shrugged – and immediately wished I had not. My body was a shrieking mass of bruises, scrapes, aches and pains but, thank God, nothing seemed to be broken. I would be entirely black and blue in the morning, nevertheless. "I am afraid I cannot discuss my lord's business, even with you, my good fellow."

The three watchmen were kind enough to escort me the last few yards to the abbey's front door, and to rouse the sleepy porter and make him admit me. I slipped Etienne a couple of coins from my purse, and thanked him again. I was in truth deeply grateful for his intervention.

"Thank you most kindly," said the grinning guard, tucking the coins away. "Remember: if you or your master need anything in Dijon, a guard or a guide, whatever you require, Sergeant Etienne, is your man!"

Robin was waiting for me in the refectory, with a face like white marble. I told him what had happened, all of it, and he listened to me in an unnervingly chilly silence until I simply ran out of words.

"So then, Alan," he said. "Let me be sure that I have this correctly. You decided, for some reason of your own, not to return to my side and deliver Lord Montbéliard's message but, instead, to go and drink wine with some tavern trollop. Then you offended two locals, assaulted them without provocation, engaged in a brawl with them in the street, during which you stabbed one, before being beaten to a bloody pulp, being apprehended by the watch and brought home in disgrace. Have I got it?"

When he put it like that I felt like the world's biggest idiot.

"I did not think the message from Lord Montbéliard was important. He was only confirming he would do whatever it was you wanted. I did not think, my lord..."

"No, you did *not* think. You didn't think at all. I've already spoken to you before about your excessive drinking. Now, I believe I have heard enough from you for one night. Do you require any treatment? Shall I summon the master of the abbey infirmary to come and look you over?"

"No, my lord, I'll be all right after a good night's sleep. It's just some bruising. A few cuts and scrapes..."

Robin cut me off. I had not seen him as angry as this for a long while. "Then go to bed, Alan. And stay there. I do not wish to set eyes on you for at least a day or two. See if you can stay out of trouble that long."

The next morning I was stiff as a fence post and covered across the back and shoulders and arms in dark purple welts. But I knew I had been lucky – no bones had been smashed and while it hurt a great deal to move about, I *could* move. I lay in my lonely cot in the empty dormitory, long into the sunny morning, alternately seething with injustice at the way my lord had spoken to me and wallowing in self-pity at my throbbing hurts.

I decided to get up. It was too late for Mass that Sunday morning but, if Robin did not require me, as he claimed, I would go for a short ride up to the village of Fontaine and see if I could find Jacqueline. She, at least, would be pleased to see me – had I not stood up for her honour in the tavern, and suffered greatly for it?

I thought I might ask her to go for a walk with me – she

could show me her apple orchard, and in some shady spot we might lie down together and she could massage my bruises with sweet oil.

So I hauled myself from my bed, washed and dressed myself. I packed my vielle in its wooden travelling box – perhaps, I thought, there would be time for some music. I could play her my beautiful new *canso* "She wakes delight" and astound her with my musical prowess.

I also strapped on my sword for the first time since I had come to Dijon. If I saw those apprentices and their fearsome friend, I'd not shrink this time from chopping them down – and to hell with the consequences.

I found Ghost in the abbey stables, saddled him and, no more than half hour later, I was riding out the north gate of the town, with the May sun warming my bruised back and a stiff breeze ruffling my blond hair.

The town guards at the gate set me on the road to the village of Fontaine, which, they told me was also the same main road that ran all the way up to Paris – it was not, alas, my good friend Sergeant Etienne who directed me onwards but one of his comrades – and this fellow told me that it was only a few miles to the charming village that had grown up around the old castle on a hill there.

Once outside the walls of Dijon, I spurred Ghost into a brisk canter and despite the initial discomfort to my own knocked about body, my horse and I were soon flying along merrily on a wide road through neat market gardens and small fields of crops – onions and leeks, mostly.

After a mile or two, I eased the pace, and allowed Ghost to walk while I contemplated my charmingly rustic surroundings. On either side of the arrow-straight main road, the wild countryside had by now closed in. The well-tended gardens and fields of near Dijon had given way to woodland, the trees thick and dark, the undergrowth dense. It felt somehow a little colder out here, away from civilization, despite the warmth of the day. And at one point, on the empty road, I thought I caught a sudden movement out of the corner of my eye and reined in. I peered deep into the deep forest to see what had drawn my attention.

I could see nothing. Was there someone there? An enemy? An apprentice? I had been ambushed only the night before for lack of wariness, and had the bruises to prove it, and I would say probably that my senses were heightened that day to a pitch beyond the normal range.

In this nervous, battered state, I thought I saw a strange shape, a man-like form, very graceful, moving behind a thick screen of trees.

I called out: "Who goes there?" but there was no reply. "Show yourself!" I shouted, my hand suddenly resting on my sword hilt.

I found I was panting, my heart beating like a battle drum.

I stared into the dimness of the thick trees and every click and scrape of one branch against another, moved only by the wind, now seemed impossibly loud. Every rustle of the leaves bore a trace of hidden malice. I could not help but think of Jacqueline's warning words – that faeries haunted the woods; that she needed the protection of a saint to pass here.

"I am not afraid of you – forest spirits, hidden folk ... whoever you may be!" I said loudly, hand still clutching my hilt. "Leave me in peace, and I shall leave you be as well. Else it will be all the worse for you!"

There was no reply; just the rustle and creak of branches in the wind. After a while, I released my sword and gathered up the reins, and walking Ghost deliberately slowly, I moved forward on the deserted road; the gentle slopping of my mount's hooves on the muddy track eerily loud.

As we rode away from that fell, faerie-haunted place, I thought I heard a cackle of demonic laughter somewhere far away to the right – but, then again, it could just have been the wild cry of some beast or a bird. I had no desire to investigate further. I urged Ghost into a trot, then into a canter and quit that awful place as fast as my dignity would allow.

Within the hour Ghost and I began to climb a small hill and I could see at the summit the stone walls and square tower of the castle of Fontaine.

I had recovered my courage from the brief fright on the woods by then and resolved not to mention the incident to any one – mainly for fear of ridicule. I had been frightened by my own shadow, most shamefully, and this wasn't something I wished to make known. I turned my thoughts instead to my lovely Jacqueline, her face, her form, her wondrous smile, as the walls of old castle of Fontaine loomed up before me. It was a fine fortress, yet it also looked as if it might be a comfortable home as well. But I avoided it. I had no plans to pay a visit to its seigneur, nor did I expect he would make me welcome if I did. I was a humble man-at-arms, in those days, despite what I had foolishly led my sweet Jacqueline to believe. Oh, my love, I thought, how I wish I could provide you with a fine castle such as this, and lands to match.

One day, perhaps, if God so blessed me. But first I had to find the girl. I did not know this village, nor any of its inhabitants save her. So I decided to go to the house of God and beg the local priest in to direct me.

I found the priest of Fontaine at the very door of his large church, which was dedicated to a holy man I was unfamiliar with called Saint Ambrosinien. It was a little before midday by then and the Sunday Mass had just ended. The small, middle-aged, kindly looking priest was standing in the doorway speaking to each of the members of his congregation as they departed, clasping their hands and blessing them.

I kept well back, tying Ghost to a convenient tree, finding a perch for myself on the low wall that surrounded the churchyard and waiting patiently. I watched as the large, loquacious congregation came filing out, one after the other, chatting happily to their friends and neighbours. And it occurred to me that it would be most amusing to greet Jacqueline as she came from the church door, to surprise her with my presence.

I thought about what I would say to her – some particularly clever remark, perhaps, about her having washed away all her previous sins at Mass, and perhaps being ready – ha-ha! – to contemplate some more.

Or maybe I'd simply begin singing to her, rather than speaking; yes, that would be much better – she'd said she would like to hear my *canso*, and I would oblige. Singing words of love I had written in front of her neighbours would surely make her blush, which would be charming...

I jumped from the wall; the last member of the congregation had gone, and the priest was in the act of locking the door with a huge key.

Where was Jacqueline?

I walked over to the priest and waylaid him as he began walking down the brick path to the churchyard gate.

"Father, forgive my sudden intrusion: but do you know a girl of this parish called Jacqueline?" I asked. "A very pretty girl, in the full bloom of her youth – with auburn hair and fine dark eyes?"

The priest smiled knowingly at me. "Naturally, my son. She's the jewel of Fontaine. The young men always ask after that one."

"Do you know where she is? Did she not attend Mass with the rest of the village?"

"No, my son. I think she is now in Dijon, that big town down the hill yonder. She has an uncle with a tavern there, I believe."

"Yes, Gregoire. He told me that she had come to Fontaine yester-eve. She told me herself she would be at Mass here today."

"That is passing strange," said the priest, scratching his tonsured head. "She was not in my church this morning. I am sure of it. I hope nothing – no, we must not rush to conclusions. Let us go to her mother Yvette, she'll surely know where she is. Come with me, young man."

The man of God and I found Jacqueline's mother in a cottage on the edge of the village, a mean construction of wattle and daub with a sagging turf roof. No wonder, I thought, looking at her home, Jacqueline choses to work with her uncle. She couldn't have much of a life here.

"She's supposed to be with me today," said Yvette, blinking stupidly up at me. "I need her to help me geld all the piglets. Oh, that good-for-nothing girl – she's probably dallying with the boys again. Or maybe she stopped on the way home to pick wild cherries or something similar."

I frowned. I didn't like the idea that she might be dallying.

"Has she done this before?" I asked. "Gone missing?"

The woman slowly shook her head. "But she's a silly, flighty girl, head in the clouds, and with no consideration for her poor old Mama. Now, who will help me with the pigs today?"

I said I would help. It seemed to me that earning merit with her mad old mother might stand me in good stead with my beloved.

So I stripped off my fine town clothes and dressed only in my braies, I helped the old woman corral, isolate and castrate half a dozen male piglets from the latest litter, animals who were only a week or two old.

It was a bloody, unpleasant job, and the squealing stayed rooted in my mind long afterwards. Old Yvette commented often on my badly bruised body and when we were done with the piglets, and I had washed thoroughly in freezing water from her well, she rubbed a foul-smelling salve made from the leaves of comfrey into my tender skin.

This was not how I had imagined this day would unfold, having an ugly, muttering old crone, smearing a nasty green paste all over my back. But that rustic salve seemed efficacious and I did feel better afterwards.

There was still no sign of Jacqueline by nightfall and so, when the sun was gone, I ate supper with the old lady, a pottage made of cabbage and bacon, and I curled up and went to sleep in one of her empty pigsties.

In the morning, after a long, deep sleep, I found Yvette weeping noisily into her porridge by the hearth at the centre of her cottage. I tried to understand what the crone was saying through all the outpouring of snot and the noise of her blubbering: "They've taken her ... I know it ... they've carried her away ... to the underworld. They have my girl ..."

I could barely make sense of her Burgundian country speech. So I went to see the priest again and conferred at length with him.

"It's just a stupid legend," he said crossly. "A lot of superstitious nonsense. But the people round here believe that there are evil spirits or faeries that live in the woods hereabouts – the grey folk or the grey riders they call them – and they carry away young men and women to their underground realm where they keep them prisoner for many centuries."

I nodded, remembering the odd eldritch feeling the day before.

" ... and, it is true, some young folk have indeed vanished from the remoter woods of Burgundy but, most of the time, they have merely gone to Paris or Troyes or one of the bigger towns to make a new life for themselves away from their lord and his land. It's nonsense, of course, these stories of the grey folk, and Jacqueline will soon show up safe and sound. You'll see, young man. She'll be back here before you know it."

I listened to the priest's rational explanation but it did not ring entirely true to me. Jacqueline had seemed content with her position at Gregoire's cook-shop – why would she quit that and go away to another town to do a similar menial role in a strange place? And if she *did* want to leave Burgundy, for whatever reason, why would she not tell anyone. She was a free woman, she had said, not at all rich, that was for sure, but no serf who was bound to her lord's fields. Something was not quite right.

"You will find her," sobbed Yvette, clutching my sleeve, pressing it to her wet face and smearing it with her slime. "You are a good man – you helped me with my pigs. You will find her and bring her safely back to me. Yes, you'll search for her in those evil woods – go, go on now."

So, most dutifully, I climbed stiffly up on to Ghost's back

and set off on the road back towards Dijon.

CHAPTER SEVEN

There was no sign of Jacqueline on the road back to Dijon – in truth the muddy track was so torn up by the passage of carts and horses, that I would never have been able to make out the steps of one light-footed girl.

My skin itched all over my body when I thought about the hidden folk – the faerie kind – that both the priest and the crone had mentioned but I mustered all my courage and explored those dark woods diligently.

I knew that Robin did not believe in these fell beings at all, or in demons or ghosts or witches. He had always maintained that it was all nonsense, fanciful stories made up by a warm hearth to frighten children into being good. But then my lord claimed he did not believe in many true things – even in God and His son Jesus. I often feared for his soul – I still do to this day. *Nothing* is more certain than God's boundless love for Man – and if God and the saints are real, why not the faerie folk, too?

Yet I was *not* wholly certain it was these troublesome beings that had snatched Jacqueline from the woods and taken her to another realm.

It seemed far more likely to me that it was men – real, flesh-and-blood men – who had abducted her from the woodland path. And I had a very good idea of who these evil men – or indeed boys – might be.

I was safely back in Dijon before the church bells rang out for noon and I went straight to the tavern on the square to find

Gregoire.

I apologised to him for my drunken behaviour the day before last and asked him if he had seen anything of his niece this morning. It was now Monday, and the dinner hour, and the cook-shop was busy once more. Little Gregoire, who was running about trying to serve all his hungry customers on his own, was not at all pleased to see me.

"I don't know where that wretched hussy is, son," he said. "No idea at all. She's supposed to be here helping me but never even showed her face this morning: it's my sister's family, all lazy, good-for-nothings."

And he trotted off to deal with some demanding diners.

When I was next able to summon his attention, I asked where in Dijon I might find the yard of Henrik the Tanner. He waved a hand in a vaguely southwesterly direction and said, "Outside the walls, of course, that's where those stinky brutes ply their foul trade, on the isle between the two arms of the Ouche."

Then he seemed to realise what I was asking. "No, no, no, young man. I heard about that stupid fracas the other night. You are to leave those two boys alone. Someone might be hurt."

He was eyeing the long sword hanging at my side.

"I only wish to ask them a few simple questions. I think they might know where Jacqueline is to be found."

This was not strictly true. I actually thought the apprentices and their friend might have captured her, to torment her – or do worse to her – as a way of punishing me. But, initially at least, I meant only to ask them some questions. Initially. If I wasn't given satisfactory answers quickly, I'd unsheathe my sword and then blood would flow like a river.

"I don't want any trouble," Gregoire said. "And I don't want you ever coming here to this cook-shop again. Don't come to eat here. I am sorry but those two – Arlo and Gerard – are, um, regular clients of mine. And their master is . . . well, never mind. But I can't have you troubling them. And I certainly won't help you against them."

"Do not fear, old man! I shall not tell them you sent me."

And I left Gregoire to his baying mob of hungry customers.

I could smell the Dijon tannery before I could see it. In my memory, a large cloud of evil-smelling smoke and stench hung like a curse over the sprawling workplace of this Henrik the Tanner, and his two apprentices.

The tan-yard was located on the northern point of a large lozenge of land, outside the town walls, where the wide River Ouche, which lapped the city there, split into two streams. The southern part of this island in the river, suitably far from the foul tannery, held a stone-built fortress.

Tanneries are almost always constructed outside towns, and by running water, for several good reasons: the smell of the rotting hides and the stale urine and old dung used in the tanning process is appalling – like the nastiest latrine behind the lowest tavern you ever had the misfortune to stumble into. Few folk would choose to live close to a stench like that.

Also, large quantities of fresh water are needed to wash the hides at the various stages of the complicated production process, and so the tannery needs a handy and plentiful source of running water. And finally the river can be used to run various large water-wheels – like those used by every village miller – which drive the big machines that pound the heavy wet leather with great wooden paddles, and turn the huge barrels that mix the wet leather with various noxious substances used to treat it.

I crossed the river by a rickety bridge and stood at the open gate of the tan-yard, gazing in at this noisy, stinking hell-on-Earth.

There were huge stacks of half-cured, slippery cow hides, placed here and there and everywhere on wooden pallets to keep the precious animal skins off the sea of foul mud that made up the floor of the yard.

In the centre of the wide open space was a gigantic chess-board of square pits filled with several different coloured liquids – browns, yellows and reds and one a vile poisonous green – I did not know if they were dyes for the completed leather, or potions to soften and treat the skins and remove the hair and fat as some part of the tanning process.

I didn't care to enquire. The quicker I was out of there the better.

Massive barrels laid on their sides rumbled, churned and slopped as they rotated round and round; other places machines with huge wooden arms bashed up and down, up and down, into soggy vats full of some foul, meaty soup. There was a vast iron cauldron bubbling and steaming over a fire in the centre of the yard, which was tended by a muscular young man with brick-red hair and a badly bruised face. He spotted me standing in the gateway and turned immediately to stare – then he let out a sharp yell of warning and surprise, and I saw most of his front teeth were missing, and that his open mouth was still wet, bloody and raw.

Good, I thought. *I hope it hurts like the Devil.* That'll teach you to try to ambush poor drunken foreigners in the darkness.

His excited yells brought an older man out from behind a huge stack of dripping hides. He had a kind of long wooden pitchfork in his right hand, doubtless used for fishing wet hides out of murky depths of the tanning pits, and he kept the heavy two-pronged instrument in his hand as he came directly to the gate to confront me. The second apprentice appeared from inside a small hut and as he limped over to join his comrades, I saw that the lower part of his left leg was freshly bandaged.

More of my handiwork, I assumed.

I held out both my hands wide of my sides and said loudly in my best French: "I have not come here to make war with you."

The three of them stopped just before their gate, the older man in the centre, the two apprentices on either side of him. I saw that the older man – Henrik, presumably – was looking at my sword but he said nothing at all. Evidently he was a man of few words.

The lad with the bandaged leg said: "What do you want?"

I ignored him and said to the older man: "You are Henrik the Tanner? This place is your tan-yard?"

Henrik nodded slowly; his hard eyes on me all the time. He repeated the wounded boy's question. "What you want here?"

He had a strange accent, I noticed, quite different from the two apprentices – who both spoke the standard Burgundian French. Henrik was leaning on his pitchfork, but he was alert, well balanced. And I knew he could fight, and fight well, that he was a man trained to arms. There was something coiled about the way he stood there. Perhaps he saw the same quality in me. "What do you want with us – speak up," he said.

"I want answers from you. My young friend Jacqueline – the serving girl of Gregoire's tavern whom your apprentices abused and molested the other day – is missing. She is not in her village, nor has she been seen at the cook-shop. Her family and friends are concerned. I am concerned. I wish to know if you three had anything to do with her disappearance."

"You say my apprentices assaulted Jacqueline?" said Henrik.

"How dare you accuse us, you big foreign bully," shouted the bloody-mouthed redhead. "Go back home to Normandy or... or it will be the worse for you! We are not afraid of you – you great pig!"

"Be quiet, Arlo!" said Henrik, without turning his head.

"We had nothing to do with it," said the other apprentice. "And you can prove nothing! Absolutely nothing. Nobody will believe your lies."

"Get back to work," said Henrik. "Both of you. Right now. I shall speak with this fellow alone."

"But, master, he is a vicious brute, a killer..." said Arlo.

"Go," snapped Henrik.

The apprentices shambled off, the red boy helping the limping one.

"You swear you mean us no harm?" said Henrik.

"I shall not hurt you if you tell me the truth."

Henrik smiled. "I'll tell what I know – truthfully. Come! Let us have a cup. We can, I think, easily settle our differences over a drink."

He took me to the wooden hut in the centre of the yard. The stench in the air made my eyes water yet I was determined not to show my discomfort to this man. As we crossed the tanyard, I looked about me – I could see no place one might hide a prisoner in this sea of mud and filth.

The revolting smell was slightly less pungent inside the hut, thank God, and I sat awkwardly while Henrik poured out a cup of strong, harsh red wine. I drank it down quickly hoping it would dull my sense of smell.

"Tell me how my boys molested that sweet girl," Henrik said.

I told him what had happened, how his apprentices had both put their hands on Jacqueline and humiliated her in public for their pleasure.

"So you stepped in and reprimanded them," said Henrik, nodding. "I salute you, man. I would have done the same had I been there. I did not know that they touched her in such a disrespectful manner. They only told me you attacked them – for no reason – in a fit of drunken rage."

"I was not drunk – not then," I said.

"I believe you," he said. "And I shall punish them for lying – I'll have the skin off both their backs – and for touching that girl. However, I think you have already taken a measure of vengeance against them, yes?"

"I don't care about punishing them. I want to find Jacqueline before, before it's too late. Do you think your 'prentices could have taken her?"

"No, absolutely not. And if they had seriously hurt her I would have cut out their still-beating hearts. They both understand that. Anyway, where would they keep her captive – here? I think not. No. It is not possible. What say her own family? What do they think has happened?"

"The old mother is convinced she has been taken by creatures called the grey riders – some kind of faeries or woodland spirits – folk who steal pretty children and take them away to their magical underground realm."

I gave a stiff little laugh to indicate that this impossibly fanciful.

Henrik just stared at me. "God forbid. I pray that it is not so."

"Do you seriously believe the faerie folk have taken them?"

He poured me more wine. "I am not from this place, this town of Dijon – but I think you already know that," he said.

I nodded – his odd speech patterns reminded me very much of my friend Hanno. "You were born a German?" I asked him.

"I come from Swabia, beyond the high Jura Mountains," he said, "and for some years I served the Duke of Zähringen as a man-at-arms. It was a good life, and I was happy – but then there was a killing, a murder and I had to flee. That was over a pretty woman, too. A stupid mistake."

He gave me a sideways glance. I nodded, pretending to understand him. I supposed that he was apologising in a round-about fashion for the attack on me the other night. I sipped the strong wine and let him speak.

"My father was a tanner, a successful one, and I was his sole apprentice. He wanted me to take over his yard when he died. But I – I thought I knew better – I wanted to be a soldier, a hero, and go off to war – for the adventure, you understand?"

I knew what he meant.

"But all that is the past. Now I live here in Burgundy and Dijon, and life here is good. I make leather and sell it, it is hard work, filthy work but . . . ach, I don't have to slaughter some poor fellow just because another man orders it. So . . ." He shrugged.

"It is a better life," I suggested.

"Ten years I have been here – I am Dijonnaise now. I am one of those fat, prosperous burghers. In all ways except one."

I shifted on my stool. I wished he would get to his point. I had finished up my filthy wine and without asking he refilled my cup.

"These grey riders – the people here think they are faeries, woodland spirits, as you said – *fee*, we call them. But I do not believe in this. They are not *fee*; they are mortal men. They are grey-clad men-at-arms on horseback. They do not take people to some magical underworld, they only take them across the river. They are men from the Free County on the other side of the Saone. Count Otto's men-at-arms. I know this for sure. I have even seen them with my own eyes. They wear cloaks of squirrel skin, black and white patches, on the cold nights. The grey riders are just flesh-and-blood men in grey squirrel-skin cloaks. I swear it."

I remembered the grey mantels tied to the saddles of the men-at-arms of the Green Knight, Raoul, the Seigneur de Beaune-du-Bois.

"You say that you have seen them? When did this happen?"

"Last summer, I went over to Vergy to look at some deer hides, which were going cheap. On the journey home, my old mare went lame and I had to spend the night sleeping in a hedge. I saw them pass me on the road at midnight, with a prisoner tied across the saddle of one of the horses – a girl, I think, I don't know who it was. Another peasant gone missing. Maybe they thought she ran off, quit her lord's demesne to find a better life – as I did."

"Did these grey riders bear any mark, any device or blazon that might help to identify them?" I asked, leaning forward eagerly.

Henrik looked me directly in the eye. "They did. Yes. And it is a device that I recognised from my time with the duke. Green and white markings; a pattern of cups, rows upon rows alternating green and white."

He drew the shape on the table in a patch of spilled wine.

"This was on their shields? You are sure?"

He was still staring at me. "Sure as I can be. I know this badge. It is the blazon of the Seigneurs of Beaune-du-Bois. I saw it many times at Besançon at the court of Count Otto, who was an ally of my duke."

"You think that these men may have taken Jacqueline?"

"What do you think?"

"But why, in God's name, why? What would they want with her?"

"What do you think they want from her? You're a young man. You know how beautiful she is. You can guess what they desire."

"Christ!" I found I was sweating and drained my cup again.

The thought of Jacqueline as a prisoner of the Chevalier Raoul and his lusty men-at-arms made me feel more than a little sick.

"Do you know where this place is, this Beaune-du-Bois?"

"I can point you in the right direction."

"Will you come? I think you have some tender feelings for her."

"No. No, I have my tannery. That is enough for me. I have my two apprentices – whom I will defend when called upon to do so, even in a wrongful cause. But I will not start a war with a lord of the County for a girl who's not my responsibility. My fighting days are behind me. I'm no hero. Perhaps I never was. I'm Henrik the Tanner. That is who I am."

CHAPTER EIGHT

When I got back to the abbey in the late afternoon, I found the place buzzing like a beehive. Hanno had arrived with a contingent of Robin's mounted men, a dozen Sherwood archers, who were making themselves comfortable in the courtyard, the stables, the refectory and dormitories.

"Where have you been?" Robin said to me. "I needed you for something and once again I could not find you anywhere."

"You told me you didn't want to see me for a day or two."

I had him there.

"I meant only that you should recover from your well-deserved beating, rest, recuperate, right here in the abbey. Where were you?"

"I was attending to a private matter, lord. But I'm here now."

Robin leaned in. He sniffed. "Have you been drinking? Are you drunk – *again*? What is the matter with you, Alan?"

I lost my temper. My bruises were aching; my head was full of worry about Jacqueline, and Robin was being even more unreasonable than usual.

"I'm not drunk. I *have* had a drink. What's it to you? You used to be a feared and respected outlaw; now you behave like a mother-in-law."

Robin stared at me. His look was icy; the eyes boring into me had the sheen of a naked knife. I immediately regretted the words I had said.

"I beg your pardon, lord," I said. "I spoke intemperately, in haste. Please forgive my insolence. Tell me, what did you require of me?

Robin drew in a deep breath. "Report to me tomorrow morning, at dawn. Sober. And I will give you your orders. Now, get out of my sight."

I spent the early evening alone with Ghost in the stables, rubbing the mud from his coat and oiling his hooves; and making sure he had a good feed of oats and barley and plenty of fresh water. I was enjoying his silent company and he was enjoying my attention, when Hanno found us.

"So, you want go drink with me?" he said with a knowing grin. "I know a good place. Cheap. We drink ale till we are out of our senses."

I declined. "I have to do an errand for Robin in the morning."

"Ja! I hear you get drunk yesterday, call him old woman to his face."

I explained to my Bavarian friend what I thought had happened to Jacqueline, and why my concern had led me to being rude to my lord.

"You must forget about the girl," said Hanno. "She is dead or all torn up inside. Those grey riders have her; nothing you can do now."

I hung my head. I knew what my friend said was true. What could I do? Chase after her? Track her down and rescue her from a powerful lord's castle in a foreign land, a man with God knew how many men-at-arms at his command. Hanno was right. I could do nothing but forget her.

Yet somehow I could not.

I dreamt about her that night. I could see her lovely face, her dark eyes pleading. She was weeping; calling on me to help her. To save her.

"Alan! Alan," she called, but these calls were no dream.

Hanno was kicking my cot in the dormitory, and trying to rouse me from a deep sleep. "It's past dawn and Robin wants to see you," he said.

My lord was frosty with me when I finally came before him, washed and dressed, in the abbey's high walled open-air cloister. He was sitting at a table in a patch of morning sunshine, reading a parchment, and when I approached he looked up and said: "Wait. I'll be with you in a moment."

He read on for a moment or two and then looked up at me.

"Are you fit to ride a distance?" he said.

I said I was.

"No lasting damage from that street brawl?"

"I'm fine," I said. While I was still stiff and sore, I was, indeed, fine, more or less.

"I want you to take a discreet message from me to Count Otto at his temporary court in Dole, will you do that for me, Alan Dale?"

"Yes, lord."

"Tell him this: 'My lord of Locksley has arranged a private meeting, alone, with the Regent of Burgundy on the Kalends of June – that is, six days' from today – at that meeting he will fulfill his promise.' Got that?"

"But surely you are not really going to mur . . ."

Robin interrupted me. "Your task is to deliver my message to Otto. Concern yourself with nothing else but that. Can you do this for me?"

"Yes, lord."

"Then you say to him: 'My master urges you to be ready to strike on the Kalends of June. Prepare all your men to ride then. After the *event*, there will be chaos in the Duchy, particularly in Dijon, and my lord Count must be ready to strike while the iron's hot.' Will you remember that?"

"Yes, lord."

"Don't tell him anything else – don't tell him what you think, or what your opinion is of my actions. Or what you surmise that I might do. Do you understand this, Alan? Just deliver my message exactly as I have relayed it to you. Then come back here and report to me. And don't get blind drunk in Dole and do anything stupid. No brawling, understand?"

I said nothing. I was feeling insulted that Robin could think that I was so irresponsible that I would discuss his schemes with our enemies or, indeed, that I might get hopelessly drunk and spoil this vital mission.

"Do you fully understand, Alan, what I need you to do?"

"Yes, lord," I said, a little sulkily.

"Off you go then," he said.

It took the best part of the day to ride the thirty-odd miles to Dole. The fine weather had disappeared and I was thoroughly drenched by a heavy rain shower around midday. But late that afternoon, still damp, I was standing in the shabby hall at the heart of Dole Castle before Count Otto of Burgundy, making my bow, and asking to speak with him privately.

I was ushered in to the solar, a small wooden walled room equipped with a large bed, at the far end of the great hall, and Otto, guarded by two burly men-at-arms, listened attentively as I delivered my message to him.

"The first day of June, are you sure your lord said that date? He cannot get himself into the regent's presence before that? That is in six days' time and he has already been in Dijon nearly a whole week."

"I am certain he said that, my lord."

"What is the delay, then?" said Otto, toying with a strand of his long red hair. "I hope my lord of Locksley has not lost his nerve. Has he?"

I shrugged, deciding not to say more. For earlier, in the great hall, I had noticed that there was a tall figure standing silently behind Otto's throne. It was the old monk Prior Gui. He seemed to flit between Dijon and Dole, between Duchy and County – making trouble for us wherever he went. He wasn't in the solar with us now but still I guarded my tongue.

"I am just the messenger, my lord. I know no more than I am told."

"Very well then. You are dismissed. Bruno will show you to

the kitchen where you will be fed. You sleep in the hall with the servants."

"May I ask a question, my lord?"

"What? What question? Yes, you may ask."

"Is the Chevalier Raoul, the Seigneur de Beaune-du-Bois... is he here in Dole; is he in attendance on your lordship at the present time?"

"Oh, the fellow who captured you? No, he is now resting his hams in his own hall, I believe. He's still sulking because I took you and your master away from him. You have a message for my grumpy *chevalier*?"

"No, no, my lord, I was merely curious. It is no great matter."

"Very well, then, if that is all you have for me..."

And Bruno, one of the burly men-at-arms, showed me out.

When I had eaten my fill in the kitchens, I went up on to the walls of the castle in the last gleams of the day and looked north. A mile beyond the boundaries of the town lay a huge swathe of thick forest, a great carpet of many hues of green that stretched into the distance as far as the eye could see. It looked like a great sea, an endless ocean of trees.

Somewhere out there, almost due north from Dole, about fifteen miles away in the middle of all that thick woodland, or so the tanner had told me, was the castle of Beaune-du-Bois, where the Chevalier Raoul, the Green Knight, as I thought of him, was holding Jacqueline a captive. The castle was close to the River Saone, Henrik had said, and there was an ancient fording spot a few miles west from the Green Knight's castle.

It would be only a small detour. I would be heading back to Robin, only by another route. I would find out if my suspicions were correct. But I would take no undue risks, nor cause offence to the Green Knight, if I could possibly help it. And I could still be back in Dijon in good time to report to my lord, only a day later than planned, if all went well...

And so the dice were thrown.

The next morning, after a soft and milky dawn, at the origin of a new and cheerful day, I mounted up on my faithful Ghost and rode out of the gates of Dole. But, instead of taking the main road west, down towards the river, I turned Ghost's noble nose towards the north, towards the loom of the deep, dark forest, and touched my spurs to his flanks.

CHAPTER NINE

It was far colder in the forest than I had expected. It was also gloomier, damper and a great deal more frightening to traverse. When I turned off the road, I rode for a while along the fringes of the tall trees looking for a road to lead me into the wilderness. I found one. Indeed, I found several.

Selecting the broadest path, a substantial track that headed due north, a direction I judged by the sun, I plunged into the trees.

A foreign wood is an unnerving place to enter alone, and I admit I was feeling more than a little apprehensive as I rode along the smooth, beaten-earth way under the dense canopy, almost a tunnel, listening to the chitter and squeak of birds and wild animals, and surrounded by the eerie rattling and scraping of branches in a light breeze.

My mind kept returning to thoughts of the uncanny – to the strange noises and flashes of movement that I half-saw all around me. In my head Robin was telling me robustly there were no such things as faeries – that the hidden folk were no more than creatures of my imagination. My Jacqueline had not been taken by magical creatures but by men, flesh-and-blood mortals, and it was my duty to save her from them. And yet...

The mind is a strange master. I saw, I definitely *saw*, a young faun that morning, a creature with the hairy legs of a goat, and the naked torso of a man staring at me from across a clearing. I cried out in fear and surprise. And looked again, meaning to challenge it. But it was gone and in its place was an old tree with gnarled bark at the base, and a patch above where the bark had been stripped away to leave a pale bare trunk by some animal, a hungry deer, perhaps. I stared, rubbed my eyes and conceded that it was a tree. Only a tree. Then I moved Ghost onwards.

Courage, Alan, I told myself. *Steady yourself now, and go forward.* But my passage through that dark wood that day was filled with disquiet. I could sense evil among the trees, an ancient evil that no amount of cold, rational thought and personal exhortations could fully extinguish.

My plan was to make my way to the castle of Beaune-du-Bois by nightfall, visiting its seigneur on the pretext that I was delivering a message to him from Robin. Then, claiming weariness after a long ride, I would beg leave of the *chevalier* to spend the night. During the dark hours, I hoped to creep out and discover if Jacqueline was his prisoner.

As far as the Green Knight knew, Robin and I were now firm allies of Count Otto, his master, who had freed us, and we were engaged on his behalf in Dijon. I planned to tell Raoul that Robin wished to speak to him about the possibility of enjoying a little hunting over his lands while he was in *Burgundia* – because I knew the chase was close to Raoul's heart.

However, I knew equally that the Green Knight was unlikely to agree to this request – for a keen huntsmen, a stranger, a foreigner to boot, asking permission to hunt his deer was almost akin to asking to bed his wife. It was a reed-thin pretext for a visit, but I judged that it should be enough to get me inside his castle for one night before the request was politely refused. After gaining entrance to Beaune-du-Bois, I had no clear idea what I'd do next. It depended on whether Jacqueline was there or not; and whether she was imprisoned in a high tower or bound in chains in some dank, rat-infested cellar. Never having seen his castle before, I had no way of knowing what to expect. I would have to improvise.

But that would happen only if I was able to actually locate this castle of Beaune-du-Bois. Henrik's directions had been horribly vague – he had told me only that it was about fifteen miles due north of Dole.

After about six or seven miles of travel, the wide track I had chosen seemed to disappear under Ghost's hooves. I had noticed that the way was getting thinner and when I had passed some abandoned huts – charcoal burners temporary dwelling, I believed – the track soon became no more than a narrow path, then a slender deer trail and, a little after the hour of noon, I roused myself from a delightfully sweet daydream about Jacqueline's gratitude to me for rescuing her, and found myself in the middle of thick woods with no visible path either before or behind me.

My first thought was that the forest must be enchanted. That it had closed in around me, trapping me with some otherworldly and probably wicked intent. But I also knew deep down that I could quite simply be lost in an unfamiliar wilderness. I kept a tight hand on my swiftly rising panic. People got lost everyday, I told myself. I tried to retrace my tracks, and instead worked my way even further into the deep, trackless woods. I could barely make out the sun by now – which had hidden behind a mass of clouds – and had to estimate my direction of travel by instinct alone.

To cut a long tale short, I found myself in the early evening without any idea of where I was or in which the direction I should be travelling. I was hopelessly lost and the light was receding fast. We had been travelling all day with few rest breaks and Ghost was very tired and hungry; his head drooping as he nosed through the leaf litter in search of a patch of nourishing grass; I was fatigued, too, and beginning to realise – with a sense of dread – that I would have to spend the night alone in these dense woods. *There are no such thing as faeries,* I told myself. *You are a match for anything you might encounter.* One night, out in the wild is nothing. Nothing at all. In the morning, I told myself, I would climb a tall tree, get a fix on north from the sun, and set off again refreshed. In the morning, I would free myself of the grip of these menacing woodlands.

I got off my mount in a small clearing, and removed Ghost's saddle and blanket, and gave him some water and a nosebag of oats while I scrubbed the mud from his silky coat with a handful of grass. I felt like the world's biggest fool as I worked. *What had I been thinking to wander the wild wood without a guide or even a proper road to follow?*

A pair of small creatures jumped into view squeaking and chirring together on an overhead branch – I jumped like a frightened rabbit, looking up wildly, dropping the bunch of grass. These beings seemed to be laughing explicitly at me. Mocking my fright and my situation. They were squirrels, I saw. Not supernatural beings, not faeries. A pair of tree rats. So I reached down and picked up a stone, which was by my boot.

I am a good shot with a hurled object – it was a skill I learnt as a youngster scrambling around the woods and fields of Nottinghamshire. I found, a moment later, that my prowess had not deserted me. I lashed the stone up at the branch, as hard and as fast as I could, and knocked the larger squirrel senseless, so that he fell like a ripe plum a yard from my feet. That raised my spirits considerably. I felt I'd struck back at the threatening forest – and gained something for supper into the bargain.

I made a small fire from dry wood and, using my *misericorde* as a spit, I roasted the skinned animal and ate it with a good deal of genuine enjoyment. I even found a large bag of salt and a heel of bread in my saddlebags – and a wrinkled old apple in there, too. *Faeries fear salt*, I remembered. *Everyone knows that fact.* And half-hating my cowardly weakness, half-applauding my luck at remembering this ancient magical protection, I sprinkled a wide circle of salt crystals around my camping site, broadcasting the white grains liberally around the clearing.

This is not so bad, I thought, as I sat wrapped in my cloak, with my back snug against a thick-trunked oak; my faithful horse was tied to a nearby bough, content and drowsing, and the flames of my fire flickering soothingly against the dark. *There is nothing to fear here.*

I sat chewing on half-roasted squirrel meat seasoned with

salt and munching dry day-old bread, reasonably comfortable, reasonably calm. I toyed with a few more verses in my mind, honing and augmenting "She wakes delight". If only I had a little wine, it could almost be a pleasant evening. The squirrel was tasty. I was lost, yes, but in the morning I would resume my journey. The castle of Beaune-du-Bois could not be far away and, if necessary, I could strike due east and try to find the River Saone.

There is no such thing as faeries, I told myself. Tomorrow would be a better day, a brighter day, a new beginning, I decided, as I snuggled down in my warm cloak, and tried to find enough peace of mind to sleep.

I awoke to the sound of the baying, and opened my eyes to see six hairy brutes growling and snarling around me, and two men on horseback, shouting and whistling and snapping whips to keep the hounds at bay.

I jumped up, still tangled in my long cloak, and a vast red-brown hound, apparently fresh from the depths of hell, sprang at me and knocked me back down with his vast weight. It was a savage creature, not far removed from a wolf, with slobber-roped jaws, yellow fangs, and breath so foul it could have stunned a Nottinghamshire sow. But this was a real beast of flesh and bone – there was no eldritch magic to this smelly, snarling, hairy animal, as I recognised with one relieved part of my mind.

I had managed, somehow to get both my hands round its thick neck, fingers buried in his loose fur and skin, and to keep its snapping teeth a few inches from my head. But the animal's strength was colossal – I felt like I was wrestling a half-grown bear – and it was hurling me left and right, left and right as I clung to its bull-thick neck, as if my whole body was of no more substance no more than some mendicant's foot rag.

I could feel my grip slipping, slipping any moment now, and the monster would be loose and his filthy jaws would be sinking deep into my face, teeth ripping me, tearing meat . . .

"Leave him, Apricot, leave that young villain be!" I dimly heard the crack of a whip. "Get away, you daft old bitch!" And the hell-hound gave me one last shake of its powerful neck that rattled my bones, then flung me to the ground and backed a few paces, still growling ominously.

I was breathless, aching, and my Dijon-beating bruises were now protesting madly at the treatment from this red demon in dog's form.

"It would be better, my good man, if you did not make any sudden movements," said a voice in French and I looked up into a lean, pale face, sweaty from a hard ride but with a trim blue-black beard and moustache.

The Green Knight himself was looking coldly down at me.

"You are that silver-tongued English earl's man," he said, surprised. "Ah, indeed, I recognise you now. But what are you playing at here in my forest? Poaching my game no doubt!"

"May I get to my feet, lord?" I said, not wishing to provoke another attack from the Bitch-Beast of Satan or her five equally fearsome pack-mates, who were slinking around the edge of clearing growling but, it seemed, all mercifully under the control of the whip-wielding huntsman.

"Gaston, keep all the hounds right back," Raoul tossed the words over his shoulder. He extended a hand and pulled me upright.

"Thank you, lord, for restraining your beasts," I said dusting myself down and feeling for any broken bones.

"Don't thank me yet, Englishman – not till you tell me what are you doing making free of my hunting grounds? You're trespassing, I think."

"I was in fact attempting to find your castle, my lord," I said. "I have a message from the Earl of Locksley to deliver only to you."

"Is this so?" said the *chevalier*. He looked as if he did not believe me. "You have not, perhaps, run away from your master?"

"No, my lord, on my soul, I swear it. I have not quit the good Earl's service. I never shall do so. I bring a message to you, that is all."

"Ah, indeed? Why then are you here, in the middle of the

Forest of Chaux? I heard your master was lodged snugly at the abbey of Saint Benignus in Dijon. Why did you not come by road? Or across the ford?"

"I went to Dole on the earl's business just two days ago; then came north seeking Beaune-du-Bois. Then I became lost. Perhaps, my lord, we could discuss this in a little more comfort somewhere else. Beside your castle's hearth, perhaps? I haven't washed this morn nor broken my fast."

"Where are my manners! Of course, you must be tired and hungry if you have ridden far and slept in the woods. Mount upon your horse, my fine friend, briskly now, and follow us. Come along!"

I did as the Green Knight bade me. I soothed, gently stroked and saddled Ghost as quickly as I could. Then I climbed up on his broad back and followed the Green Knight and his huntsman as they walked along a barely perceptible inches-wide path through the trees.

I was glad to have their horses' wide rumps to follow, since the way was twisted and through some of the most overgrown forest I'd ever seen. I was grateful for their company, too, in a strange way. My night-time fears of faeries and fell beings had been utterly banished by the sunlight and the solid presence of these two Burgundian men – and even by their slinking, slobbering hell-beasts. Yet, after about half an hour of travel, I gave a groan of frustration, I realised that in my early morning haste I'd left my *misericorde* at my camp, skewering the cold, half-eaten squirrel.

However, it was too late to go back now. I would have to do without my favourite dagger. I did, at least, have my long sword in the scabbard at my waist, and in my saddlebags there was a fine Arab knife, a thick, curved, deadly weapon, that would serve me well, if it came to it and I was forced to cut my way free of the *chevalier*'s castle with Jacqueline.

We plodded along for an hour, with me trailing their two horses, on near invisible game tracks, with branches brushing at my elbows and the six hounds crashing though the undergrowth all around us, occasionally howling or barking, too. More than once I wondered if the Green Knight had become lost in his own forest. But I recognised this was an absurd notion, and indeed after a mile or two, three at most, it was difficult to gauge the distances with our lines of sight restricted to a few feet, we came out from the trees and undergrowth and into a cleared space and a road.

I say road – it was a narrow, weed-covered, deep rutted cart track that ran roughly west along the edge of the forest wall. I guessed that it led down to the river and beyond that to the Duchy of Burgundy and Dijon. But it was not the neglected thoroughfare that drew my eye. On a piece of rising ground beyond the track lay the castle of Beaune-du-Bois.

I reined in instinctively when I first saw the castle, checking Ghost abruptly. I had thought that the dark forest contained a definite air of danger and menace. But that was as nothing to this fell place. The castle squatted on its small hill like some evil brown toad. Long, low and dark, somehow flabby, its timbers black with age, dirt and decrepitude, it seemed to suck in all available sunlight with its crouched malevolence.

I shook my head to clear it and looked again. No. I was wrong. It was just an old fortress made of ancient wood, no more than that. Walls and towers and a solid gatehouse. Like many I had seen before. I spurred after the distant figures of *chevalier* and his huntsman as they rode up the hill towards the entrance of the castle, the six hell-hounds gambolling merrily around them as they anticipated home, food and well-earned rest.

As I rode in under the long gallery above the double-gated entrance, I looked up and noticed that a rather small human skull, encrusted with years of accumulated filth, had been nailed to the wood. Below it two blackened thighbones were fixed, one crossed over the other, in a symbol of Death itself. This was not an uncommon configuration: I had often seen the same grim device carved on gravestones in consecrated ground – but it seemed to me an evil omen. I had never seen actual human remains fixed above the portal of a lord's castle before. I shuddered for no reason.

The Château de Beaune-du-Bois was roughly square in shape, fifty paces long on each side, with four wooden towers, of varying sizes, one at each corner of the crenulated walls. The castle ramparts were made of double thicknesses layer of oak logs, no doubt cut from the Forest of Chaux in decades past. It also possessed a large two-storey stone hall at the rear of the sandy courtyard, with the entrance to the main chamber up a set of stone steps on the first floor, and with farmyard animals housed beneath the human living space. This, I later discovered was known as the Logis de Seigneur, and was the beating heart of the castle.

There were a dozen other smaller wooden buildings inside the walls – kitchens, stables, store houses, kennels and so on – and that was all.

It was a rough, unfussy, utilitarian place. I'd been in many similar castles before – but none quite so remote from civilisation, and none that left me feeling so ill at ease, as if my very soul was itching.

However, the castle if small and crude did seem strong for its size, well appointed to defeat any attacker without a decent-sized force at his command. The heavy oak gates would give even an iron-tipped battering ram a good deal of difficulty. And I reckoned a company of forty hard fighting men, prepared and provisioned, could defend this fortress for a month at least – by which time, presumably, aid would have arrived from the defender's lord. No castle is impregnable. And all any sensible defender can hope for is to delay attackers long enough for help to arrive.

There was a stone chapel beside the largest tower, in the northwest corner of the courtyard, and this small house of God, too, I saw, was adorned with the skull and crossbones motif in its small, arched oak door. Not the actual bones of a long-dead person, this time, but a representation of them carved deeply into the ancient timber of the door.

There were three other smaller towers in the corners of the castle, which I discovered later held storerooms, lesser halls, dormitories and lodgings for the few male servants here on the ground floors. The windows in all four wooden towers, and in the thick stone walls of the Logis, too, were mere arrow slits, though which no man or woman, however slender, could pass. I noticed that the gatehouse also served as a place of accommodation for some of the *chevalier*'s many men-at-arms, of whom I saw at least a dozen wandering about the yard at their leisure.

There was something else that was odd about this fortress – quite apart from its grim atmosphere and ghoulish decorations above the gate – and it took me a moment to realise what it was. There was no village sheltering beneath its high walls, no settlement of humble peasant huts and hovels spread out in the surrounding countryside. The pieces fell quickly into place in my mind. This meant the land around here must be uncultivated. No fields, no pastures. Crops, of course, require gangs of serfs to grow and harvest them; and hard-working serfs require villages to live in, and villages require the protection of a well-fortified castle.

This place was, I quickly realised, more of a strongly built hunting lodge, than a true knight's castle. The deer of the Forest of Chaux were the lord's only cattle, and the folk who lived here, apart from doubtless growing a few kitchen vegetables, sustained themselves by the chase.

It also meant that the lean, dark-haired *chevalier* who was getting down from his horse in the courtyard, this Green Knight, was not, in truth, master of this place. He was its guardian, its temporary steward; he held this fortified forest outpost for his lord Otto, Count of Burgundy.

As I got down off Ghost's back, and handed the reins to a waiting stable boy, I thought about what this might mean. I realised very soon it changed nothing. The *chevalier*'s word was law out here. I was in his power, whether he was lord or not. He must have two score of men-at-arms here, perhaps more. They would do his bidding without question.

I wondered where Jacqueline was being kept, and then – suddenly, in a flash of insight – whether she was actually here *at all*. I'd leapt to the conclusion – a common failing of mine – that she must surely have been captured by this Green Knight, and this deduction was based on Henrik's description of a prisoner he had seen a year before being forcefully carried away by the grey riders. I already knew these folk raided across the river into the Duchy but it did not necessarily mean they had captured Jacqueline or that, if they had, that she would still be here now. She could indeed have fled to Paris or Troyes or Nevers – or somewhere else – for very good reasons that I didn't know about and probably never would.

The Green Knight could be quite innocent of the crime I suspected him of . . . or he could equally be guilty as sin – but had sent Jacqueline to another place. I felt like a fool. My sweet girl could be in Dole – and I never even saw her there – or at Besançon or . . . anywhere on Earth!

There was certainly no sign of Jacqueline in the courtyard, and when my host politely invited me to wash my face and hands and change my chemise – in preparation for the castle's dinner at noon – I saw no sign of my girl in the small wash-house, or in the damp chamber at the base of the tower where I changed my clothes.

I instinctively avoided the stinking kennels, a large caged enclosure by the east wall: if she was in there, I reasoned, she was no more than a rag of chewed up gristle and bone fragments by now. Nor did I spot her in the stables when I checked on Ghost's comforts, nor was she in the many different storerooms, which I happened to "accidentally" stumble into while seeking the latrines. Nor was there any sign of her in the stone hall at the rear of the courtyard – the Logis de Seigneur – which I entered up the stone steps and passed all the way through on my way to the *chevalier*'s food-laden table at a little before the canonical hour of Sext.

My confidence was now shaken. Had this been a bad mistake?

There were, in fact, no women at all present in the Logis at dinnertime. Neither had I seen any in my vague wanderings around the courtyard. Only the Green Knight and a dozen of his more senior men-at-arms were gathered round the long wooden trestle table for the midday repast. They were seated on benches and, as I approached, already tearing at the food – a whole haunch of bloody venison, barely cooked – without the slightest restraint. There were bread trenchers to soak up the meat juices, and cheese and fruit and plenty of wine, too, and pies of various game birds, and a sauce made of sorrel to go with the venison, and I must confess I fell to with a will, eating like the others with unabashed greed.

The men at the table were mostly Burgundians but the language they spoke was predominantly a kind of German, with a few French words added to the odd mixture that I could occasionally catch. Some spoke a kind of French but with a strong Teutonic accent. It was clear that both basic tongues were broadly understood by almost all the men present. However, since they all seemed to speak with their mouths full of half-raw venison, and mainly in gruff manly grunts and guffaws, I was able to follow only a little part of their conversations. This seemed no great loss to me then, for all the growling talk seemed to be about their own hunting exploits, the possible locations of future game and other forest matters.

I stopped trying to follow their dull talk and concentrated on my surroundings, looking for some clue that Jacqueline was indeed held captive here. The Logis itself was decorated in the usual traditional style of a hunting lodge – it was, I surmised, perhaps the original stone building of this whole fortress, which had been more recently enclosed by the castle with its wooden towers and ramparts.

The dusty horns of wild animals were mounted on small shield-shaped plaques, and adorned the Logis's interior walls. The moth-eaten pelts of a dozen wolves and bears, too, were also hung on the walls between the plaques. There was an unmistakably masculine air to the place, too – by which I mean it was scruffy and dank. It smelled of sweat, stale animal grease and old farts, and just a tint of fresh urine. And high up, almost obscured from view in the dim light of the hall and a covering of filth, was another human skull above a pair of crossed thighbones.

The macabre emblem seemed to be the distinguishing mark of this dark, depressing castle – its unholy blazon, if you will.

When I was full to the brim of raw meat and strong drink, I wiped my greasy mouth and hands on a napkin and sat back on the bench with a loud, contented belch. The Green Knight then shoved a jug of red down the table in my direction, and said: "You claim to have a message for me, Englishman. So I had better hear it, I suppose."

So I got slowly to my feet and delivered the wholly fabricated message from Robin, which I had prepared in my mind over the past few hours. It was full of extravagant phrases about the nobility of the hunt, with the chase as an obvious metaphor for the glories of battle and the brotherhood of men-at-arms. The *chevalier* listened in silence, picking his teeth with a sliver of wood.

"He wants to hunt my deer over my lands, that's it, is it?"

"Yes, my lord, if you will graciously grant him this great boon."

"Nothing else?"

"No, lord."

"He doesn't have a proposal, or an offer, or a suggestion?"

"No, lord – why would he?"

The other men-at-arms, now also heavy with meat and wine, were getting to their feet, without the slightest ceremony, shoving and joking as if they were equals, and stumbling out of the hall. Some instead went over to the side of the hall to slump on benches and sleep off their dinner. Beaune-du-Bois, it occurred to me, was as informal a court as I'd seen since I lived in an outlaw den. They shared the same degree of courtesy.

"We might be a little out of the way here, Englishman," said Raoul, "but we do hear things. Your master in Dijon has been whispering to men who owe fealty to Otto, murmuring in their ears. Holding secret meetings with disaffected lords and grasping churchmen, or so I'm told. There are tales of fiefs and plum positions being offered for favours, titles dangled here and there before their eyes, and pressures applied. I wondered if he had a bribe to offer me, perhaps some of his fabulous hoard of Moorish gold we've heard so much about since you came to these parts."

I went cold at the *chevalier*'s words. Robin thought he was being cunning with his stratagems, his quiet meetings with the local lords. Yet this near-hermit knight living in the wild seemed to know all about them.

"Ah, um, no, my lord; he just wants to . . ."

"Because I don't believe for a moment that he simply wants to hunt my game in the Forest de Chaux, and I thought he might want to offer me a great big sack of gold to do him some little favour. No? No gold? He does owe me a huge ransom, you know."

I said nothing to this ill-tempered enquiry. To be honest I had nothing to say and I was feeling embarrassed. It seemed that both Robin and I had underestimated the intelligence of these Burgundian lords.

"Well then, Englishman, you may rest here in my hall tonight, but tomorrow I desire you to ride off to Dijon and deliver a message to your lord – one of my men will put you on the right road. It's not a complicated route, even for someone who is as prone to getting lost as you. My message to your master is simple. I'm sure you'll be able to remember it. It is this: 'No.' However, you may also tell him that, if he wishes to come here with a cart full of gold coins, I'd be more than happy to discuss any other discreet little proposals he might have up his *sleeve*."

I blushed, made my bows and left the table, reeling slightly. This backwoods knight, this impoverished steward of a hunting lodge, was clearly mocking us – teasing me for my obviously made-up message; and jeering at my lord for his attempts to pull the levers of power in the two Burgundies. At least, I thought he was mocking us. The reference to the sleeve was a dig about Robin's dramatic revelation in Dole before Count Otto – surely. It was most unlikely he was actually admitting in front of his own men that he would betray his lord for a glittering pile of gold.

Either way, I would leave the Château de Beaune-du-Bois the next morning, after breaking my fast, and return as swiftly as possible to my lord with some hopefully plausible explanation as to where I had been.

That was tomorrow. Tonight, when the whole castle was fast asleep, I would search the place from top to bottom, as best I could, quietly, without raising any fuss, to discover whether or not Jacqueline was here.

I slept all that afternoon in the stable next to Ghost, after checking that my horse was happy and had been properly cared for; and I confess I had no difficulty in falling asleep. I was tired, and I'd gorged mightily at dinner. I awoke some hours later when the shadows were lengthening, refreshed and ready, if necessary, to spend all night creeping about the castle on my quest to discover the whereabouts of the woman I loved.

My quest did not take me all night. Not long at all, in fact.

I went into the Logis at dusk to take a cup of wine, and perhaps find a bowl of hot soup, and the first person I saw, sitting by the hearth like a grandmother and mending a torn pair of hose, was my sweet Jacqueline.

CHAPTER TEN

I was so surprised to see her that my mouth actually fell open. She looked so completely relaxed and at home, with a needle and thread in her fingers, that I was shocked speechless. I had been prepared to find her in chains, bruised, bleeding, torn, weeping, perhaps having been subjected to the appalling desires of these brutish men-at-arms, or the cruelties of the chevalier himself, but she looked as if she was at her own fire-side.

She stared at me with a strange expression on her face – a frown of incomprehension, but also, I think, one of surprised pleasure at seeing me in this place. She opened her mouth to speak but I put a warning finger to my lips. I drifted over to the sideboard, where there were a number of men-at-arms drinking wine and laughing together. I collected a cup of red and went back to the hearth, which was two-thirds of the way along the hall, set in the wall between the main part of the hall and the solar, the lord's quarters. As I returned, I saw the Green Knight striding towards me down the hall, as if he meant to prevent me from speaking to his prisoner.

I bent close to her. "I've come to rescue you," I whispered. "But, for now, just pretend that we mean absolutely nothing to each other."

Then I made her a low, courtly bow. "Beautiful lady," I said a little too loudly. "I don't believe I've had the pleasure of your acquaintance. Allow me to name myself: I am Alan Dale of the manor of Westbury, a visiting Englishman in the service . . ."

"But Alan . . ." she said.

The *chevalier* was upon us then. He glared down furiously at Jacqueline: "What in the name of the Devil do you think you're doing here, girl? Get back to your own quarters. Now!"

Jacqueline blushed prettily to the roots of her auburn hair and rose, gathering up her mending basket and the pile of torn clothes. He dipped her head to Raoul submissively and hurried away. As she passed him, the Green Knight slapped her buttocks playfully, making her gasp. I boiled with fury – but knew I could not show it or I'd risk ruining my plan.

"Who is that pretty thing?" I asked, nonchalantly.

"Nobody. A servant. She shouldn't have been here this evening. But never mind her. There's something I want to ask, Englishman. A boon."

"You told her to go back to her own quarters. Do female servants in Burgundy not live in the hall with everyone else?"

"What? No. Not the women. Not in this castle. They live and sleep in the east tower, near to the kitchens, to keep them safe from . . . But never mind that. I want to ask about something else. I think your English earl said you were a trained musician, a *trouvère*, is that true?"

"I have that honour."

"Well, we are deep in the wild woods here and don't get much entertainment. So I wondered if, as a personal favour to me, you would perform for us this evening – sing for your supper, if you will. My men would surely appreciate it."

I looked at the scruffy, boorish crew of iron-hard men-at-arms, who were drinking and laughing and shoving each other like unruly apprentices by the wine jugs on the sideboard, and seriously doubted it. But I could hardly deny my host the pleasure of my music when he had offered me shelter in his hall.

"I shall be delighted to perform for you, when I have taken my supper, but not just for your men. I would much prefer to sing, if I may be allowed, for every soul in the castle – for all the men-at-arms, the maids, the servants, even the huntsmen and the grooms..."

He frowned at me, and I wondered if I'd been too obvious.

"Very well, I shall pass the word. In, perhaps, an hour?"

"In one hour," I agreed.

I sank my wine, wolfed down a piece of bread and some cheese and went out for a walk around the castle courtyard. I wandered past the east tower where I now knew Jacqueline was being kept prisoner. I stared up at the arrow slit windows and, although I saw several with yellow candlelight behind them, I could not see any sign of my beloved.

I decided that it would not be a clever idea to try to force entry into the women's quarters at this hour, so I wandered casually away, circling the entire courtyard. At least I knew she was in the castle, and *she* knew I was here to rescue her. That should raise her spirits. I went to the stables on my next circuit and, after greeting Ghost with an apple purloined from the sideboard, I rummaged through my belongings and removed the vicious curved Arab dagger and the long vielle box from my saddlebags.

I tucked the dagger in my belt and went to the back of the long row of stables where I had spotted an old tack room earlier that day. After checking that nobody was nearby, I searched the recesses at the back of the space and swiftly found exactly what I needed. Rope. Lots of it. I stole a sixteen-foot length of thick hemp line from a dusty coil in a chest at the back of the space and wrapped it around my waist, hidden under my tunic. Then I climbed up on to the castle walls by the staircase.

I found a comfortable spot on the north wall, not far from the east tower. Once there, removing my vielle from its travelling box, I tuned the strings of the instrument, twisting the wooden pegs at its head, and played a few slow, sweet notes, putting some music into the front of my mind.

There was a sentry patrolling the wall, a young man in mail with a spear, shield and helm, and he nodded at me in a friendly fashion as I plucked the strings and practised a few simple combinations. He watched me for a while, clearly very bored, then eventually, he disappeared into the large western tower at the far end of the north wall.

There was no one else about. Acting as quickly as I could I laid down my instrument, unwrapped the rope from around my waist, making a large loop in the end and fixing it around one of the wall's crenulations, I dropped the rest of the rope down the outside of the high wooden wall.

Then, checking once more that I was not observed, I smeared some muck and dirt over the visible loop, making it the same colour as the dark wood, then peered over the edge of the wall. The end of the rope had fallen into the wet, filth-filled ditch that ran around the perimeter of the castle. In the gloom of dusk, the line, flush against the wall, was hidden from any casual glance. You'd need to know it was there to spot it.

Now that I had a viable route for escaping the castle with Jacqueline, I strolled along the wall, pretending to admire the last light of the day, and plucking a few notes on my instrument as I paced.

To the north of the castle the dark forest was just as dense as to the south – the way I had come. A black carpet of trees stretched out as far as the northern horizon. I wondered what creatures – magical or otherwise – lurked out there in that vast arboreal desert. Truly this was an island of men surrounded an ocean of wilderness. I decided on the spot that, when it came to the escape, I would not chance the forest again. I'd take the road west. And go hell for leather to evade the inevitable hot pursuit.

The young sentry reappeared suddenly, giving me something of a shock and making me actually jump a few inches in the air. However, I think I managed to hide my guilt and surprise just well enough.

The man-at-arms nodded again in a friendly fashion. I guessed that he had popped into the tower have an illicit cup of wine, or a bite of bread, or just a rest from his long, dull spell of patrolling the castle walls.

"Tell me, my good fellow," I said in my best French. "How

far is it to the River Saone from here. A goodly distance, I would guess."

"You'd be quite wrong," said the soldier. His accent was Germanic but his French was entirely comprehensible. I noticed that he had a large ugly red birthmark marring the whole of his right cheek.

"It is no more than five miles along that old road yonder."

I looked down at the weed-choked path that ran across the front of the castle. "Indeed? Five miles to the ford?" I guessed I could travel that far in an hour, an hour and a half, if Jacqueline slowed us. "And beyond the ford, how far beyond the river to the town of Dijon. Fifty miles?"

"Why, it is less than twenty miles. But beyond the river is the Duchy, out of our lord's domain. It is a strange, foreign, benighted land."

"I travel there tomorrow with a message from your lord to mine."

"Is that so? I've never been across the great river myself. I hear they're a sinful lot over there. Hardly human. Much given to sodomy."

I assured him this was true and urged him to stay this side, if he valued his soul. Then I bade him a good evening, and went down to the hall to sing for my supper.

I had hoped to get a brief opportunity to speak with Jacqueline alone but, when I saw her, she was with two other women, both dressed plainly like servants, chattering by the interior wall of the Logis. These were the first females I had laid eyes in the castle of Beaune-du-Bois – apart from Jacqueline herself – and their ordinary doughy features made her face all the lovelier. Word had clearly spread that I was to perform my music and the hall was now full of bodies, drinking and joking, friends chatting with their friends. At a rough count I thought I could see forty men-at-arms, and about twenty male servants, of varying ages – as well as the two serving girls and Jacqueline in a group apart from the men, by the door.

Very few women in such a multitude of young men, I thought. *If Jacqueline has not been ravished, it cannot be long before some drunken lout tries his luck.* There was no lady of the castle, so far as I could see, no chatelaine to order the household, and when the Green Knight took his place alone at the head of the table in a chair, he swung one muddy boot up on the wood, as if he were in some low whorehouse, not his own hall.

I stood up then and played a loud, dramatic chord on my vielle, with a great flourish of my bow. The entire hall fell silent.

Since the audience was largely made up of rough-hewn men-at-arms, I began my performance with a tale of warfare, of Roland and Oliver, two Christian heroes who fought the Saracens in Spain many hundreds of years ago, and who died bravely doing their duty at the pass of Roncesvalles. The song has a moving passage about Roland refusing to blow his famous elephant-tusk horn to summon help because he believed it would be an act of cowardice, and this part of the song was a huge success, greeted with cheers and quite a few doleful sighs.

By the time I had finished its recital, the hall was bellowing its warm appreciation for the tale; and I saw that more than a few of these tough Germanic men-at-arms had unashamed tears in their eyes.

Naturally, I followed up this triumphant beginning with another song of glory and honour and death in combat, this time a tale of a duel between two lords, who both loved the same beautiful lady.

This was also well received. *They must be starved for entertainment here*, I thought. And wondered how long it had been since they had a musician of my quality in this hall. Then I decided to change the whole tone of the performance. I played them a love song about a young squire who was in love with his lord's wife, but who tragically can never possess her – and this theme I noted was popular with the two servant girls. I thought I saw Jacqueline, too, wiping her eye when it was done.

After that, I asked for a moment or two to wet my throat with a cup of wine, and to use the latrine, and the Green Knight, who was all affability by that point, urged me to drink up and piss to my heart's content – then return to make more of my excellent music for his men.

I downed a cup of red and walked to the door of the Logis. I had spotted that Jacqueline was there, alone for once. The other two women had gone off on some errand or other – perhaps also looking for a similar relief. As I passed her, I paused, pretending to adjust the ties of my tunic, and muttered: "Meet me on the north wall. The wall right next to your tower. At midnight. Be sure to wear your warmest travelling clothes."

Then, without waiting on an answer, I left the hall, and trotted down the steps and into the courtyard, heading for the common latrines.

As I came back up into the hall, just a few moments later, I passed her again, and quickly winked. She was staring at me wonderingly – I thought I detected a look of deep yearning, perhaps even adoration, in her beautiful dark eyes. I do not think she had ever seemed so lovely to me. The firelight caught the fiery golden lights in her auburn hair beneath her simple white headdress; and her eyes seemed huge in its shadow, deep, dark pools of love. Once again I whispered to her, "This next *canso* – this next song I will play, I composed it only for you, my dearest love."

I quickly retuned my vielle, quickly drank down another cup of wine, nodded at the *chevalier*, who was sprawled in his chair but beaming ruddily at me, and with one quick, meaningful glance over at Jacqueline, I plucked a note and sang:

"She wakes delight in me once more
That's too long lain asleep,
Unearthing stirrings buried deep
She does my heart restore."

The response from my darling girl was more than just satisfactory. I saw Jacqueline gape and put her hand to her mouth. The two servant girls, now returned to her side, were all a-twitter, too. Even the men-at-arms seemed to like the *canso*'s jaunty tune. I struck a few more notes and sang another three elegant verses, lines that I had composed in my head on the lonely ride in the forest. I ended my Jacqueline's song with:

"A love that grows with each new breath
Fresh hope that blossoms sweet
I'll find my heaven when we meet
My hell her frown, her scorn my death."

The applause was a veritable storm of sound. The men were banging their clay cups in the tables and sideboards, the endless clatter seeming to shake the whole structure of the Logis. The Green Knight absolutely had rivers of tears running down his lean, black-bearded cheeks.

"Wonderful," Raoul said, "simply wonderful, Englishman!" I saw that Jacqueline, too, was overcome with emotion. She covered her lovely face with the long flap of her white headdress, turned, said something to her companions and made her way out of the hall.

I ended my performance that night – a fine exhibition, even though I say so myself – with a pair of hilarious and bawdy songs, about a lusty fox, a foolish old badger, a weasel thief and a coy lady rabbit, and had the entire hall in peals of laughter, the tears flowing freely once again, for a more joyful reason. Then I put down my vielle, and sat down at the table.

"Bravo, Englishman," boomed the Green Knight from the far end, "you have earned yourself another jug of wine at least. I was unsure about offering you my hospitality, at first, I thought you might be a spy, or be up to some mischief, but you've repaid my generosity tenfold. Here, take some wine, drink, be merry – you've brought us all joy tonight!"

So I drank and laughed with my host – since I could not refuse him. But as I smiled, and the wine slipped down, and he began to speak of his lonely life in this place, I found myself hating him and thinking: *"You cur – you foul despoiler of women. How dare you hold my love, my darling here against her will, with who-knows-what evil in your corrupted heart."*

"I envy you, Englishman," slurred the Green Knight a little while later, "you will be gone from here in a few days, travelling the world – and you've already seen much of it. You have been to Outremer, you've fought for Christ against the *paynim*. I've not left *Burgundia*, not once!"

He was very drunk, this Green Knight. And maudlin. And while I too could feel the wine stirring in my blood, too, I had not lost my self-command. I smiled and said: "This is not too bad a place, *chevalier*. You have the forest – rich in game; and no overweening king to bully you; or force you to war. I'll warrant your taxes are lighter, too, than in England."

"Hunting, that is all I have. That is all. I have no money, no lands, my family has guarded this castle faithfully for hundreds of years as the hereditary stewards of the Château de Beaune-du-Bois, yet it remains the Count's own demesne . . . all this is Otto's. He calls me his Forester! As if I was some cloddish woodsman, wielding an axe, stacking up logs for the winter. Where is my family's reward for all the decades of loyalty? The bones of my ancestors have been interred here for three centuries, yet still it is Count Otto's castle to do with as he chooses. I pay him no taxes, except in service – that is written into our charter, a deed from the time of Old Charlemagne himself – and Otto takes a full measure of service from me, you may be sure. I have no fields to grow crops in, no peasants to raise my wheat and oats and barley. If I want fresh meat for my men, I must catch it myself. If I want new clothes on my back, a ring on my finger, a fine horse and accoutrements, I must raid across the Saone."

I made a sympathetic noise but drunken self-pity is always tiresome.

" . . . I thought my troubles were over when I took you and your earl prisoner last week. I thought I would finally be rich as Midas! But even that plum was snatched away from me – and by Otto. I am left, as always, with nothing. Nothing. You say I have no king – and you are correct – I have something worse, the Free Count, the *Freigraf*, as he styles himself. He answers to no one but his brother the emperor – and so I say this to you again, if your English lord wishes some favour from me, and will pay well for it, or grant me a castle of my own and a title, let him ask..."

Despite everything, I *was* moved to pity for this drunken oaf of a knight. I hardened my heart. This sot had kidnapped my Jacqueline, snatched her from her hearth and home, and God only knew what cruel indignities he had made her suffer, or planned to inflict on her innocence.

"I will pass your message to my lord," I said. "Perhaps he can find a way to help you. But I must sleep now, *chevalier*. I shall be on the road all day tomorrow. With your permission, I shall withdraw to the stables."

"Sleep here. There's plenty of room. It will be warmer, too."

"The snoring of your men would, I fear, keep me awake long into the night," I said. Many of his wine-sodden men were already stretched out on the long benches around the hall, honking and sawing like hogs.

"As you please," said Raoul grumpily. He seized the jug and sloshed half a pint in his cup, spilling a goodly amount on the wooden board, too.

I gave it an hour, brushing Ghost down in the stables and saying a fond goodbye to him. There was no way I could take him away from the castle that night. And though I was saddened at the prospect of losing my faithful friend, I felt a grain of satisfaction: I knew that the Green Knight would look after him very well. And there was some measure of justice in leaving Ghost here. A sort of recompense. Raoul might be losing a pretty girl from his household that night but he was gaining a very fine horse.

When I judged it by the rising half moon to be nearly midnight, I crept out of the stables and went across the courtyard to the stair that led up to the north wall, circling the locked kennels, from whence I could hear the sleepy snorting of the six hell-beasts within, and climbed quickly and silently on to the battlements. There was no sign of a sentry – for which I was grateful. I'd have had to put the fellow down, knock him out or kill him, and I wished, if possible, to do this without bloodshed.

The Blessed Virgin Mary was with me. There was no one up there. There was *no one* up there. No sentry, but no Jacqueline either. I sat with my back against the wall, making myself as small as I could and I waited in the darkness. Half an hour crept slowly past, then an hour. I wondered if perhaps she could have misunderstood my message. I had delivered it in something of a hurry. No, that could not be true. She was a clever girl. Perhaps, then, she was bound with stout ropes, or chains, in her high tower. That seemed more likely. Or the doors to her rooms were bolted.

I would have to break in and rescue her.

I got up, uncoiling myself cautiously, and went down the steps to the dark, empty courtyard. Until this point I could have talked my way out of any encounter with one of the Green Knight's men. Taking a breath of night air or stretching my legs, I could have used any number of excuses to explain my nocturnal wandering. Until this moment, that is. I was about to cross a line. A point of no return. I checked that my sword was loose in its scabbard and the heavy Arab dagger was to hand in my belt.

I meant to do this without spilling any blood but, by Christ, if they tried to stop me freeing Jacqueline from her chains, they would get what was rightfully coming to them – and in full measure.

The half moon was emerging from its blanket of clouds, lighting the courtyard with an eerie glow. There was no one around – but for the buzz of soldierly snoring coming from the hall, the castle seemed deserted.

I twisted the cold iron handle on the arched outside door to the east tower, and it turned, and the portal swung open silently. I sent up a prayer of thanks for the man who had recently oiled the hinges. God reward him.

I stepped inside, into a dim red glow like a forge. I was inside the lower chamber of the east tower, and a small, banked fire glowed in the hearth by the wall. There was a man sleeping on a pallet by the coals, covered with a blanket, muttering in his sleep. A spear was leant against the wall, next to a sword. A coat of mail was hanging on a wooden stand.

Ahead of me a wooden staircase disappeared upwards into darkness. Ignoring the sleeping man-at-arms, and moving as quietly as a mouse, I began to climb the stairs. I had not taken more than three steps upwards, when the fellow by the fire gave a loud cry and half-sat up in his pallet.

I froze, my hand on my hilt.

But the soldier was not truly awake. He gave a low groan, or moan, as if he were in pain, and rolled over, pulling the blanket more firmly around his shoulders. I stayed stock still for a dozen heartbeats, listening to his breathing turn to regular snores. When I was sure he was asleep, I continued upwards, placing every foot carefully to avoid making the slightest squeak. I reached the first floor, which was largely occupied by a small chamber. The door was half-open and I peered cautiously inside.

There was a canopied bed in the centre of the room and two girls were lying next to each other, their heads on the pillows. I looked hard, aided by a shaft of moonlight that sliced through the arrow-slit window. Neither of these was Jacqueline. They were the servants from the hall.

I retreated, leaving the door open and the two girls undisturbed, and began to climb the stairs again to gain the upper storey, to the topmost part of the tower. Of course, I thought, where else would a rascally lord lock his damsel prisoner but in the highest chamber in his tallest tower.

I wondered for a few mad moments whether there was a *canso* to be found in this midnight tale – with myself as the dashing hero. And scolded myself silently for frivolity in a time of danger. I was on a mission. I had a vital task to perform. I had a flesh-and-blood damsel to rescue in real life, not in some silly ballad. The door to the chamber was closed, and I grasped the handle and turned it. And the door swung open.

I pushed the door to the upper chamber wide, and poked my head around the jamb. There was another bed, and resting on the white pillow I saw an auburn head, the glossy locks shot through with fine lines of gold.

It was Jacqueline, of course, her pale face just visible in the dim moonlight from the arrow slit. She was fast asleep; her features much softer, more blurred and vulnerable in repose. Yet, to me, she was still as beautiful as ever. I called out her name softly, hardly more than a whisper. She did not move. I called to her again, more loudly this time. She remained insensible. Dead to the world. I wondered if the *chevalier* had incapacitated her in some way, ensured her total lack of consciousness with some powerful sleeping potion or apothecary's drug.

I tiptoed closer, tripping over some tangling female garment in the darkness, stumbled, and shot out a hand to the small table next to the bed to steady myself. My fingers stabbed into a heavy earthenware water jug, which wobbled alarmingly, and I had to swiftly seize it with both hands to stop it falling with a crash and raising a hellish racket. I caught the jug, thank God. I steadied it. I let out a long relieved breath. Once I had recovered my calm, when my heart had ceased its reckless pounding, I spoke Jacqueline's name again, in a normal tone this time. Surely she must wake. Nothing. I stroked her downy cheek gently with my fingers.

She did not respond.

I grasped her slim right arm which was poking outside the warm covers and which felt strangely cold under my warm fingers. A sudden wave of panic drenched me: she was dead. This was a lifeless corpse. The Green Knight had killed her. Murdered her in her bed. Why? Why would he do such a thing? Was it my fault? Had my arrival sealed her fate?

Jacqueline opened her eyes, saw my deeply concerned face looming over hers, only a few inches away.

She screamed.

She yelled like a tormented soul from the depths of hell. I had to slap a palm over her mouth to shut down her terrible noise. I held her there, clamped to the bed, one hard hand over her open mouth. My other hand was at my own face; a commanding index finger at my own lips.

"Shush, Jacqueline; shush now. I need you to be very quiet."

She stared at me, eyes huge with uncomprehending terror.

"I mean you no harm," I said. "No harm at all. I've come to rescue you – remember? I told you in the Logis. I've come to take you away from this place, from the *chevalier*. I'm going to take you home. Now, I'm going to release you in a moment. But you must promise not to scream. You won't scream again, will you?"

I took my hand away from her face and moved back on the bed to allow her to sit up. She raised herself up. I saw her take a large, steadying breath, and another one, her bosom rising and falling. Then she took another breath – and screamed, much, much louder this time than before.

I was on her like a leopard, my hand slapping round her jaw, cutting off all breath. I pinned her down to the bed, using both my arms and one leg, although she was squirming, wriggling like a trapped eel in her terror. I had to use all my strength to subdue her madly writhing body.

"Jacqueline, stop it!" I hissed in her ear. "Just stop it now. Be still and quiet. Be calm. I'm here to help you escape this place."

She ceased struggling, mainly I think because she couldn't breath with my big hand over her face. I cautiously released her.

"No more noise," I said. "Promise you'll be quiet. I need you to get up and get dressed. I'm taking you away from here."

Her expression was unreadable in the dim and shadowy room but, thank God, she finally seemed to understand that I meant her no harm and she began to do as she had been told. I half-turned away to give her some privacy, as she pulled on a gown over her thin linen chemise, and threw a woollen shawl gathered from the floor over that. I was listening hard for noises down the stairs – but I heard nothing untoward. God Almighty was with us that night, it seemed, for no one had paid heed to her screams.

I turned back to face her. "Are you ready?" I said.

"What do you want with me, Englishman?" she said.

"I told you," I said, somewhat testily. "I'm here to rescue you. I'm here to take you back to your old mother in Fontaine."

She stared at me. Struck dumb with gratitude, I assumed. Previously I had alarmed her – that was clear. Now she had grasped the truth.

"You will need your shoes," I said helpfully.

Then I heard the clatter of heavy boots on the stair, several men pounding upwards, and through the open door the red flicker of torches.

I gave Jacqueline a long, disappointed look. I shook my head sadly and drew my sword. I had not wanted to shed a drop of blood this night. Now, it seemed, I would have no choice.

An instant later the Green Knight appeared in the doorway and behind him I saw two big men-at-arms carrying burning brands.

"Step aside, *chevalier*," I said, pointing my naked sword at him. "Step aside and let us pass. I mean to get the girl away from here safely."

The Green Knight was glaring at me like a demon. He had his own shining blade out. "You filthy snake!" he said. "You greasy slithering reptile. You came into my house, as an honoured guest in my hall, and I welcomed you. And this, *this* is how you repay my kindness, with low treachery and foul lust."

Something exploded. I felt a sharp pain in the back of my head. The chamber slowly expanded into bright sparks of blue and red and gold, and then shrank back to a ring of pitch black around the tableau of the three men-at-arms by the door.

I could feel my legs collapsing under me, a sinking feeling, and I twisted to look behind me as I fell, a slow descent to the floor more than a sudden tumble. I saw Jacqueline holding the handle of the shattered water jug in her hand, her pink mouth open with the shock of her violence.

Then the world slipped sideways and slid into nothingness.

CHAPTER ELEVEN

I awoke in the chapel of the castle of Beaune-du-Bois. It was not a swift process: a slow dawning, a creeping sense of awareness, as my whirling mind eased back into my broken head and I realised I was indeed alive.

They had tied my hands and my feet and, judging from the fresh agonies on my back and shoulders, overlaying the bruises I had earned in the dark streets of Dijon, they had dragged me roughly down the stairs from Jacqueline's chamber and across the courtyard and thrown me into the chapel with maximum force and minimum thought for my comfort.

I lay in agony, head splitting, my whole body throbbing – the ropes too tight around my ankles and wrists making bands of cold fire – and I wondered if the Green Knight meant to kill me this day. For it *was* day, I saw, the faint light in the chapel told me so. I looked up at the large wooden cross hanging on the wall of the chapel, above the altar, and prayed for my soul. My sword was gone; and the Arab dagger too had been taken away. My purse full of silver had disappeared from my belt.

None of that was a surprise.

Yet Jacqueline's actions had been. It was certainly my fault. Of course, it was. There was no point blaming my sweet Jacqueline for our discovery by the Green Knight and his two men. She had been frightened out of her wits – God know what the *chevalier* had done to her these past few days. I suddenly popped up in her chamber like a demonic apparition and she panicked. She screamed; she lashed out wildly with the heavy water jug. Any woman might have done the same. My fault, I told myself once again. But, as my head pulsed and my aching body protested, all my muscles screaming at being held in such an unnatural position, other less noble thoughts bubbled up inside my mind. Was she stupid? Was she, in fact, a total fucking imbecile? I had very clearly told her to meet me at midnight on the north battlements. Then, when I was in her sleeping chamber, I had immediately told her I meant no harm, that all I wanted was to rescue her from the *chevalier*. What was wrong with the girl?

I pushed these unkind thoughts away – with some difficulty.

I loved Jacqueline, of course I did. I held fast to that notion. If I could only get myself out of this situation, I would sit down and quietly explain everything to her. And she would understand. One day we would both laugh about this and tell our children of our misadventures. First I must survive whatever foul torments the *chevalier* had in store for me.

I lay on the cold stone floor of the chapel, in sheer, spine-racking agony, for another long, long hour at least. The grey light seeping into the low building was growing stronger and I saw that the entire right-hand wall of the chapel had a strange cobbled texture, as if it was constructed of small round boulders, and there seemed to be short thick sticks placed under each of the boulders. I looked again as the morning light grew steadily brighter. Not sticks. Not boulders. They were bleached, fleshless skulls and the crossed thighbones of long dead men and women.

I gave an involuntary gasp and shiver of terror, all the way down from my blood-crusted nape to my sadly bruised toes. Then I steadied my nerve and attempted to control my fears. I knew what this chapel was. I recognised soon enough it as an ossuary, a place where the bones of the dead are stored, awaiting the resurrection of the bodies of the faithful on the blessed Day of Judgment.

I recalled then what the Green Knight had said in his interminable drunken ramblings the night before, that the bones of his ancestors rested in this castle. There was nothing sinister about it. Nothing. These were the remains of many generations of stewards of the château de Beaune-du-Bois. I knew that. I also knew it was common practice in many lands.

They were merely dry old bones, the piled remains of long-dead men and women. Yet for some reason I continued to be gripped by a sense of fear, deep in my core, a terror that grew, and which I could not shake it off. I was looking at my own death. Those old bones were a *memento mori* – a message from God to remind me of my fate; that, shortly, my living, breathing body was to be reduced to a skull and a few dry sticks.

Then the wooden door banged open, a vigorous young man in hunting leathers put his head though looked at me for a few moments, and then turned and bellowed over his shoulder in their own crude German dialect. Words that I could only assume meant something akin to: "The prisoner is awake now, master!"

"Bring me water for the love of God," I gasped in French.

The man ignored me and went away, the door crashing shut.

A little while later the chapel door opened again and this time it was the Green Knight himself. He came and stood over me, tall and forbidding, trembling slightly. I realised that he was simmering with a vast rage.

"Water, for God's sake," I said. "And loose my bonds..."

The *chevalier* kicked me hard in the face, his riding boot splitting my skin over the cheekbone.

"You do not speak to me, you snake," he said. "You never speak to me again, if you understand what's good for you."

"My lord, I have done nothing wrong. If you would only let me explain..." I was pleading like a coward. Fear had me in its claws.

He kicked me again; this time his boot caught me under the chin, bruising my throat. I decided to keep my mouth shut and listen to what he had to say. Which was nothing for a long time.

"I should string you up, right now," he said, "for what you tried to do to the girl. I've hanged better men for lesser crimes."

I opened my mouth but before I could utter a syllable he kicked me in the belly. I let out a groan but no actual words.

"You even think about speaking and I *shall* hang you!"

Two men-at-arms came into the chapel, and behind them a nervous priest. One of the soldiers said something I didn't catch.

"Carry him out and cut him loose," said the Green Knight in French, addressing the priest. "Have him say his final prayers."

The two men-at-arms picked me up. I heard the priest say: "I must hear his confession, grant him absolution. It is only right and proper."

"He claims he has done nothing wrong," sneered Raoul. "So he has no need of your absolution. If he goes to hell, so be it."

In the courtyard they untied the ropes that bound me and one of the men gave me a bowl of filthy water from the horse trough.

I drank every last drop.

There were a dozen men on horseback, circling round the courtyard, and the six of the enormous hell-hounds had been released from their kennels – horrible, shaggy monsters, appearing to be more wild bear than tame dog to my terrified eyes. Their whippers-in came nearer to me and I began to edge away until I felt the prick of a spear point in my back.

"Stand and let them get your scent," said the Green Knight. I knew, then, I knew with a dread realisation, like a bucket of icy water hurled in my face, what the *chevalier* had in mind for me this day.

The six massive hounds sniffed my legs, my hose, my boots, taking great hungry gulps of my scent.

"We will patrol the main road to Dijon with horsemen. If they see you they'll ride you down without mercy. Men will be on the riverbank, too. Your one chance of success, your one chance to live, is to get all the way through the Forest of Chaux down to the town of Dole."

The Green Knight smiled nastily as he told me this.

"No," I said. "I won't do it. I'm Christian. An Englishman. I will not be hunted down, pursued like some beast of the forest."

"You'd rather hang? Very well, fetch the ropes, Gustav."

"Wait!" I said. "Wait just one moment..." I found I was panting madly, as if I was already being pursued. "If I escape. If I make it though the forest, if I can get clear away, you will let me live? You swear it?"

"You do not deserve to live a moment longer, snake. And were it not for the fact you favoured me with your music, I'd have stripped all the skin from your living body by now and pissed on the raw wounds. But, yes, if you can touch the walls of Dole with your right hand, you may live. I swear this on my honour."

"If you kill me, my lord of Locksley will have your head on a spike," I said. It was quite true. Yet it did not scare the Green Knight.

"Your message from him is false – and obviously so. I do not think you still serve the cunning English earl. I believe you have fled from him. When we catch up with you in the forest – and we will catch you – when my dogs have ripped your living body into rags, and chewed your bones to splinters, no one but us will ever know what became of you."

Raoul smiled again. "The Earl of Locksley shall never know where your torn remains moulder. He will simply think that you, like so many other low-born, cowardly scum, have run away from your rightful lord."

I could think of nothing useful to say to that.

"You may have the quarter part of one hour," the *chevalier* said, "then I shall release my hounds. The man-gate is open, you see..."

I turned to look and saw that the small man-sized door in the much bigger castle gate had indeed been flung wide. All around me were hard, unfriendly foreign eyes. Some filled with a savage glee in anticipation of the pleasures to come. I looked up at the east tower and saw a small white face framed with auburn hair watching from the arrow slit on the third storey. One hound, the bitch called Apricot, growled – a terrible sound.

"Time is slipping through your fingers, Englishman," said the Green Knight. "Do not tarry. If I were you, I would run, run as fast as you can."

So I did.

I pelted straight out of the castle gate, flashed across the east-west track and plunged into the Forest of Chaux. I ran with heart and legs pumping, ignoring my pounding head, my poor aching body. I put all my strength and courage into sprinting as fast as I could away from the château de Beaune-du-Bois and into the deep gloom of the woods. I found a narrow track, a deer path no more that that, which wended through the close-growing trees and followed it, gasping, thumping along, hobbling, staggering, stumbling sometimes, but concentrating only on putting one leg in front of the other as fast as possible, staying upright, moving forward, and getting precious air into my poor burning lungs.

I do not know for how far I ran, for a mile perhaps, maybe even two, but eventually, inevitably, I tripped on an unseen root and crashed forward on my face in the tangle of an alder bush; scraping my cheek painfully against the rough branches. I lay in the bush, panting like a bellows in a leaf-filled bowl in the earth, my chest rising and falling, trying to listen to the forest above the hectic noise of my own breathing.

My stomach heaved and quickly turning my face to the side I vomited. And again. I pushed myself up on to my hands and knees with difficulty and puked once more, until my belly was empty as an upturned bucket. My head was spinning now, my vision flashing red, yellow and black. My body felt as if it had been crushed by boulders. Then pulled apart by wild horses. Every inch of me seemed to burn.

But, eventually, my breathing returned to near normal.

I cocked an ear to take in all the sounds around me. No birds, no animals. No God-damned hell-hounds. No noises at all. Could I have escaped the hunters? Was that even possible?

I wiped my sick-wet mouth and got shakily to my feet. I did not want to get up. I wanted a drink of water, and I wanted to lie down and sleep for a year. Then I heard it, faint but quite unmistakable.

The sound of baying behind me.

I had no idea where I was, and only the faintest notion of where Dole was – somewhere south of me. But I knew it was about mid-morning then so I decided to head directly into the sun – if I could find it under that gloomy green canopy. I heard the sound of the pack belling again, closer this time, and louder, as I stumbled about looking upwards through the branches and leaves for a hint of the great yellow orb that would show me the way. I heard a snatch of mocking laughter – a faerie? A faun? The hidden folk held far less terror for me now. There were real monsters after me. I could hear the sound of those evil dogs clearly, crashing through the undergrowth. I caught a flash of the sun, and seeing it, I fixed on a direction, and began to run once more.

I burst through the branches, blundering forward, following no path at all now, just bulling my way through the green, face scratched, all my fine clothes ripped to sad rags. The terrible hounds were closer now – it was clear they could easily outpace me in this forest – and I thought I could hear the excited calling of hunters, too, and the jingle of equipment and the sounding of jaunty horns.

I forced myself to increase the pace, from a shambling loose-footed trot to something closer to a proper pounding sprint. On and on. On and on. I found a path, roughly heading south, and pushed all my remaining strength into my legs. But my limbs seemed to have turned to jelly and I was zigzagging madly between the unforgiving trees, panting with wild fear and exhaustion, stomach sick and cold, bashing into trunks like a drunkard, swiped across the face by low branches, tripping over vines and tussocks of undergrowth, sprawling on my face, again, hauling myself upright, cursing, crying quietly and continuing to stumble onwards.

I staggered on for the best part of an hour – I had no true

knowledge of time – my legs now almost folding beneath me. I realised that it had only been six days since I had been badly beaten with wooden clubs in Dijon; since then I had ridden fifty miles, been smashed over the head with a heavy jug, dragged down the castle stairs and now I was being hunted by a pack of savage hounds through these accursed woods.

God was clearly very angry with me for some reason.

The dogs were very near now and as I turned and snatched a glance behind me I saw two low, black, streaking forms, bounding effortlessly between the trees only thirty paces away.

Would it hurt very much, I wondered, as I tottered onwards, my speed getting slower as exhaustion crept up my spine and turned my muscles to water, when the first horrible beast sank his fangs into me? It occurred to me that I should try to find a stout branch somewhere to use as a make-shift club. Should I turn and face them? Make a stand? No, I thought, while it would be good to have weapon – any weapon – I could not afford the time it would take to stop and find a suitable bludgeon. I'd have to dig for a branch in the leaf litter; or try to snap a limb off a tree.

I glanced behind me and saw a flash of a huge reddish-brown object leaping lithely through the trees just ten yards behind me. It was that Satan-spawned bitch Apricot, I was sure of it. I pushed myself to make more speed, somehow summoning a final burst of strength from I know not where. I was not even sure if I was still heading south, towards Dole and safety. There was no sign of the sun. The baying behind me was now very loud – but one canine voice was sounding louder, deeper than all the others. That hell-bitch Apricot. She was in front, leading the whole devilish pack, seeking to have the first bite of my frail exhausted body.

I saw a patch of forest that was partially cleared, lighter that the shadowed rest, and stumbled towards it, more falling than running. I needed to see the sun one last time. I needed to find the way south.

I burst out of the trees and into the clearing and looked up at a patch of clear blue sky. The sun was there, yes, cheery, bright – and behind me! I had been running in circles. How could that be? I had run a huge arc.

I'd been heading north all this time.

My heart sank. I was now further away from Dole, even further from salvation, than I had been half an hour ago. I crumpled to my knees, head drooping in defeat. I was beaten. I was finished. My swollen hard-battering heart was trying to burst its way out from my chest; my gasping lungs were filled with liquid fire. I opened my eyes, and saw the lead hell-beast clearly – Apricot – her fur as red as fresh blood, eyes gleaming with a pure malice, a mere twenty yards away across the little clearing.

She stopped lifted her massive head and howled, a huge noise, a deafening death knell, summoning the rest of the monstrous pack and all the fell huntsmen who followed it. I surged to my feet – I must find a weapon, I must, a stick, anything to keep that foul beast's jaws from my soft flesh. I scanned the clearing for something, anything, and saw the remains of a fire, a black patch in the green grass with some slender, half-burnt sticks, remains of a human camping place.

Not all of them were sticks. One of them held the tiny, blackened carcass of a creature, gnawed meat, and a steel handle shaped in a cross.

Not a stick – it was a blade. My own *misericorde*.

I scrambled over to the remains of the fire and snatched up the dagger, stripping the bones of the squirrel off the iron spike with my left hand. The handle felt cool in my right palm; fitting in to it snugly like a beloved old friend. I turned to look at the massive red-brown beast on the far side of the clearing. It was crouched low, creeping forward slowly. The red-brown monster was stalking me. Yet I was ready to take her on.

"Come on then, you ugly bitch!" I said. "Let's be having you."

Apricot rushed at me. A series of long low bounds and they she was on me, rearing up. Her yellow jaws were wide, her breath searing my face like a flame. But I got my own left hand up just in time, desperate fingers gripping her thick muscular throat. Her weight and power were astonishing, hurling me irresistibly backwards, slamming me hard into the bole of an oak tree. I managed somehow to keep her madly snapping teeth from my chin – but only just.

My right hand shot out. I rammed the needle point of the *misericorde* into her lower ribcage. It crunched through the giant hound's ribs with no difficulty, the tip raking through her lungs and heart, ripping through soft organs, tearing the life-giving arteries and puncturing veins.

I pulled out the slim blade, now bloody to the hilt and punched it home again. And again. And again. My right arm working like a piston, the blood splashing and pulsing right up my forearm. The dog sagged against me, its head thumping hard on to my shoulder, a pathetic whining sound squeezed from her finger-compressed throat. I dropped my aim and spiked the blade into its taut belly, slamming in once, twice, three times.

Then I thrust the limp weigh of the dying animal off me. It crashed to the ground and the hell-bitch kicked once and was still. I spat on the corpse, turned and sprinted away into the trees, this time towards the sun.

There is a great deal of difference between being unarmed and fleeing in terror of your life, and having a good bloody steel blade in your fist and the hot coursing joy of having dispatched an enemy singing in your veins.

The slaying of the hell-bitch Apricot filled me with a fierce new energy. My lungs still burned with an icy fire and my poor legs were as limp as sops of milky bread, but I had fresh purpose in my wobbly stride.

I had a plan. I knew what I would do.

I jogged slowly and painfully south for a half-mile, then turned due west, heading towards the River Saone. I could still hear the monstrous dogs and the bastard hunt-riders, crashing through the greenwood somewhere behind me, and the oddly merry tootling of their horns. They were surely more wary now, after the killing of Apricot. And my heart was filled to the brim with a fine, hard, killing rage.

The cold power of righteous anger.

The *chevalier* had clearly thought that he could pursue me like a poor, panting hart. He may have believed he could treat me like prey. But I was no longer the hunted. Blade in my fist, I was now the hunter.

After a few hundred yards, travelling through the dense wood, I turned due north. At least I believed it was north, I was orienting myself not by the noon-high sun now, but by the sounds of the dogs and their riders. The remaining hounds would follow my scent anywhere, I knew, and the riders would follow the hounds.

I was trying to get round behind them all.

I stumbled into a small stream in the woods and paused for a moment to clean the blood off my blade and drink a few much-needed mouthfuls of water. I had no feelings of hunger at all. When the cold water hit my empty belly, I felt a shock of a pure joy jolt through my veins like lightning. I offered up a prayer to my personal saint, Michael, the warrior archangel: "Grant me proper vengeance, holy one, watch over me and ward me as I mete out justice to this arrogant band of evildoers."

I caught a glimpse of a rider through the trees then – a young man in hunting leathers wearing a green woollen hood. He was alone and alternately drinking from a wine flask, and calling out plaintively, trying to locate to his lost companions. I saw the red birthmark on his face and realised it was the sentry from the north wall. It seemed he had become separated from the rest. *All praise to you, Saint Michael,* I thought.

I stalked that poor young man for an age, moving closer to him, step by step, keeping behind trees and bushes, and occasionally scuttling along on my belly like a rat when his back was turned. I had regained my ragged breath, and my exhaustion was now fuelling my hatred. My friend Hanno had spent many hours patiently teaching me all the tricks that he knew for stealthy movement in a wide variety of terrains – and thick woodland is one of the easiest to traverse. Lines of sight in the forest are short at the best of times; and this young fool was a little drunk, and also a bit slow-witted and inexperienced.

I killed him as swiftly as I could – but I must admit I did it without the smallest shred of remorse. I leapt on him from out of a low-growing limb on an oak tree, bundling him clean out of the saddle with my weight and momentum, and stabbing him several times in his belly and thighs as we struggled together on the leafy woodland floor.

He tried to scream but I clamped a hand over his yelling mouth and slipped the blade of my *misericorde* up under his ribs, through his lungs, probing for his heart. As I did so I was reminded, painfully, of my silly struggle with Jacqueline in the chamber at the top of the east tower.

When the young man was finally still, I got up and I cleaned myself as best I could. I took off his green hood and cloak, caught his frightened horse and secured the animal to a tree. Then I took stock of my situation. I pulled the fellow's corpse into a patch of bushes and kicked leaves over it. It would not stay undiscovered long, not with hounds on my scent, but with luck it should remain hidden long enough for me to get clear.

He had a falchion, a kind of short, cleaver-like sword, and a hunting crossbow slung from his saddle, with a handful of bolts in a bag beside it. Best of all, he had a long spear held upright in a deep leather socket on his horse's withers. That would serve me admirably well, I thought.

I could hear the hounds, very close now, a mere few hundred yards away, as I swung up into the unfamiliar Burgundian saddle. Soothing the skittish horse, patting it, I turned its head north and kicked it into a trot.

The animal was eager to run, to escape the smells of blood and death in the forest, and it seemed to know where it was heading. I concentrated on staying on its back as it went into the canter, avoiding being brained by low-hanging branches, and keeping one ear open for sounds of pursuit. I was gratified to hear the noises of the hunt soon fade away behind me – the trumpets dying, and the mad howling of the hounds growing quiet.

Soon there was near silence. As we rode along, the only noise was the horse's breath, and my own, and the thud of hooves on the leaf litter.

It felt wonderful to be mounted, and well armed, after such a day of helpless terror. After two or three miles I stopped and patted the horse's neck, dismounted and I took a swig from the dead man's wine flask. I found some dried sausage and bread from his saddlebags, and ate like a wolf. The forest all around me was silent as the grave – no birds, no animals, and no sight or sound of that infernal hunt.

I realised that I had escaped them.

We were, I soon discovered, only about a mile from the main road. The horse found its way there without much help from me, instinctively heading back to its stables and, a little after noon, I found myself on the weed-covered track that led from Beaune-du-Bois west towards the river.

In the distance, about half a mile to my right, I could even see the dark, forbidding walls of the castle itself. I was filled then with a strange icy bravado: a part of me wanted to ride up to the castle, and enter it, and kill every miserable, motherfucking bastard inside, before riding off with Jacqueline over my saddle bow. But I managed to quell this mad, suicidal instinct. It would have been lunacy. There were forty armed men in there. I'd throw away all I'd gained in the past hour, and my own life with it.

So, reluctantly, I turned the stolen horse's head west and, sticking to the old weed-covered road, I cantered off into the golden afternoon.

CHAPTER TWELVE

There were three of them at the ford. Mounted, all with shields bearing the green and white pattern I had seen on the warriors of Beaune-du-Bois. I knew who they were and why they waited. Yet they did not know me.

I pulled the dead man's green hood further forward over my face, so they would not recognise me. Yet I was confident that they would not expect their beaten, frightened, unarmed fugitive – their God-damned *prey* – to be mounted and armed. I trotted towards them straight backed, looking beyond the three riders to the wide, brown, shallow stretch of the Saone, which was marked by several large stones. This was the crossing place that Henrik the Tanner had told me about. Beyond it was the safety of the Duchy, Dijon and my friends. First I had to pass these enemies.

I showed them no mercy. None at all. When I was twenty paces away, I lifted the loaded crossbow from where I had concealed it against my leg, levelled it and shot the leading rider through the lower abdomen.

He yelled out in agony and shock, the short black quarrel sticking out from his belly, just above his groin. The blood already beginning to ooze. I snatched the spear from the holder, flipped it under my right armpit, and with my lance couched like a knight, I kicked my horse on. The other two men were shouting warnings to each other, hauling out swords – and I admit they were good soldiers, very quick off the mark.

But I was quicker.

A few instants later, I thrust the spear deep into the centre of mailed chest of the second man, transfixing his hard-beating heart as I galloped past, and, releasing the long shaft, I left it wedged in his sternum.

Then I ducked. The third man was on me, his sword hissing just an inch over my green woollen hood.

I got past him unharmed but I was now in trouble, struggling to get the heavy falchion out of its leather sheath. It was an unwieldy blade – thicker at its square end than at the hilt – and the third man-at-arms was coming at me again, sword flickering out towards my face. I managed to dodge his lightning lunge the blade hissing past my shoulder. Then he lashed at me backhanded, a blow that would have sliced half my skull away, had it landed. He was snarling and spitting at me as he made his stroke. I left the falchion in its stout leather sheath, and held it up two-handed, above my head, as if it was no more than a flat steel bar.

His sword clanged into the falchion's middle section, slicing right though its thick sheath. But he did not cut into my body. I swung the falchion at him, hard at his ribs, and heard a crunch as the blow landed.

He yelled out, cursed me in German. Hunched over in his saddle, obviously in great pain. So, as his horse passed me, I hit him again, a smashing sweep of a blow across the back of his steel-helmeted head.

The ring of iron on steel was shockingly loud – but more surprising was that it did not fell the man. Astoundingly, he shook off the blow, seeming to recover astonishingly fast. Now he was coming back at me. Shield held high, sword cocked and ready to strike again, guiding his horse only with his knees. A good warrior, this one, skilled and deadly.

I had finally got the ripped leather sheath off the falchion blade, and hurled it away. The weapon's weight and balance was quite unfamiliar and felt horribly unnatural in my hand. The falchion is a big, bludgeoning weapon, best used by untrained men, who are unskilled in sword play.

But it *is* a formidable one. As the third Burgundian man-at-arms came barrelling at me on his horse, I smashed the cleaver-like blade straight down into the poor creature's long forehead, aiming the heavy tip at the big white blaze between its huge liquid eyes.

The blow landed. The horse reared up, snorting and whinnying, its long nose now drenched with blood, while I hunched under the Beaune-du-Bois man's wild swing – made inaccurate by the horse's dying antics. His beast was done beneath him, its front legs collapsing; meanwhile I circled back, spurred back, came in hard, swung and sunk the falchion into the fellow's mailed back, just as he was trying to kick both his feet free of the stirrups, and extricate himself from the fast collapsing beast.

The blade crunched though mail, ribs and spine and he gave a great coughing yell, his back arching, his whole body flopping like a fish.

I hauled my red blade free of his flesh, catching a glimpse of his bluish, opened lungs. Then, knowing him a dead man, I kicked my horse on, towards the wide ford, leaving three dying souls in my bloody wake.

I had thought to go straight to Dijon. Robin would be worried about me – although I suspected that *furious* would be a better word – and this may have had an impact on my decision. Instead, I rode directly to Fontaine on the stolen horse and, as the shadows began to lengthen, I found myself climbing the hill with a view of Dijon town spread out to the south.

I rode past the low wall by the churchyard, looking out for the kindly little priest but seeing no one around, and finally I came to the gate of the little enclosure where the old woman Yvette lived with her pigs.

Jacqueline's mother was overjoyed to see me and delighted when I said her only child was safe and, as far as I knew, quite unharmed.

She hugged me, kissed me several times, and sat me down

and fed me a pottage with bacon and cabbage and a cup of strong cider, and while I told her what I knew, she kept making delighted cries and comments.

"So, my pretty minx has caught the eye of a lord of the County – a knight with his own castle. A-ha, a forester, you say! She *has* fallen on her feet! I always knew she would – luck of the Devil, that little cat."

I did not like to say that I believed that she was being kept against her will and might perhaps even now be being brutally ravished by the Green Knight or one of his many lustful henchmen. If *Maman* chose to believe her sweet daughter was happy and had found the love of a fine, rich man, well ... who was I to bring her painfully back down to earth.

Neither did I mention that *I* had been cruelly beaten and bound and humiliated and hunted like a wild creature through the forest and had been obliged to kill four men this very afternoon. Frankly I was too tired and sore to try to make her understand the truth and, when I had eaten my pottage and drunk my cider, I begged leave to sleep the night in one of her empty pigsties.

She kissed me again and insisted that I show her my bruises, and she tutted over the fresh marks on my skin and once again wielded her pot of comfrey, then she stitched my cuts, and when I finally managed to escape her attentions and curl up in the straw, I was asleep in the blink of an eye.

I did not awake until noon the next day, as stiff as a plank of oak. The first thing I saw was a small, bald, man-at-arms in well-worn leather armour, sitting on the wall of the pigsty and cleaning his fingernails with a long, vicious-looking dagger.

"You snore even louder than these hogs, youngling," said Hanno.

I was overjoyed to see him, leapt up and hugged him, and felt only a little apprehensive when he continued: "Robin's here. He wants to speak with you when you wake. But first wash – you stink just like your pigs."

I washed thoroughly and made myself as presentable as

I could. The rich-man's clothes I had purchased in Marseilles were in a wretched state by now, not much better than tatters and rags after my helter-skelter flight though the thick woods. But there was nothing I could do about that. I found Robin with the crone at a table in her garden, a dozen yards from her cottage, sipping a big cup of her cider and eating bacon and eggs.

"So Alan . . ." he said to me. "This is what has become of you. You've chosen the life of a humble Burgundian swineherd, is that it?"

I said: "Why not? Congenial company, if rather pungent, no lord to constantly scold you, plenty of sleep, and all the bacon I care to eat."

Robin laughed then and I was so relieved he wasn't angry I almost burst into humiliating tears. But I kept my composure – even at the tender age of seventeen, I cherished my dignity. The old lady got up then, mumbled an excuse, and hobbled off towards her tumbledown cottage.

Robin said: "You had better tell me, Alan, what you've really been doing then. I take it you *did* deliver my message to Count Otto?"

I told him everything: the sudden disappearance of Jacqueline; the rumours of the grey riders; my journey through the forest to the castle of Beaune-du-Bois; the attempt to flee the fortress with Jacqueline; and being hunted like a hart through the forest by Raoul and his hounds.

Robin listened without interruption – a fine quality he had always possessed – and, when I had finished, he said: "There is a reckoning to be made with this presumptuous *chevalier*, that's for sure. First he attacks us in the Duchy, captures us and puts us in a difficult position in Dole, now he hunts you for his sport like some wild animal. It's quite unforgiveable. You threatened him with dire revenge, didn't you? You told him I would surely make him pay with his life if he hurt you, yes?"

I admitted I had. But I also said that the Green Knight didn't seem to be very concerned about any retribution from my lord.

"Hmm. Is that so?" said Robin, and something glinted in his

eye.

"When Little John comes up," I said, tentatively, "when he gets here with all the men and the wagons, could we go back to the castle, besiege it, take it, and rescue my sweet love from his evil clutches? Could we do that, Robin? And reduce the whole place to a pile of burning rubble."

"That is one option, certainly," said Robin. "But tell me honestly now, Alan, are you completely sure that you love this girl Jacqueline?"

"I love her with all my heart," I said. "And she loves me."

Robin looked cautiously around but the old woman had disappeared inside her little house, and was well out of earshot, in any case.

"Are you quite *sure* she loves you in return?"

I frowned at him. "What do you mean?"

"I mean no disrespect, Alan, for sure. And I'm not trying to be clever, or hurtful, or to make you feel bad . . . but Jacqueline *did* hit you with a heavy water jug. And knocked you unconscious."

"She was frightened. I surprised her in her chamber . . ."

"Yes, well, it's just that, ah, from the way you tell it, she never actually *said* she loved you, or that she wanted to be rescued by you. Or that she was not, in fact, perfectly happy to remain in this remote castle with this young, handsome and desperately lonely *chevalier*."

I stared at him. A horrible realisation began to dawn on me. I had assumed that just because I wanted Jacqueline, she must reciprocate my tender feelings. Now that I thought about it clearly, unemotionally, she had never given me any indication that she sought my affections – none at all. She had been friendly in the cook-shop but I had been a paying customer there, a young man with a purse full of silver and time on his hands – I searched my memory for anything she had said to show even a jot of feeling for me. Even when I had stood up for her honour against the two pawing apprentices, she had not been particularly grateful to me.

She did not love me. The realisation crashed into my mind. She hadn't wished to be rescued by me from the castle. I had told her to meet me on the north wall, and she had ignored my instructions. When I went to her room, she had screamed for help, not once but twice, then knocked me down with the jug. She *did not* want me. But did I still want *her*?

Suddenly I wasn't even sure about that. How could I love someone who was happy to remain with a monster, a cruel man who hunted men?

"We don't have to do anything *now* about the Green Knight," said Robin. "I've had word from Little John saying he'll be in Dijon in a day or so. We can decide what to do then. Meanwhile, I'd like your company. I'd to talk to you about something important. Are you fit enough to ride?"

I said I was – although in my head I was cringing from my stupidity over Jacqueline. I was also asking myself why. *Why didn't she love me?*

We bade farewell to Yvette and her pigs, and Robin, Hanno and I rode away. On the brow of the hill, before we descended on the road towards the town of Dijon, Robin told me that he would now explain to me how we might be able to further the cause of King Richard in this region.

"That great, slow, green river twenty miles yonder," said my lord, waving eastwards in the direction the Saone, which was of course quite invisible at this distance, "is the natural frontier between two kinds of peoples, Germans on the far side and Frenchmen on this one. This is the juncture, the line, where the two great tribes of Europe meet. They are blood enemies – different both in tongue and in temperament. There had been enmity between then since Charlemagne died three hundred years ago. And I believe there will always be bad feeling between them."

"What has that to do with our cause? King Richard's cause?"

"Richard will soon be at odds with Philip of France," my lord continued, "and war between them is now inevitable. The

Duchy of Burgundy will support the kingdom of France. Lord Eudes, son of the duke, the current regent and heir to the Duchy, spent much happy time as a child at the French court of Philip. They are childhood friends and now allies. Together, the combined strengths of France and Burgundy are more than a match for Richard's knights in all the Angevin lands in his demesne. If those two managed to combine together with the Holy Roman Emperor's German knights to attack Richard, the war would be over before it even began. We English would surely be expelled from the continent. Richard would be ejected from his patrimony. So, clearly, our task must be to try to prevent Burgundy from supporting the kingdom of France in the coming war, and also to stop the emperor from joining in on their side against us. Now, how can we best achieve that worthy aim?"

Neither Hanno nor I had any answer to his question.

"We achieve that aim," Robin said, wagging a comic finger at me like a dusty old schoolmaster, "by involving the Duchy of Burgundy in a costly and protracted war with their rivals across the river in the County of Burgundy. We get the duke's Frenchmen to fight the count's Germans because while they are doing that – with luck for many months or even a few years – they cannot give their aid the King of France. Do you now see, Alan, how this war-making profits our own cause?"

I nodded. "If all our enemies quarrel amongst themselves they cannot combine to attack us. But how to get them to fight each other?"

"It all begins," said my lord, grinning like the wild and reckless outlaw he had so recently been, "with an act of homage."

"So when will this act of homage take place?" I asked

"If all goes to plan, on the Kalends of June," said Robin, with another bandit-like smirk. "In two days. In the ducal palace in Dijon."

Our friend Sergeant Etienne of the guard was manning the northern gate in the walls of Dijon that day, and greeted us with a joyful shout, as our little group came into trotting into view.

By the time we were within twenty yards of the gates, they were swinging open and Etienne had paraded the sixteen men of the guard in two lines to welcome us to his town.

I was astonished to receive such a warm welcome from the beaming men-at-arms, who snapped out a salute as we trotted past. Then I realised the reason for such an effusive greeting. As he rode up to the good sergeant, Robin tossed him small leather bag, which chinked sweetly as Etienne caught it in mid-air. "What fresh tidings, man?" called out Robin.

"Your friends and followers have arrived at the abbey of Saint Benignus, my lord," said this cheery fellow, bowing very low. "More than a hundred of them, I'm told, well mounted, well armed, a truly gallant sight. Their captain or commander is a great big blond warrior, a massive fellow, a giant, I heard, with a face both scarred and scarlet."

"Good," said Robin. "And did they have with them a cumbersome wagon train? Three large, heavily laden ox-drawn vehicles?"

"No, my lord. About ninety mounted fighting men. Plus a few raggle-taggle camp followers, some children, pack mules and hand carts."

"No heavy wagons at all?"

"Not a one."

The grin slid off Robin face like water off a trout. He suddenly looked old. My stomach felt hollow. I knew what those wagons carried.

"Quickly, Alan!" my lord snapped at me. "To the abbey!"

CHAPTER THIRTEEN

We galloped through the streets of Dijon, heedless of the crowds of citizens going about their business, and knocking several of them over as we forced our horses through the press. It was a Saturday, a market day, and the town was full of merchants and farmers trading their goods. Our rapid progress through the streets was punctuated now and then by the outraged cries of the slow-moving Dijonnais. We paid them no mind.

Very soon we were at the abbey in the western part of the old town, and I could already see familiar faces among the mass of men and horses, milling in some confusion in the street outside the huge stone walls.

Robin jumped off his horse – leaving Hanno to gather up his reins and, when I dismounted, mine too – and he plunged into the throng, cutting thought the mass of his own men like a pike though a fish pond. I followed more slowly after him, slapping backs and nodding and grinning at comrades as I went, but I caught up with Robin in the familiar cloister where he was standing nose to nose with Little John.

". . . and you just handed over the gold, gave the bulk of our hoard to Mordecai the Jew – without bothering to consult me?"

"He had all the correct passwords, Robin, in the letter he showed me from Reuben – he does not seek to rob us; and he says he will hold on to all the gold for one week in Chalon in case you countermand my actions. He's trustworthy. He will hand it back, if I've made a terrible mistake."

"He'd better or I'll rip out his living bowels with my bare hands." Robin was calmer now, despite the violence in his words.

"Tell me again how it happened, John, from the beginning. You arrived at Mordecai's mansion in Chalon and he showed you a letter..."

I stood quietly by while Little John, a huge, red-faced man, as Sergeant Etienne had described, who was Robin's chief lieutenant, told his odd story. John was unsettled by Robin's anger but stood his ground.

The story he related our lord was this: the Sherwood men and women under Little John's command, along with the three heavy ox-drawn wagons – which carried the boxes of gold ingots, the barrels of silver coin and other precious items – had all arrived in Chalon two days ago. They had travelled up the Saone Valley without incident, taking the old Roman roads but going very slowly, following in our footsteps.

On arrival in Chalon-sur-Saone, they had presented themselves at Mordecai's house, which was large enough to accommodate all Robin's followers with ease, and had been warmly received and given much lavish hospitality by the old Jew. After they had been fed and watered, given wine and allowed to wash themselves, Mordecai drew John aside and said he had some disturbing news from the Holy Land. The Jew then produced a letter from Reuben, Robin's partner in the frankincense trade who had remained in Jaffa, after Robin's departure in October last year.

Frankincense is burnt in every church, at every holy Mass, every day in the whole of Christendom – and the profits from this trade are simply staggering. Robin had used violence, persuasion and barefaced trickery to gain control of the incense networks in Outremer and Arabia, and had left Reuben, a tough, clever fellow from Yemen, in charge of all his interests.

Reuben's letter, which Little John produced there and then in the Dijon cloister and showed to Robin, was written in Reuben's fine, bold, recognisable hand, and apparently contained various code words that vouched for its authenticity. The letter itself was a desperate cry for help.

Robin's long camel trains, coming up from southern Arabia, and laden with tons of frankincense, had been targeted by local bandits – twice, it seemed – and on both occasions, the trains had been overrun, the guards slain, and the entire cargo stolen away.

Robin's frankincense business had been utterly destroyed and Reuben, who had also pledged himself and his own goods as surety to raise the funds to hire camels and guards, and to buy the incense from the Yemenis, was completely broken by this double catastrophe.

Reuben – a good man I was very fond of – had been arrested by his powerful creditors and imprisoned. Only money, a very great deal of money, an absolute fortune, in truth, could extricate Reuben from his dank cell and allow him to resume his incense trading on Robin's behalf.

"You do not think Reuben played us false?" Robin asked, when he had read the letter, and discussed it soberly with Little John. "It is not a trick, is it? I trust Reuben with my life but . . . all men are corruptible."

"I don't believe so – but you know him better than me."

"So you lodged our gold with Mordecai, so that he could relay the money through his friends and colleagues to the Holy Land?" said my lord. "And so that Reuben could be freed when it was delivered to them?"

"Not all of it. I kept thirty ingots for our use – about four hundred and twenty *livres* worth of precious metal. But there was no need for the big wagons for that quantity. I sold the wagons in Chalon and have the remaining treasure on the mules, here in the abbey stables under guard."

"That is something, I suppose."

"Did I do wrong, Robin?" John seemed embarrassed by his question. "I reasoned that the sooner I lodged the money with Mordecai, the sooner Reuben would be released from his debts and could pick up the pieces of our trade again. The sooner he is free the sooner he can make our money back. That was my thinking. But I will ride back to Chalon, if you require it, and retrieve the gold myself. Give me the word."

"You did not do wrong, old friend," said Robin, and he sighed. "I'd have done exactly the same. We could not leave our friend to languish in his chains. Reuben is one of us. One of mine. And our frankincense business may well revive under his tender care. But get word to Reuben, will you, and tell him that he now owes me the mother of all favours."

Robin caught sight of me loitering near by, obviously listening to these dismal tidings. "Not a word of this to anyone else, Alan," he said. "I'd much prefer people to continue to think me as rich as Croesus."

I promised I would keep my silence.

"You better give up your dreams of entering the wine trade, too. I daresay you will receive your share in time but for now – and I can't believe I'm saying this to you of all people, Alan – you'd better make the most of these Burgundian vintages. Drink deeply, while you still can."

Then he actually laughed.

"Come then, let's go and take a refreshing cup in the refectory. I need a drink after this bad news and there are matters I want to discuss."

It might seem strange but the sudden loss of the bulk of our fortune in gold did not strike me with the same crushing force that it had Robin. We were very different people, of course, and I was ten years younger than he, and had never experienced the pampered upbringing of a lord of men, the servants, the gorgeous tapestries, the fine foods and wines, but as I recall it now, I was surprisingly unruffled by this blow to our fortunes.

It was good to see Little John, and I realised I had missed his massive presence and rock-like certainty in his own prowess. I greeted many of my other friends too. Owain the Bowman, one of Robin's senior officers, gave me a huge bear-hug that lifted me off me feet. I believe, in truth, that it was being reunited with the Sherwood men – my comrades – that lifted my spirits and acted as a counterweight to the gold's sad loss.

More than that, I felt as if some great weight had been lifted from my shoulders. And that weight's name was Jacqueline. I felt rather foolish, naturally, I *had* made an idiot of myself. I had mistaken my own desire for love. And more stupidly than that, I had assumed that, because I persuaded myself that I loved her, she must return my youthful ardour.

She was with the Green Knight now, willingly or not – and so be it. She had made her choice when she cracked me over the head with that water jug. It was painful to admit she had chosen that bastard over me but, once I had recognised this, once I'd firmly grasped this nettle, I got to work on forgiving her, forgetting her and healing my own torn heart.

The Green Knight himself, this lonely *chevalier*, was another matter entirely. I would not be forgiving him. Nor forgetting what he had done to me. We might bide our time, take our ease in Dijon for a day or so, but there was a reckoning to be paid. He had hurt me, humiliated me, and hunted me like a beast through his forest. And I would have my revenge.

Yet there was no hurry. Robin had agreed to help me punish the Green Knight – in due course – and I could wait a day or two before I made him pay the price for his cruelty. It would allow me to savour it. They say that revenge is a dish best served cold. Well, I could allow mine to cool for a little while.

After the ceremony of homage, which was to take place at noon on the Kalends of June, the first day of that glorious first month of summer, which fell on the day after tomorrow, we would take action against the Green Knight. Until then I was at liberty to take my ease in Dijon and to sample the wines of Burgundy with enthusiasm – as Robin himself had suggested. After I left my lord and Little John arguing like the old comrades they were in the abbey refectory, I went to the main square of Dijon, and took my place at one of the long tables at Gregoire's tavern.

The cook-shop had long since ceased serving food and when

little Gregoire brought me a jug, I solemnly told him of the fate of Jacqueline, sticking to the benign tale I had told her mother. That she had caught the eye of a lord from the County, and was living in his castle over the river.

"Ah, is that so?" said the little ogre. "I am not surprised, that saucy young trollop always did have a fine nose for a rich fellow."

I drank my wine slowly, and watched the absurd antics of the other evening drinkers. To a sober man, I reflected, a drunkard cuts a perennially ridiculous figure. I watched placidly, almost bored, as two young men taunted each other face to face, their language becoming increasingly violent until one of them punched the other, and an amateurish fist-fight began. As I watched the absurd struggles of these two silly young men, I was struck with a vast weariness of my own spirit. I realised I had been beaten with clubs by Henrik and his two apprentices only one week before – yet such a great deal had happened to me in the intervening time that it seemed like a full year had passed.

My bruises were turning yellow already but my body still ached from top to toe – I was exhausted, quite done in. I got up from the table, leaving half the wine still in the jug, and stepping carefully round the still-brawling youngsters, now writhing furiously together on the terrace floor in a tangle of limbs, I made my way back to the abbey and my bed.

The next morning, a Sunday, I slept in very late but rose just in time to attend mid-morning Mass in the fine, old abbey church. Then I dined at noon with Robin and the whole Sherwood contingent – nearly a hundred exuberant souls – in a tithe barn belonging to the abbey near the town's western walls. Somehow, Robin had conjured up a pair of roast oxen, and fifty golden capons, as well as fresh bread, pies and tarts, cheeses and fruit, and even a vast sallet of green leaves. There was much good wine and joy aplenty. We ate and drank and made merry together.

Then, in the afternoon, a warm and sunny Sunday afternoon in late spring, full to the brim with good food and wine, I drowsed in the courtyard, and watched our men-at-arms testing each other's skill with sword, dagger and shield. I was in my bed and asleep before sundown.

The next morning, as I was soaping my body in hot water in the abbey's wash-house in preparation of the homage ceremony at the palace, Arlo, the red-headed tan-yard apprentice, came to call on me.

No man likes to be surprised when he is naked – no women either, I presume – and particularly by someone with whom you have a history of violence. So I flung on a chemise, and shoved my feet in my boots, grabbed the falchion and, with a good deal of ill-grace, I went out to the street to see what this importunate fellow wanted. Hanno, fully dressed and armed to the teeth as usual, came with me. However, it seemed a resumption of hostilities was not on the apprentice's mind that morning.

"Master wants you," he mumbled, looking sullenly down at his filth-encrusted shoes.

"What does he want?"

"Wants to speak with you."

I eyed this ginger lout with disfavour. "What about?"

Arlo shrugged. "He's got a girl," he muttered.

"I am delighted for him. But what has this to do with me?"

"She's in a bad way. All scratched and torn. Dirty. Cut-up. The master found her wandering like a madwoman in the market at Dole. She said she'd been hunted by huge dogs in the forest."

An icy shiver ran down my back. "Is it Jacqueline?" I said.

The boy frowned at me.

"Tell me, you imbecile, is it the pretty girl from Gregoire's tavern – you know her. You grabbed her breasts. *Jacqueline*. Is it her?"

"Why would it be her? She's gone off somewhere, I heard."

"Wait here till I get dressed. We'll go and see your master."

I reckoned I had an hour to spare before I was supposed to be at the palace in the main square. Little John and I had been ordered to wash thoroughly and wear our finest clothes and accompany Robin to the ceremony of homage, which would begin at on the stroke of noon.

I reckoned I just had time to see Henrik before then.

"Tell Robin where I've gone," I said to Hanno.

"It is best you don't go running off, Alan," said my Bavarian friend. "You get caught up in some nonsense, Robin will not be pleased."

"I have to find out what happened," I said. "Won't be long."

Henrik had brought the terrified girl by mule cart from Dole to his tannery the day before, and fed her and given her somewhere to sleep. But she was still in a bad way, shivering and twitching like a lunatic, and her thin face was so raw, bruised and bramble-scratched that it took me a while to remember where I had seen her last.

Then it came back to me.

She was one of the two servant girls I had seen sleeping in the chamber below Jacqueline's in the east tower in the castle of Beaune-du-Bois – one of the two girls who had been with Jacqueline in the Logis when I had made my music for the Green Knight and his crew of ruffians.

We were sitting in the small, reeking hut in the centre of the tannery, on the island between the two arms of the River Ouche. Henrik had given the girl an old blanket to cover her badly torn clothing and a cup of wine to steady her nerves – I had politely refused one, as I meant to attend the ceremony at the palace sober – but she was barely able to speak, so great had been the horror and shock of her experience in the Forest of Chaux.

The story emerged slowly, painfully so, but I was able to fill in the gaps from my own experience. It was this: the very day after my own misadventures in the forest, this girl, Pauline, and her friend had been given the same instructions as me, to run from the dogs, and the same cruel promise, that if they could put their right hands on the walls of Dole, they would be spared. I assumed the *chevalier* and his men, denied their sport with me, had created another opportunity for their amusement.

Pauline had actually managed this difficult feat, after being pursued by the Green Knight's men and their hell-hounds through the thick woods for most of the day. But her friend, Minou, had not been so lucky.

"I saw them, master, I watched with my own eyes as those terrible great dogs brought her tumbling down. I was up an oak tree, hiding, frightened. Only a dozen yards from it . . . We ran together all day but I was faster, I was swifter and . . . I thought they would eat her, those monsters; I thought they would tear her flesh from her bones with their great big yellow teeth . . . Oh, but it was so much worse than that . . ."

I poured her some more wine, and glanced at Henrik, who shrugged.

"You need not speak of it any more, if you do not choose to," I said.

Pauline was silent for a little while, then she said: "They took her, one after the other, all of them, even the *chevalier* . . . They whipped the great dogs off her, held her down and forced her legs open . . . I watched from my tree and I did nothing. I could do nothing to help her. I was too frightened, frozen . . . Why, why did they – we never did anything to them. We didn't complain . . . we were good girls. Even when they captured us, we did not scream or try to run away. . ." She began sobbing wretchedly. "After . . . after the sixth man took her, Minou stopped screaming . . ." She took a slurp of wine and I saw her hand trembling.

"When they had all taken their pleasure . . . the last fellow, Jehan, a little fellow with a squint, who had sometimes said kind things to me in the Logis . . . he sliced open her throat with his knife."

"Filthy bastards," growled Henrik. "They'll pay for this . . ."

I put a hand gently on her arm. She flinched away in fear.

"I'll make them all pay, and the *chevalier*. I shall punish them."

"What . . . what does it matter? It will not bring back my friend . . . It will not restore poor Minou to life . . ." The girl was sobbing. She seemed inconsolable. Neither Henrik nor I knew what to do with her. We gave her some more wine, muttered soothing words, tucked the blanket around her, and went out into the rank and fetid yard to talk privately.

"Do you know where she comes from?" I asked the tanner.

"She's from a place called Champlitte," said Henrik, "about thirty miles north of here. Apparently they snatched her a month ago, while she was gathering wood, and carried her across the river. They told her if she behaved and did not try to run, she'd be well treated; a servant but safe."

"Safe?"

"The other girl, Minou, had been there a week or so before that. God rest her soul. They knew nothing about this cruel manhunt till you . . ."

"There'll be a bloody reckoning. I shall bring down such a terrible vengeance on them all. I hereby swear it, I vow that . . ."

"That's not what most concerns me," said the tanner. "Jacqueline is still there. How long before they seek more of their . . . sport?"

I hadn't considered this. I had blocked Jacqueline from my mind, perhaps to protect my own bruised heart. Rage now came roaring back.

Robin was outside the door of the abbey, dressed magnificently in a scarlet tunic, embroidered with gold thread at the neck and sleeves.

"Is that what you're going to wear?" he said, eyeing my scratched old leather jerkin and grubby green hose, my boots, which were liberally splashed with unmentionable tan-yard filth.

"I should send you off with Owain and all the other old sweats."

I looked around and saw the master bowman was standing

with a group of twenty archers, all of whom I knew as veterans of many a hard battle. They stood by their horses' heads, most with long unstrung staves in their hands, some chatting to their neighbours, but most waiting quietly for the order to mount up.

"Where are they going?" I asked.

Robin said: "I can give you a little time to change – go and put on some clean hose at least, and wipe whatever that muck is off your boots."

"We need to go across the river," I said. "Right now."

"Why?"

"We must go and take the château de Beaune-du-Bois. Sack the place. Capture it. And we need to do it now. The Green Knight and his men are hunting people for sport."

"We know that. They hunted you – what is the urgency?"

"Jacqueline's there. They'll hunt her, rape her, kill her."

Robin looked at me for the longest time. I was bouncing up and down on the balls of my feet, feverish with the urgency of the matter.

"Are you still enthralled by that girl?" he said.

"No, but I can't abandon her to the *chevalier*'s huntsmen."

"No," said Robin. "Not today. It's the Kalends. I have made plans."

"We must go and get her! If you won't help, I'll go alone."

"No," said Robin again. "I require you to be at my side today in the palace for the homage ceremony. I've had more than enough of you running off to attend to your own concerns, deserting me and ignoring my explicit commands. You serve me. You made me an oath when we met that you would serve me until death. I require you to honour that oath."

"But Robin, they will do terrible things to her, I *must* go ..."

"I cannot compel you, Alan. I cannot force you to serve me. But I will say this to you: if you do not go, immediately, and change out of those disgusting clothes and report back here within the time it takes to say ten paternosters, then accompany me, clean and cheerful, as my liegeman and *trouvère*, to the ducal palace, I shall dismiss you from my service – for ever. And

I mean it. Do not test my will in this matter. Now, Alan, choose!"

CHAPTER FOURTEEN

I went and changed my dirty clothes – of course I did. But, when we presented ourselves at the doors of the palace a little while later, I was seething with rage and self-pity at the dressing down I had received.

Little John, who was scrubbed and shaved and squeezed into a jerkin that was too tight for his huge frame, his hair washed and arranged in two fat blond plaits on either side of his red face, offered words of comfort.

"He needs to have attendants, Alan; it's important for his status. No great lord can appear at an important ceremony like this unaccompanied. He has to be seen to have his loyal men around him. But don't fret, Alan. When all this tricky business of Robin's is done with, I'll round up some of the lads and we'll go to this Castle of Bones and we'll kill every pig-fucker in the place. Cut off all their shrivelled cocks, if you want to."

I muttered something and glared at the back of Robin's scarlet tunic – hating my lord, in that moment, and wishing I had the courage to tell him to his face that I would do the right thing whether he liked it or not.

Then the doors swung open and we are admitted to the palace.

Robin was not the only important lord in the great hall of the dukes of Burgundy; there were dozens of important men crammed into this huge, high ceilinged room, whose walls were adorned with colourful, finely wrought wall hangings depicting scenes from the Holy Bible. In front of each woven work of art, stood a stern man-at-arms, standing stiffly and holding a spear. I saw that one of them was our friend Sergeant Etienne, who gave me a grin of recognition, but otherwise did not move from his post. Although it was a warm June day, and I was already too hot in my best green woollen mantel – my baggage had come up to Dijon with the rest of Robin's men and equipment – a large log fire was burning in the central hearth of the crowded hall, which had been scattered with expensive incense filling the space with sickly sweet-scented fumes. The smell brought back the disaster of the lost gold. I wondered whether Reuben realised the enormous sacrifice that Robin had made for him.

Most of the nobles here to witness the ancient ceremony of homage were natives of the Duchy, yet there were several from further afield. I recognised the slender, saintly old man who was the Archbishop of Lyon, who also held the title of Count of that region, and who had entertained us lavishly as we travelled north through his territory. I heard a boisterous young man introduce himself to his neighbour as Viscount of Troyes, a wealthy town just north of the Duchy in the kingdom of France.

There were men present from the County of Burgundy, too, invited to come across the river to witness what was to occur. There was the older nobleman I had met before the painful incident with the tan-yard apprentices – what was his title again? I struggled to recall. Montbéliard. Amadeus of Montfaucon, Lord of Montbéliard, that was it, and he was in conversation with another old fellow who looked eerily like him.

It was that meddling monk, Gui, the Prior of Cîteaux.

The resemblance between them was so clear, and their ages were so close, that they could only be siblings. As I looked at them again, I sensed Robin standing at my elbow. He leant in to me and said quietly in my ear: "Do you know who that man is?"

I turned to look at him, a little surprised by his remark. It seemed that Robin wanted to end the argument between us, to sooth my rage. It was an olive branch. I accepted it: "He is the churchman who denounced us to Lord Eudes when we arrived here," I said. "And who knew about the gold when we were captured by the *chevalier* and taken to Dole."

"Not that meddling monk; the other man, his older brother."

"I delivered your message to him. He's Lord Montbéliard."

"Yes, obviously. Did you know he is also Tanisha's uncle."

I had to think for a moment to remember that name too. Clearly, all the wine I had been enjoying in Burgundy was dulling my memory. Tanisha – of course – a princess of the Almohad, the rulers of Spain.

Robin had flirted with her and formed some kind of relationship. She had delivered over to us the hoard of gold ingots as a ransom for her father Prince Khalil, after he had fallen prisoner to us after a bloody fight at a Hospitaller castle called Ulldecona. She spoke very good French, I remembered, and had said she had some relatives in Burgundy.

"That explains how Brother Gui knew we had the gold," I said. "He plucked that valuable information from the family grapevine."

"Maybe we can reap a sweeter harvest from the same vine."

Amadeus of Montfaucon saw that we were staring at him and he bowed slightly then gave my lord a significant nod of the head. Then he seemed to be making his way through the crowds towards us but, instead of coming over to speak, he veered towards the door and, paused there, to give Robin another unsubtle head bob, before disappearing out of it.

"Wonder where he's going?" I said, fishing for more information.

"If all is going according to my plan," said Robin, "he will be heading for his own lands around the castle of Montbéliard, in the County of Burgundy, on the other side of Besançon."

My fishing had landed a catch, yet I was still none the wiser.

I was about to speak up and ask my lord exactly what was the significance of this, when a nervous young man suddenly appeared in front of Robin. He was sweating even more than the warmth of the hall merited and was plainly agitated. He tugged

Robin's sleeve and pulled him away from Little John and me.

I made to follow but my lord held up a restraining palm.

"That fellow looks like he has swallowed his own chin," said Little John. I laughed. I found I had lost much of my earlier ill-humour.

"He's called Stephen of Auxonne," I said quietly to John.

"The man of the hour," he said. "The reason we're all here."

"What?"

"Did Robin not tell you? Stephen, Count of Auxonne, will do official homage today to Eudes, Regent of the Duchy of Burgundy."

"What?" I said. "But he's a vassal of Count Otto, isn't he?"

"By God's baggy, brown-stained braies! Have you not talked to Robin about this at all?" John seemed outraged by my ignorance.

"Lord Stephen is switching sides. He's coming over to the Duchy!"

"I've been rather busy," I said. "I haven't seen much of Robin."

"Busy with the girl? The wench at the Castle of Bones?"

"Mostly. But tell me, John – what is happening today?"

"You'll witness it all soon enough. That chinless young idiot will repudiate Count Otto today, and do homage to Lord Eudes for his lands. He is adding his fiefdom – Auxonne, which lies between here and Dole, just on the other side of the River Saone – to the Duchy of Burgundy."

"But that's treason!" I said. "Otto cannot allow this. Lord Eudes is suborning one of his own vassals, annexing a large part of his County!"

"Yes, that's the point. And keep your voice down, Alan."

"This is Robin's doing?" I was beginning to grasp my lord's cunning scheme. But I kept my voice low. "I see. He wants to make Otto angry, so blindly furious he's prepared to go to war with the Duchy."

"Not only that," said Little John, grinning at me, "but he wants to control *where* and *when* Otto will attack Eudes. The town of Auxonne is right on the river. The first thing Otto will do when he hears the news of the betrayal today is to seize young Stephen's ancestral seat. It has a decent castle but, I'd wager Otto can take it pretty quickly if he brings his full force to bear. Then, of course, the most logical thing to do, would be to cross the river at the old bridge at Auxonne and take the main road west directly to Dijon. To come straight at us. And we're counting on that. Owain and his men are watching over Auxonne from this side of the river as I speak, we have scouts scattered up and down the west bank."

"Wait, John, wait a moment ... *Why* is Stephen of Auxonne doing this? It doesn't make any sense. Why would Stephen openly betray Otto? He must know he is going to lose his town, his castle, his ancestral lands. How can that possibly benefit him?"

Robin had finished speaking to Stephen and he had obviously reassured the nervous young lordling, who was now looking far more confident, perhaps even enthusiastic about the move he was to make.

There was a general stir in the hall. Lord Eudes, Regent of the Duchy of Burgundy, in a long purple robe, had entered to applause and was taking up his place at the great gilded chair at the far end of the hall. He arranged himself in the throne – for it was a throne, in truth – and gazed serenely out at the great throng of lords and their attendants in the hall. He said nothing, made no gesture or sign but, gradually, the hall fell silent. Only then did a herald give a triple blast on his brass trumpet, and announce the ruler of this realm in loud, sonorous tones.

Eudes began to speak: "My lords and ladies, I warmly welcome you to the court of the Duchy of Burgundy. We are gathered here this special day to witness the ancient and holy ceremony of homage, the sacred bond between a lord and his vassal, decreed and sanctified by God Almighty."

There was a long pause, but not a man spoke. The Regent finally said: "Well then, who is here to witness this important act of homage and to make a lasting record of this binding promise?"

Prior Gui, of the abbey of Cîteaux, stepped forward.

"I am here as a representative of God Almighty, the Lord of Hosts, and Holy Mother Church, I stand ready in the Name of His only Son Jesus Christ our Saviour, as well as on behalf of my own humble order of Cistercians. I stand ready this day to bear witness to and record in the annals of my House the solemn oath made here today by my lord Eudes of Burgundy and Stephen, Count of Auxonne. But let us first piously invoke God's blessing on the sacred rite we are about to perform here."

There follower a series of long prayers led by Prior Gui, in which every man in the hall was expected to join. Many did so devoutly, a few did not, some stared into space or muttered with a friend or neighbour.

"I don't understand this at all, lord," I whispered to Robin, who, needless to say, was not taking part in any of these interminable prayers.

"Why does Stephen of Auxonne seek to switch allegiance?"

"Tell you later," whispered back Robin.

"Tell me now, lord, I beg you. I'm always kept in the dark."

In a few terse whispered sentences, Robin explained to me all the complicated dynastic reasons why Stephen of Auxonne was willing to transfer his loyalty from Count Otto to Lord Eudes and the Duchy. The exact details are as vague to me now, so many years later, as indeed they were then, but it as I seem to recall that Robin told me that Stephen's family had once been the Counts of Burgundy, rulers of the lands on the far side of the Saone. The Holy Roman Emperor, Frederick Barbarossa, had with a combination of a canny marriage and sheer, naked might, taken the County of Burgundy entirely for himself. Then he had died and passed it on to his son Otto. Now, Stephen of Auxonne, wanted it back.

Robin outlined the case as it stood in law but boredom had, by then, robbed me of most of my powers of comprehension. I yawned.

"You insisted on knowing, so I told you," hissed Robin angrily, when he saw me smother another yawn. "To put it simply, Stephen has been promised control of the County by Eudes, if he does homage to the regent for Auxonne. After the war, if it all works out, Stephen will rule most of the lands over the river, under his overlord Eudes of Burgundy."

The prayers had finally ended, and Gui fell silent; his tonsured head reverentially bowed. "Let my new vassal step forward," said Eudes.

The young nobleman took a step into the centre of the hall a few paces before the regent's throne. He was bareheaded and carried no weapons at all. He took another hesitant step towards the high throne.

"Do you Stephen, Count of Auxonne, son of Count Stephen, grandson of Count William, of the noble House of Ivrea, hereby renounce all former ties and obligations," said Lord Eudes, "and repudiate all other claims on your loyalty and honour from this day forward and for ever?"

"I do," said the young man.

"Do you freely choose to become my man, my vassal, my sworn soldier under God for the fief of Auxonne and all your other lands, and do you look to me, and only to me, from this day on for justice and mercy?"

"I do," said Stephen. He came forward the final few steps and knelt before the throne. The silence in the hall was absolute.

Stephen placed his two palms together in the attitude of prayer and extended his hands up towards Lord Eudes who was seated above him, who placed his own pale hands around the younger lord's fingers.

"By this ancient rite, you are confirmed before God as my man," said Lord Eudes. "Do you accept this burden and this great honour?"

"I accept and embrace my condition. My life begins anew."

The regent released his hands and smiling at his new-made vassal, he took his right hand and raised him up from his knees. Then Eudes kissed Stephen on the mouth, in the holy gesture known as the "kiss of peace".

"God, Mary and all the saints be praised," said Prior Gui loudly. He began leading the audience in the Lord's Prayer in Latin.

When that most familiar prayer was completed, Gui beckoned to another monk, who approached with a red velvet cushion on which rested a small golden box with crystal sides. I could just make out through the crystal a tiny, shrivelled dark brown object inside it.

"Behold," said Prior Gui, "the toe of Saint Ambrosinien!" I heard Robin give a loud disbelieving snort but the sound was mercifully masked by the gasps of the assembled lords, who eagerly craned to look.

"You will place your right hand on this most sacred and holy relic," said Prior Gui to Stephen, "and repeat after me this most solemn oath."

Stephen put his palm on the golden box and, echoing the words of the old prior, he intoned: "I promise by my faith in Jesus Christ our Saviour that I will in future, and for ever, be faithful and true to my new lord; that I will never cause him harm and that I will diligently observe my homage to him completely, and against all persons, including any man to whom I have made an oath in the past, dealing always in good faith and without falsehood or deceit. Amen!"

The ceremony was over. The hall was filled with the sound of applause, although, I thought I heard one voice mutter darkly "Filthy turncoat" amid the clapping and calls of appreciation. I turned to look and see who had spoken thus, but I couldn't make out the culprit in the throng.

"That should do it," said Robin, with an air of satisfaction.

"Time for a drink!" said Little John. And I could see that he was not the only man to have had this excellent idea. Many of the lords were heading for the door of the hall, slapping friends' backs and grinning happily at each other. As well they might; their homeland, their Duchy had just increased significantly in size and power.

More than that, for these belligerent Burgundian fighting

men, the prospect of a good, bloody war was now closer than ever.

"Not yet," said my own lord. "Stay close by me both of you."

He stepped forward and walked towards the throne where Eudes and Stephen were now embracing like reunited brothers.

"My lord Regent," said Robin. "If I might have a moment."

Eudes released Stephen from his bear hug and looked over at Robin. But I could see he was most reluctant to engage with my lord.

"Locksley, isn't it? The English earl, if I'm not mistaken."

"Quite correct, your grace. May I compliment you on your excellent memory for foreign faces and strange titles. Most impressive!"

"Thank you, if you mean that. What do you want with me?"

"I must quit your beautiful land soon, too soon, indeed, for my liking. I have grown attached to your fine Duchy; indeed, I feel it has become almost like a second home to me. However, alas, I must soon return to England. Yet before I depart, I would crave a boon or a favour from you. I should like to thank you personally for your kind and generous hospitality over these past few weeks, and would appreciate an audience with you, alone, perhaps somewhere more private than this chamber? I'd like to discuss a matter that is, in truth, a little delicate."

"Can't you just say whatever it is to me here?"

Robin looked around the great hall. Most of the lords of Burgundy had left but there were still a dozen here and there, talking with their close friends. "I think it would be better to conduct our talk in your solar, perhaps, where no inquisitive ears may overhear us."

Lord Eudes looked at Robin. I could see the previous suspicion in his eyes. He opened his mouth, I believe, to refuse Robin's request.

My lord said quickly: "I would speak to you of gold, a vast quantity of gold. A hoard that I wish to make a gift of to a dear friend."

Eudes closed his mouth.

"I would take it very kindly indeed, *my friend*, if you would consent to meet me privily," said Robin, smiling like a hungry wolf, "only for a brief moment. I would consider it a mark of the highest honour."

"Oh, all right then," said the Regent of Burgundy. "If you must. You may speak with me very briefly in my solar. But I should like Count Stephen and Prior Gui, to be witness to this private meeting. And you, sergeant," he said pointing at Etienne of the town guard, who was standing spear-straight by the wall, "I want you standing by with half a dozen of your men. Come on then, Locksley, let's get this over with!"

We all followed the regent as he stalked to the back of the hall and disappeared thorough a doorway into his private room.

The solar was a large room, with comfortable chairs and a broad table with wine and goblets and a large bowl of apples set out by the regent's servants. And a large canopied bed in the centre of the space, with finely carved posts and hangings of some rich purple cloth. This was the place where the lord of Dijon could relax after the official matters of the Duchy were concluded. Lord Eudes went to the table and poured himself a goblet of wine. I noticed that he did not I offer refreshment to the others.

Sergeant Etienne's men lined the wood-panelled walls of the solar – six of them and the jolly sergeant himself. Stephen of Auxonne stood next to the table – I could almost see him wondering whether he would be allowed to help himself to a drink. Prior Gui stood near the door, his hands thrust into the sleeves of his simple white monk's robe. He was watching Robin most attentively.

I stood at my lord's right, with Little John on his left flank.

"You mentioned gold," said Eudes. "I confess I have heard rumours of your wealth. So, come on, Locksley. Say your piece."

"*Did* I say something about gold?" said Robin. He sounded quite uncharacteristically vague. "Perhaps I did . . . but first you must allow me to show you something far more interesting, your grace."

He took a long stride towards Lord Eudes, shook his right wrist, lowered his hand and a shiny blade dropped into his waiting palm. His left hand snaked out and he seized Eudes by the purple mantel at the shoulder, suddenly tugging hard and spinning the regent around, so that the ruler of the Duchy tumbled into the crook of his left arm.

Robin now held Lord Eudes in a grip of iron. His right hand, holding the knife, slashed across once, very deeply. A thick spurt of blood, red as treachery, jetted from the wildly struggling regent's neck.

Lord Eudes gave one long, loud, gurgling moan and slumped in Robin's arms. And the whole chamber instantly exploded into movement.

CHAPTER FIFTEEN

A man-at-arms standing by the solar wall, the one nearest to Lord Eudes and Robin, started forward, bringing his spear down to the horizontal, but before he could bring the pole-arm into play, Little John stepped across, swung fast and belted the fellow hard in the face with a meaty fist. The unfortunate fellow was sent flying backwards and crashed into the wall.

Stephen of Auxonne, Lord Eudes' new vassal, threw both his hands up to his lower face, the place where his chin ought to have been and began to scream like a little girl. A man-at-arms surged towards Robin, and I intercepted him, seized his two shoulders and stopped him with a hard, slanting butt from my forehead, a savage blow that crunched into his nose, flattening it and making him to reel away stunned on jelly legs.

By then I was also struggling to get my falchion out of his heavy leather sheath – a stupid clumsy weapon, too difficult to draw in a hurry. Sergeant Etienne, snarling like a bear, was coming towards Robin in low, gliding steps. He had dropped his spear and had a naked sword in his hands – an intelligent move, since the room was too cramped for efficient work with pole weapons. I stepped in front of Etienne, held out a palm

Robin shouted, "Seize the monk, John, don't let him escape!" and I saw that Prior Gui, quick as a hunting weasel, was already fleeing via the solar door. He paused for a half heartbeat at the portal, turned and I saw him staring in blank horror at the blood-drenched scene: Lord Eudes now unconscious and limp in Robin's arms; the wink of gory steel in Robin's right fist; Little John red and roaring with rage, sword in hand, charging directly at him. Then the monk was gone – the man of God was out the door, free and clear, calling for guards to come in and save their lord.

Three men now opposed Little John at the door with spears and swords, and Sergeant Etienne, all friendliness now utterly blown to the winds, was sliding in under my guard to come at Robin. I swung at him with the heavy falchion, a heavy round-armed blow, and he blocked me smartly, our blades ringing as they clashed like a hammer-struck anvil.

Robin released Lord Eudes, who crumpled to the floor to the solar, still bleeding, his limbs twitching a little. There was a flurry by the door, Little John exchanging ringing blows with two of the men-at-arms, and dodging the other fellow, a spear-men, who was trying to spike him in the ribs.

Then there were more men, all in the livery of the Duchy, blue on gold, bursting through the door, five men, six, and more. Now we had a proper fight on our hands. I parried another lightning-fast strike from Etienne. Forced him back with a hack at his hip, which he sidestepped.

Robin, now free of his burden, had his own sword out – but bizarrely he was now shouting: "Hold! Hold! Put up your swords! Let no man be killed here today." I didn't know if he meant us – his loyal friends – to put up our weapons or was attempting to command the Burgundian men-at-arms to surrender *en masse* to us.

Sergeant Etienne cut at my head, a fast deadly blow, but I blocked and swiped back at him with my chopper; he danced away in plenty of time from the clumsy swing. There were more men now pouring into the room, a good score or more of Burgundian soldiers were in the solar. Robin was now yelling: "We yield, messires; we yield to your mercy!"

Little John booted a fat man-at-arms in the stomach, turned to Robin and yelled: "What? Are you mad? We can take them!"

"Drop your sword, John. Now! You too, Alan. We must all yield!"

As if to show us what he meant, Robin released his own blade and it clattered loudly to the floor. John shouted: "God's great hairy bollocks!" and hurled his sword away angrily; it clanged into the corner of the room.

Then the big man lifted both hands in surrender. There was a sudden stillness in the chamber. I dropped my falchion and suddenly the Burgundian guards were swarming all over us, raining down punches and kicks, flattening us, and putting their boots on our necks to keep us down. "I acc . . . accept your surr . . . surrender, on behalf of my lord," warbled Stephen, Count of Auxonne. "Tie their hands . . . securely, you . . . men!"

We were swiftly bound, the three of us trussed up on the floor, and one or two of the men-at-arms got in a few belated punches and kicks while they were doing it. I did not hold it against them. They had just seen Robin slit open their master's throat without the slightest reason.

With a hard boot squashing my face into the dusty floor, I saw Etienne, kneel beside Eudes, who was lying no more than two paces from me. I heard Stephen call out quaveringly: "Shall I fetch a physician, sergeant? The barber-surgeon? Or should I perhaps call for his chaplain?"

Sergeant Etienne looked past me up at the trembling Count of Auxonne and shook his head. "He has no need of any of them, my lord."

Etienne stood up. "Get these murdering scum into the cells," he said, gesturing at the three of us, all bound like hogs. "They will go before the town council first thing tomorrow morning. They shall decide their fate."

As castle dungeons go, the one in the west wing of the ducal palace of Dijon, was remarkable for its cleanliness, and its light, almost pleasant atmosphere. It had three brick walls and the entire front of the prison cell was a row of bars, with a small barred door set into them.

There was a large window at the back, barred, but still admitting a good deal of late afternoon sunshine. There were buckets set out for our bodily evacuations, and a large jug of clean spring water and a loaf of fresh bread and even a large round of yellow cheese on a side table, in case we might suffer either thirst or hunger.

I can honestly say that I have been an honoured guest in castles that were less welcoming. But all that counted for nought beside the hard, certain knowledge of our impending doom. We would be taken before the town council in the morning, we were told, and put on trial – and what other verdict could the worthies of Dijon reach for the planned murder of their sovereign lord but immediate death?

I knew the rest of my life could be measured in a handful of hours. And, for once, I was blameless of the crime for which I was imprisoned. I could not understand why Robin had taken it into his head to cut Eudes' throat before so many witnesses. Some kind of madness, perhaps, or a fit.

I knew that Robin was perfectly capable of murder – and much worse besides – that was not what surprised me most about the day's bloody events. It was that Robin had never been so crashingly inept or clumsy before. He had, in fact, been downright incompetent. There was no way on this good green Earth that my lord could have accomplished that public murder and escaped with his life, or with our lives. And there was something else that was very odd about the situation in the solar – why had he surrendered to Sergeant Etienne's town guards so meekly?

Admittedly, there had been more than a dozen of them against three of us, but we were all decent fighters, skilled and experienced, and I could not say the same for every man of the town guard. We three had faced worse odds before, more than once, and survived – even triumphed. Little John alone could have accounted for four, five men, maybe more. I could easily have dropped a few. Yet Robin stopped us defending ourselves before we had wounded a single Burgundian man-at-arms.

I was so angry with my lord in that gloomy, doom-filled hour, in that oddly well-kept, comfortable cell, as I awaited my inevitable ignominious death, that that I could barely look at him. I was seething again, in truth. I felt that he had thrown my life away along with his and Little John's. And for what? While Robin and his giant lieutenant sat with their backs against one of the walls and stretched their legs out on the surprisingly clean, straw-strewn floor, talking quietly, even joking in an infuriatingly relaxed manner, I found a far corner, turned my back on them and began to pray. I called on God to save me; I beseeched Saint Michael to come down from Heaven with his great fiery sword and lead us all out from this prison of woe and despair.

Yet I found I could not fully concentrate on my prayers. I had something I had to say to my lord and I could not rest until I'd said it.

I got up and walked over to Robin and Little John. They both looked up at me, cheerily grinning from the floor as I loomed over then both. I knew Robin favoured insouciance at all costs – but this was insane.

"I forgive you, my lord," I grated. "I want you to know that serving you has been a privilege and an honour, and while your ill-thought-out, blundering foolishness, your selfish disregard for all consequences, has undoubtedly caused my death – I want you to know that I forgive you."

"He forgives you, Robin," said Little John, "Isn't that nice?"

"Such a relief," said my lord. "I can die a happy man at last."

They were both smirking up at me in such an intolerable manner, that I felt a red vessel of rage boil over inside me.

"Your behaviour on many occasions, my lord, has been callous, even downright wicked – I still remember the slaying of Sir Richard at Lee for no good reason except to make some more of your beloved filthy lucre. Yet I think this is the most egregious act of sheer, selfish, bloody-minded, unnecessary evil I have ever seen you perform since I have known you. Lord Eudes had done you no harm, no harm at all, yet you opened up his throat like a slaughter-week pig. And yet . . . I forgive you, my lord, I forgive you for our crimes! I only pray God will do the same."

Little John let out a chuckle and instantly smothered it.

"Do you have anything else you wish to say to me, Alan?" asked Robin, getting to his feet. "Anything else troubling your tender little heart?" I thought for a moment he would strike me – perhaps I even wished he would. I would retaliate. I could feel a huge, hot, pressure of anger deep inside me, aching for release.

Little John was getting up too. "You have to tell him now, Robin," the big man rumbled. "Come on, you've had your fun."

"Tell me what? What should you tell me?"

"That all will be well, Alan. Do not fret. It will all be fine."

"What in the name of God do you mean, all will be well? In the morning, we three will all be hanged by our necks until . . ."

"I would be grateful, young man, if you would not take our Lord's name in vain in my house," said a new voice.

I spun round to look the barred front of the cell to see a tall, thin, aristocratic man standing there smiling. There were several men behind him, one of whom was a broadly grinning Sergeant Etienne.

"When Lord Locksley says that all will be well," said the tall man, "he means simply that – and all *will* be well."

The man speaking was none other than Eudes, Regent of Burgundy.

I was lost in a daze of confusion as I saw Etienne using a large iron key to open the cell's door. The sergeant said casually to Robin: "Our friend was seen leaving by the town's southeast gate less than an hour ago, taking the direct road towards Dole. I'm told he was in something of a hurry."

Robin said: "That's a relief. It's not all been for nought then."

I looked closely at Lord Eudes, at his neck. There were a few black, crusted lines of dried blood, remnants of the gore he had failed to clean off, but there was no gaping cut, and no recently sewn or bound wound.

It was not until we had all convened in the solar once more, where a small table had been laid out for supper, that I began to understand what had happened. Amid much merry laughter and slapping of thighs, Little John apologised to a Burgundian man-at-arms for breaking his nose; and I nodded and smiled cautiously at the fellow I had head-butted – who grinned at me in a friendly manner and displayed a bloody gap in his lower jaw where he was missing a tooth. Then we all sat down to eat.

"Pig's blood," said Robin, through a mouthful of leek soup and bread. "I obtained a pint or two of fresh pig's blood from our friend Yvette, and a pig's bladder to hold it all in. I had that up my other sleeve and squirted it out lavishly when I pretended to murder our noble host."

"Utterly ruined my best linen chemise," said Eudes with a smile.

"And the point of all this bloodthirsty mummery?" I asked.

"Gui of Montfaucon, prior of the abbey of Cîteaux, and the secret eyes and ears of Otto of Burgundy in my capital," said Eudes.

"The old monk is a spy for Otto?"

"Certainly he is," said Robin. "You remember Otto boasted of his agents who would be watching our every move?"

I nodded. "How do you know this?" I asked. But I could tell immediately that Robin did not like *that* question.

Robin frowned down at the table, then and looked over at Lord Eudes and then at Little John. It was only the four of us seated at the supper table. Sergeant Etienne and a couple of his town guards were dispersed around the solar but they were well out of earshot.

"The boy deserved to know the truth," said Lord Eudes, "after the shock he suffered today. Do you not fully trust him, Locksley?"

"I do," said Robin. "But this must go no further, Alan, yes? You're not to spill my secrets to the next willing tavern wench you tup."

I promised that I'd guard my tongue but the reminder of

Jaqueline's dire plight made it hard to concentrate on Robin's words. But I nodded along most attentively as my lord revealed his devious ploy to me.

It appeared that Robin and Eudes had been plotting together in secret from shortly after our arrival in Dijon. While the regent had kept up a pretence that Robin was excluded from his court at the palace – for fear of assassination – they had, in fact, met up together discreetly half a dozen times at the abbey of Saint Benignus, after the service of Vespers, which Lord Eudes attended almost every day. They had decided between them that Stephen of Auxonne's defection to the Duchy, while it would be deeply humiliating for Count Otto, might not be quite enough to spur him into making an attack on the town of Auxonne and then the Duchy.

"He's quite not as stupid as he appears," said Robin. "There was a tiny chance that he would simply swallow the humiliation of Stephen's repudiation of his overlordship. Or that he would attack Auxonne, burn it down, but remain safely on his side of the river.

"On the other hand, he was also *expecting* me to assassinate our good friend Lord Eudes here. So we agreed that, if he believed the regent had been murdered, and the Duchy was suddenly leaderless, the chaos that would result would surely be enough to entice Otto to attack us here. So we set up the false assassination, the pig's blood, the bladder and all, and arranged for Prior Gui to witness it himself. Then we encouraged Otto's spy to ride straight to his master in Dole and pass on the glad tidings. Do you see now, Alan?"

I did. Stephen of Auxonne, I learnt, had also been kept in the dark about Robin's plans for the day of his homage and been informed of the false murder by Lord Eudes only afterwards. He was thoroughly shaken by all the bloody play-acting and had since retired to a quiet chamber in the palace to restore his nerves with a large jug of wine.

"How did you know Prior Gui was Otto's agent?" I asked.

This was the question that Robin had been trying to avoid.

"This is even more of a secret than the rest of it, Alan," said my lord, after a small pause. "You must take this to your grave. Do you swear it?"

"Please, just tell me," I said.

"Lord Montbéliard let it slip during our several long talks. He said his brother had recently gained a great deal more sway with Count Otto. He boasted that Gui had his private ear. It wasn't hard to work it out."

"I see. So why then did he denounce you to Lord Eudes here when we first arrived in Dijon. Prior Gui claimed you were an assassin out to murder the Regent! If he was truly acting on Otto's behalf, as his spy, he would have held his tongue and allowed you to cut down our host then."

"Count Otto surely believes that Prior Gui is his creature," said Robin. "And Gui *does* diligently report back to Otto from Dijon about the affairs of the Duchy. But Gui truly serves only one master – and that is his conception of the divine. His loyalty is, in this order, to God, to the pope in Rome, to the Church, and to his superior the Abbot of Cîteaux, and then far down that list comes his loyalty to Count Otto of Burgundy."

"His brother told you this too?"

"More or less. Gui will serve Otto as far as he is able to because he believes Otto's promise that, if he does so, he will be granted lands on which to build a Cistercian house in the County of Burgundy. So, by serving Otto, he is serving God. But Gui is a devout monk, and a good Christian and he would never condone an actual cold-blooded murder."

"Which I'm very pleased about," said the regent.

"Indeed. I believe Prior Gui hopes that you, my lord, will also endow him with lands in the Duchy on which to set up a new house."

Robin was looking at Lord Eudes as he said this.

"We've had some discussions on those very lines," said our host.

"Well, that covers everything, I'd say," said Robin smiling at me. He took a piece of bread and began to wipe out his soup bowl.

"Not quite, my lord. What were your long discussions with Lord Montbéliard *about*? You did not say."

"You do ask a lot of questions, Alan."

"Because you avoid answering most of them, my lord."

"Very well. Amadeus, Lord Montbéliard, might seem like a kindly buffoon, and loose with his secrets, but he is, in truth, a very ambitious old man – ambitious for himself and for his extended family.

"He wants the County of Montbéliard to be an independent fief – a free county, rather like the two Burgundies. He wants to take control of the whole of the eastern part of the County of Burgundy and join it to his own extensive lands; to renounce his age-old fealty to Count Otto and to the emperor. He wants his own little private mountain kingdom. He also backs his brother Gui's plans to build a new house for the Cistercian order across the Saone. Furthermore, he wants his favourite nephew Walter, who is now fighting the Saracens in Outremer, to be given a plum post in the Holy Land. He favours making him Constable of Jerusalem and Lord of Jaffa – and I have agreed, in Richard's name, that this shall be done. In exchange, Lord Montbéliard has promised that when Count Otto come across the river to attack the Duchy of Burgundy, he will rise up with his knights and seize the town of Besançon, Otto's capital..."

"So Otto will be crushed between two stones!" I exclaimed. "On this side, by the Duchy's knights, and behind him by his own disloyal vassal Lord Montbéliard. That *is* very clever, my lord. Otto is surely doomed."

"That's the general idea, yes," said Robin, just a little bit smugly.

"You mean to divide up the County of Burgundy, like a vast apple pie, between you – between you Lord Eudes and old Lord Montbéliard."

The image of apple pie brought the fate of Jacqueline once more to the forefront of my mind.

"Precisely, young Alan," said Lord Eudes. "For years Otto's

greedy knights have been raiding my lands, kidnapping our women, stealing my sheep, cattle and helping themselves to my crops, treating my demesne as their private larder. My father, Duke Hugh, is in Outremer, fighting for Christ and his fief should be protected, free from attacks by neighbouring lords. The pope has said all who break the rule will be excommunicated."

"And you have the pope's blessing for this enterprise?" I said.

"We do – but only privately," said Lord Eudes. "I have a personal letter from his Holiness confirming this agreement. By Christmas, the County of Burgundy will cease to exist. Otto's territory will be divided between the Duchy of Burgundy and the Free County of Montbéliard. With a generous grant made to the abbey of Cîteaux for a new house."

I was rendered speechless. This was a grand design indeed.

"So what is the next step?" I said, finally summoning my wits. My mind was whirling with the scale of Robin's ambition, stunned by the casual way he and Eudes seemed to be redrawing the old fiefs of Europe in the spilled wine on the supper table.

"Our next step," said Robin, "is to make ourselves ready."

"Ready?" I said.

"Yes," said Robin. "Ready for war!"

CHAPTER SIXTEEN

I went to see Henrik the Tanner the next day, and made a gift to him of the purloined falchion. It was not the blade for me but in skilled hands I knew it could be a fearsome weapon. The girl, Pauline, was much revived by the care that the tanner had lavished on her, and she was now up and about and able to undertake the less arduous duties around the tannery.

"Is it true?" whispered Henrik. "It is true that your English lord murdered the regent in cold blood? Cut his throat with a hidden knife?"

I did not know what to say. I'd promised Robin that I would keep his secrets and yet this man Henrik was a friend, and I did not wish to lie to him. Anyway he'd soon discover the truth.

"I may not talk about what truly happened yesterday," I said.

"It is all over town," said Henrik. "Lord Eudes is said to be dead. The duke is in Outremer, and he may be dead, too. Folk are panicking."

I fell back on parroting Robin's line "All will be well," and winking conspiratorially, which made the German tanner even more confused.

I longed to gather up half a dozen good Sherwood men – Hanno at least would come with me, I was sure of that – and gallop off to Beaune-du-Bois to rescue Jacqueline. It was like an itch deep in my bones – but I would do it properly this time, with a gang of seasoned men at my back.

I no longer believed that I was in love with Jacqueline – some tenderness remained, of course, but nothing more ardent – however, I could not bear the thought of doing nothing while she was hounded like a desperate animal through the woods by the Green Knight's whooping, jeering men before being casually murdered when the lustful hunters had all taken their pleasure on her innocent body.

However, there was nothing that could be done for her now. Robin had given me command of a contingent, known as a *conroi*, of twenty mounted men-at-arms, with Hanno as my sergeant-at-arms, and I dared not abandon my duty yet again to go off on another unlicenced excursion. Jacqueline's rescue would have to wait. I just hoped not for too long

I was far too busy in those days anyway for another lone adventure. I had to kit myself out properly for the looming conflict. I needed to pick out a well-trained warhorse from the Sherwood herd to replace my faithful Ghost, select a bridle, trapper and other bits of equipment for the unfamiliar animal. Then I had to dig out my own full set of mail – hauberk, chausses, coif and aventail – and find a decent new shield and a steel helm that fitted my head properly. Most important, I had to procure myself a first-class arming sword from our company's stores.

Not only had I to do all that for myself before we rode off to battle – I had to do something similar for twenty other men, some of whom were old comrades I'd known since the outlaw days, but a many of whom I did not know at all.

Robin had recruited dozens of new men-at-arms to his wolf banner in Marseilles – English, Normans, some local Provençal men, even a lone Fleming. They were a tough lot, all experienced men, the flotsam and jetsam of the Great Pilgrimage – and I was a boy not yet eighteen years of age. So I was glad to have Hanno at my side to back up my orders.

Some of the new men were knights fallen on hard times, who were forced to sell their swords; some were sergeants, low-born men but with all the deadly skills of a knight, who found themselves without a leader; others were little better than bandits who found life outside the law too dangerous and had chosen to join a powerful lord's retinue and swear an oath of fealty. All of them could fight as well on horseback as off it: Robin always did have an excellent nose for a competent man-at-arms.

My *conroi* of twenty riders was one of two in Robin's travelling force. Robin himself commanded the other mounted squadron, which was slightly larger in number. There were also two companies of archers, fully equipped, and each consisting of two dozen seasoned English and Welshmen; one was commanded by Owain, the master bowman, who had left Dijon the day before to scout the western river bank and watch for Count Otto's crossing. The second archer company – of twenty-six men – was under Little John's control. The big man was not a natural bowman, although he could shoot well enough; in truth, his favourite weapon was a big double-headed axe, which he wielded with a truly appalling ferocity.

The second morning after the feigned assassination of Lord Eudes – while rumours were circulating through Dijon and the surrounding territories, and the regent himself was keeping to his solar, out of sight to all but his most trusted servants – a rider in a moss-green cloak, with an English war bow hung over his shoulder, galloped through the streets of Dijon, and came skidding to a halt outside the big doors Saint Benignus.

I was in the street outside the abbey, sparring with Hanno and two of our new Provençal knights, and getting the feel of the balance and weight of my new arming sword. I knew the rider, a grizzled archer called Samuel who had been a friend of mine for several years now, and called out to him asking for his tidings.

"Otto has taken Auxonne," he said breathlessly. "He fell on it yesterday with two hundred knights and his banner – a golden lion rampant on a blue field – is now flying high above battlements."

"Any sign of his men trying to cross the river?" I shouted.

"I'm bound to report this first to our lord, young Alan," said Samuel. He waved cheerily and disappeared inside the abbey.

"Better get ready to ride, Hanno," I said. "Rouse the men."

I could see the burning town of Auxonne clearly from the Duchy side of the Saone. The small, low settlement – strung out between the curtain wall of the castle, on the eastern bank of the river, and the large stone church a little to the north and east of it – was shrouded in a shifting grey cloud with a few flickers of red and orange visible in the gloom of dusk.

The priory of Saint Vivant, I had been told by Robin, owned much of the town of Auxonne and the surrounding land. The rest belonged to Stephen, who was in command of the Duchy troops we brought with us.

This priory was a daughter house, or an off-shoot, of the great abbey of Cluny, a bitter rival of Cîteaux, which was situated to the south of the Duchy of Burgundy near Mâcon. Not that this had much bearing on the present conflict. Once the town of Auxonne had fallen to Otto's troops, I doubted that the blood-drunk men-at-arms unleashed by the vengeful Count would have given a soggy fart whether it was Stephen's steward or the monks of Saint Vivant who collected the rents due on the houses, shops and taverns that they robbed, ransacked and gaily put to the torch.

Yet Stephen of Auxonne, apparently, did care very much indeed. The chinless fellow had tears glistening in his eyes as he sat on his horse a few yards from me and watched the smoke drift over the river towards us from his burning town. On the walls of his ancestral castle the blue and gold flag of his former lord flapped boldly against a smoke-wreathed sky.

Our men were hidden in the thick woods about a mile back from the wide, green river, on either side of the main road that slanted down from Dijon to Auxonne. Another rutted track, meandering north, coiled up through open farmlands along the western side of the river bank, and I could see a few horses and carts piled with cut hay toiling south towards the old bridge that crossed the river, heading with their towering burdens towards the wooden gate in the stone walls of Auxonne on the far bank.

It had taken us most of the day to form up our army – including Stephen's large contingent of well-equipped Burgundian knights – and ride the twenty miles southeast from the capital of the Duchy to this place of concealment less than a mile from Stephen's smouldering castle walls.

Owain had greeted Robin, Little John, Hanno and me when we joined his small band of scouts in the woods near the bridge.

"Otto hasn't moved since he took the castle this morning, my lord," the Welshman said. We had all ridden to a spot just behind the fringe of the trees and were peering out cautiously at the smoke-obscured town across several fields of wheat and rye, and the waters of wide slow river.

"He's letting his men run riot in the town – to the cry of havoc! He is giving them some sport after all the blood and horror of the assault."

I winced, thinking of the poor, defenceless women of Auxonne.

"What then. . . has happened to my poor garrison?" asked Stephen. He sounded diffident, even rather shy, which was odd considering that Owain had no rank beyond captain of Robin's scouts.

"Can't say what happened to them *all*," said the bowman, ducking his head respectfully. "But Otto hanged more'n a few."

Owain pointed to the high southern walls and I realised that I could make out a dozen black dangling forms under the grey stone battlements. I shuddered. They must have quickly surrendered to the Count – certainly Stephen could not have ordered them to defy the attackers. Yet Otto had executed them anyway. A message to his disloyal former vassal, perhaps.

"Perhaps Otto won't come over the river this way," I said. "Perhaps he will think that sacking and burning poor Auxonne is revenge enough."

"He'll come," said Robin. "And he'll come up this very road.

He's pandering to his men today – letting them have their fun, which good news for us, if not for the townsfolk. His men will all be sore-headed in the morning and, with luck, tired and unwary. But they will come up this way if they want to take Dijon. It makes no sense to take another road."

We spent a cold and cheerless night in the wood. I allowed my twenty men no fires, following Robin's general decree, and although we were a good mile from our enemies, I barred all talking too. Sound travels well across water, particularly at night – and there was a great big stretch of black river between us and our enemies. We lay in the chilly darkness of the wood, wrapped in our thick cloaks, chewing dried meat and bread, and sipping nothing but spring water from our flasks.

The men of my *conroi* took this with ill-grace but Hanno snarled at one of the more mutinous men-at-arms, a big Norman hedge-knight called Bertram. With my Bavarian friend's hard, unshaven chin stuck out, and a hand on his hilt, Bertram offered me no further argument.

My greatest fear was that we would be discovered by some passing peasant – a man or woman gathering firewood or feeding the pigs under the trees or hunting hares for the pot – and the ambush would be spoiled by bad luck. It is something of a feat to hide nearly two hundred armed men and a slightly smaller number of horses for an entire night in a wood just three bow-shots from your roistering enemies. Yet we managed it.

In the chilly pink light of dawn, as I stood behind an oak tree and emptied my bladder, I looked out on the town of Auxonne on the far bank once more. The scorched houses had finally been quenched of their flames and its sky had been almost entirely cleared of the smoke-fog by a brisk west wind. I wondered what this day would bring.

Watch over me in the battle, Saint Michael, I prayed. *Keep me safe so that I may do my duty here, then go and rescue poor Jacqueline.*

Robin was right, as usual. They came out of the gates of the town about mid-morning, a fat column of men-at-arms on foot, iron mail and helms glinting in the light, a forest of spears waving and clattering above their heads, and began spilling across the old stone bridge into the Duchy.

The first wave were only humble infantrymen, so far as I could see, with only a couple of grey-bearded sergeants on horseback to marshal them and relay the count's marching orders. There were about a fifty men-at-arms, at a guess, in this vanguard, spears in hand, and knives in their belts, not a gaudy banner, nor a well-born nobleman, among them.

However, their superiors were soon emerging from the town gates, hard on their heels. Scores of knights clattered on to the bridge on their huge warhorses, with pennants fluttering above and the heralds' *buisines* squawking out their brash notes, a joyful promise of the victory to come.

In the June sunshine, the knights' polished metal gleamed, and their richly dyed surcoats and the trappers of their horses – purple, red, silver, gold and blue – struck a festive note. This was the heart of the Count of Burgundy's army – knights and noblemen, and all their squires and pages, at least two hundred folk in all, excited, cheerful, a noisy mass of colour and movement that dwarfed the drab block of spearmen in front.

Otto himself rode in the very centre of this brilliant throng. I could just make out his bright red hair, held back by a thin golden circlet on his helmet-less head. I saw that his long blue surcoat was embroidered with lions in glittering thread. Otto had drawn his sword, a sliver of pure silver, and he seemed to be shouting encouragement to his followers – I was too far away to make out the actual words – and gesturing with the shining blade, urging his bold knights on, forward to fight and conquer.

Yet his army made no attempt to be stealthy or to proceed with any caution whatsoever; there was, indeed, little attempt at military order at all. They came surging out of the gates in a mob, clattered across the bridge and launched themselves straight up to road to Dijon as if they were in a tearing hurry to reach their destination. They were no more than a mass of spoiled, arrogant men advancing swiftly in the knowledge of success, forging ahead into a wide open, wealthy land – a land whose leader had been murdered at their count's order only days before.

The whole Duchy lay at their feet, ripe for despoiling.

Or so they believed.

My *conroi* was the nearest to the river. When I was certain Otto's army was advancing up to road towards us, I pulled my fellows back a dozen yards from the edge of the wood but ordered every man to mount.

The main road ran in a northwesterly direction directly up to Dijon, the capital of the Duchy, which was about twenty miles distant. Our concealed ambushing force was split into four unequal parts. The cavalry units commanded by Robin and myself were both on the northeastern side of this wide, muddy thoroughfare. I was in the front of the position, nearest to Auxonne; Robin and his similar-sized force lay two hundred yards further up the road, and was equally hidden in the thick woodland.

There was a good reason for this two-hundred-yard space between our two small *conrois*. On the southwestern side of the road, the far side of the track from Robin and me, stood the combined force of Owain and Little John's archers, fifty men in all, and dispersed around the thick woodland in their pairs. Two men to each unit – one to spot, one to shoot

Bowmen hidden in forested areas are the prefect troops for ambush – and the skills of these Sherwood archers, many of whom were former poachers or outlaws, made them particularly lethal. But you don't want to be on the other side of the road when bowmen loose their deadly shafts.

While some of the men could shoot the eye out of a bird on the wing, not all of them were quite so accurate, and there would be arrows flying thick and fast when battle was joined. So Robin and I, over the road, had posted our companies well clear of the archers' killing zone.

The final contingent of our ambushing force was commanded by Stephen of Auxonne and was made up of the proud knights of Burgundy who owed allegiance to the ducal house, a full company of Dijon's town guard, and the few knights who followed Count Stephen himself. I knew that Robin had argued against Stephen being placed in command of this strong force of ninety mounted men, but Eudes, who decided to remain at his palace with the rearguard, in case things went awry, overruled him.

"Stephen of Auxonne is now a nobleman of the Duchy. He must command my troops. It would be an insult not to give him this honour. You, my dear Locksley, are my friend and ally, but you're not my man."

Robin had accepted this decision with good grace. But I suspected that Eudes, for all his emollient words, did not entirely trust my lord.

However, Robin *had* insisted on overall command – it was, he said, the price of his participation in this conflict. He'd posted the Burgundian contingent a quarter of a mile up the road on the same side as the archers. Their task, when the battle was at its zenith, Robin said, was to sweep down the road, overwhelm the surviving enemy troops and carry straight on over the bridge to Auxonne, and recapture Stephen's ancestral town.

Stephen, understandably, was enthusiastic about this role for his knights. And I believe Robin was pleased to have them initially out of his way. There was a discrepancy in the strength of the two warring sides, I saw: there were two hundred of Otto's knights and squires coming up the road, and a fifty spearmen in front of them, while we had fifty archers, and some forty of Robin's men-at-arms. Stephen's force of ninety knights might ultimately prove crucial, if mere surprise didn't allow us to prevail.

I made a final signal to my men for absolute silence, as the first of the enemy spearmen came swinging past. There were singing, something jaunty in a their own German dialect that I did not comprehend, although I saw Hanno grinning, and wagging his index finger in time with the beat.

Then they were past us, and we were still mercifully undetected. I let out a long breath. Now came the jingling of harness, the creak of leather, and the slop of many hooves in mud. There were shouts from wine-sodden voices, jests and boasts roared in Burgundian French – the language of nobles, which I *could* understand. I found I was holding my breath once more and trying to keep my madly beating heart in my chest.

One of our horses gave a loud whinny, a greeting, perhaps, to the mass of strange equines he could scent on the road twenty yards away, and I swung round in my saddle, glaring, finger to my lips, and saw one of my men dismounted and holding his hand over his horse's nose. He raised his eyebrows in apology, and I snapped back round to look at the road. But that one explosive snort had not, thank God, alerted the enemy to our proximity. It had been lost in the general hubbub of the advance.

Otto's knights seemed to take an age and a half to pass by our leafy hiding place. I peeped out through the branches only once more to view them passing and saw the redheaded Count of Burgundy, slumped in his saddle, his eyes shifting from side to side. He had a premonition, perhaps, or some low instinct warned him that these woods held hidden dangers.

As I watched, I saw the first strike of a yard-long shaft. It came flashing out of the trees in a streak, and sank into the chest of a knight who had only that instant spurred up beside his lord. I suspected that Owain had loosed the arrow himself, hoping to put Otto down in the mud.

The knight yelled out, pawing at the pale shaft sticking from his ribs, and suddenly there were arrows slicing out of the trees all around them. Fsst. Fsst. Fsst. The archers hammered their missiles into the ranks of the knights. Such was the crowd on the track that they could scarcely miss.

The only patch of the road I could see through the trees was now filled with plunging, stricken knights, the horses screaming as often as the men, rearing up in pain, shaking loose their riders. This was a stretch of hell. Yet I knew it must be the same on a hundred yards of thoroughfare. The count's men all seemed to be shouting, screaming, calling on God and the saints to preserve them, trying to control their panicked mounts as the arrow storm ripped and sliced into them without mercy. The shafts kept on coming, on and on – punching into flesh, skewering limbs and torsos. The road now a mass of movement and confusion, chaos, kicking horses, splashes of scarlet blood, white-faced bellowing knights with their steel swords out, looking for someone – anyone, anyone at all – to attack.

There were more empty saddles now than occupied ones. I saw one unfortunate man take a shaft to the right eye, his head knocked right back, and the arrow protruding half its bloody length from the back of his skull – such was the power of the six-foot bows Robin's hidden men wielded.

They had no trouble sinking their shafts through iron mail, steel helmets, rib cages, skewering the soft organs beneath. The mud of the road was now thickly stacked with dead and wounded. Still Owain's bowmen lacerated the writhing column of knights – fsst, fsst, fsst, fsst – their barrage relentless. A rain of horizontal death. But it could not last.

One richly clad knight, in scarlet and gold, a gold coronet atop his steel helm that marked him as a lord of men, pointed his sword towards the trees to his left, and calling for his liegemen to follow, he put back his spurs and charged headlong into the thick wood.

Three arrows smacked into his body, one after the other, in a short rippling tattoo, and he screamed in anger. More knights, raking their horses bloody, followed the dying lord into the trees on the far side of the road, and I knew when the horsemen reached our bowmen, some of whom lacked mail, shields, even helms, there would be a great slaughter.

I shouted: "Ready all! On my command!" and felt a wild stirring, the vast jostle and stamp of twenty eager men and horses all about me.

"Charge! A Locksley! A Locksley! Charge!"

CHAPTER SEVENTEEN

We came out of the wood like a ravening wolf pack, spilling out on the muddy, bloody track. We each had a nine-foot ash-wood lance couched under our right arms, with a razor-edged leaf-shaped steel blade at the tip. And my mounted warriors used them with a cold, merciless efficiency.

There were targets aplenty, although our horses' hooves were very often tangled by the corpses and still-squirming bodies of the victims of Owain's arrow storm. My *conroi* sliced into our foes with a glee that was, indeed, positively lupine. The count's men were in shambling disarray on the road after the onslaught by the bowmen, no formations, no discipline at all, just a mass of horsemen, lost in gory, stumbling chaos, trying to discover what was happening and where the enemy was.

About half of them had been struck though with arrows. Some even looked like giant, man-shaped pincushions. We came at them anyway, wounded or not, at a fast canter, and using the momentum of the charging horses, we slammed our long, lethal spears into their bellies and chests.

I saw one on my older men, Bertram the troublesome Norman hedge-knight, plunge his lance directly into the shouting open mouth of a Burgundian man-at-arms, the tip bursting out the side of his face in shower of blood and fragments of a broken jaw. I slotted my blade into the belly of a squire, a fool who was half-turned away from me and looking the wrong way up the road – there is little honour or glory in an ambush – my lance entered above his right hip and sliced through the front of his stomach, eviscerating him. The lad screamed and slumped in the saddle, his surcoat instantly drenched in red.

The lance tip snagged in his mail and stuck. So I abandoned it and pulled out my sword, thinking that I would now seek out the Count of Burgundy and engage him myself, man to man. He was a far more worthy opponent for me. I would slay him myself, as Owain the bowman had tried to do, for personal glory and the greater good. Yet I might also condescend take him prisoner – if he yielded swiftly enough to my sword.

It would be fine revenge to make him pay gold for his life.

But the crush was so great, the melee so confused, that I could not make out Otto anywhere on the crowded road. A Burgundian knight swung at me, a big fellow, cursing in German, and I blocked his sword blow and swung him laterally with my shield, which was newly painted with Robin's emblem of a snarling wolf. He reared back but the bottom point of the shield caught him in the mouth, smashing his teeth and lips, and he reeled back, spat blood and boldly hacked down at me overhand.

It was a hard, full-strength blow, and I caught it neatly near the cross-guard of my sword. Yet even so it came perilously close to slicing into my mailed shoulder. I flung his blade away from me, and lunged, in the same movement at his head, the sword struck his cheek, slicing flesh.

His ripped and snarling face was now a mask of blood, but he still would not yield to me. He was still spitting curses and gore at me in equal quantities as the surging crowd of horsemen swept him out of my reach.

There were occasional arrows flitting lethally between the riders but the barrage had mostly ceased. Owain's men must see us fighting hand-to-hand in the road. I looked quickly up the track and saw that Robin's two dozen men-at-arms were also battling, fifty yards away, and that my lord was alone and surrounded by enemy horsemen, all hacking at him.

I decided I must go to my lord's aid but, even as I watched, he stabbed one of his foes through the thigh, spun his blade, sliced another across the face and, with a roar, he burst out of the circle of his enemies.

I felt a ringing blow against the back of my helmet, and I turned to see a lone footman, jabbing at me from the ground with his long spear.

There were few of these infantrymen on the churned up road. Many had fallen to the arrow storm, but the bulk, I suspected, had merely fled.

The spearman thrust at me again, boldly but inefficiently, and I parried the weapon with my sword and then twisted in the saddle and chopped his leather-clad skull wide open with the backswing, dropping him into the mud in an instant. My surviving horsemen were all about me, now, battling for their lives. Hanno was killing like a fiend only a length away from me, axe in one hand, a sword in the other, his shield slung over his back, controlling his mount with his knees. I saw him slice the lower jaw off a man, then run him though his belly with his sword.

I cut at a mounted man-at-arms, who appeared out of nowhere, aiming at his head. He blocked, reposted strongly, but got himself badly off balance, whereupon I lunged, struck and dug my point into his belly – and immediately had to block a savage sword swing with my shield from another knight, who was then swept away in the whirl of the battle.

The noise of steel grating on iron mail, shrieking, grinding, and clashing with other blades, was almost deafening; shouts and crude oaths, in German, French and English, cheers, bubbling moans, screams and jeers filled the air. I could smell fresh blood and runny shit comingled, tasting it as strongly as if it were coating my tongue.

The fight had carried me by now to the far side of the road, pushing me out of the churning melee and into the light scrub before the true dense woodland, and I saw that figures were coming out of the trees, walking slowly forward, big, broad fellows in long green cloaks, carrying six-foot yew bows and arrow bags at their waists – there was old Owain himself, with a deep bleeding cut on his dirty, lined old face, and a set expression, very grim, leading his dozen surviving Sherwood men.

The archers were still formed in pairs, usually stopping next to a tree, one man spotting, one shooting down the foes picked by the other.

A knight in a pale blue surcoat, twenty yards from me, with a black eagle imprinted on the chest, pointed at the line of bowmen with his blood-spotted sword, screamed a challenge, and spurred towards them. I made to intercept him, calling out in French for him to come and fight me, answering his challenge to Owain's men on foot, but there was no need: the first hissing shaft took him right through the throat, the second smacked into his left side with such force it swept him out the saddle.

I saw Otto then – he was fencing with one of my men. It was Bertram the hedge knight, I realised, and while he was madly fending off the count's quick silver blade, a second Burgundian knight spurred forward and rammed his sword deep into Bertram's back. Then I heard a hunting horn sounding further up the road, and turned to see Robin fifty paces away with the instrument to his lips. It was the agreed signal, the call for help. The blast from the brassy horn was supposed to summon Count Stephen and his Duchy knights – ninety well trained horse warriors – urging them all to come out from their hiding places and help us.

It dawned on me that Stephen should already have been in the thick of the battle – yet he was not! Robin's small force had taken on an army more than twice their size. And while we had fought valiantly and slain many foes, we could not possibly hope to defeat them all. I saw one of my men cut down by two of Otto's knights attacking him from both sides – and felt the first cold creep of despair.

The element of surprise, the power of an ambush well sprung, had given us a temporary advantage. The arrow barrage had taken its toll on the enemy ranks. Yet in the ripped-up road we still faced a hundred-odd surviving knights and squires of the County – the cream of their army.

The balance of the battle had shifted. I could feel it. It no longer tilted in our favour. We were tiring, most of us exhausted, in truth, and I'd lost perhaps a dozen good men already.

We were losing this fight.

We were dying. And Otto's men now seemed to be everywhere, slicing, hacking, hurling my poor fellows from the saddle. Where in God's name was Stephen? A pair of Otto's mounted squires had reached the tree line and they were busy hunting down the dozen or so archers still there, lashing their swords down at them from the height of their saddles, shouting like wild schoolboys in their terrified excitement.

More Burgundian knights rode over to join the fun – four, five, six horsemen. The bowmen were forced to duck behind the bulk of the trees, evading the swinging blades of the enemy knights, and the trampling hooves of their warhorses. The archers, scurried and dodged, sometimes managing to loose a quick shaft before haring away into the safety of the wood. Robin was blowing his horn again, it sounded more urgent this time. It sounded, in truth, utterly desperate. Where *was* Count Stephen – where was the aid we so badly needed?

The truth hit me then like an avalanche: the Count of Auxonne was not coming to our aid. The coward Stephen had foully betrayed us. His master the regent doubtless had no qualms at all about Robin's men lying dead in this muddy, bloody road, dying for the Duchy, dying for him. But his own precious knights – why would he sacrifice them in this minor skirmish? I could easily imagine the secret orders whispered by candlelight by Lord Eudes to his new vassal Stephen of Auxonne: "Let Locksley's men fight it out with Otto, eh? Let the English kill the foe and die in the mud. But save our own knights for the battles to come!"

Stephen wasn't coming to our aid. He was leaving us to die.

Then I heard another sharp blast – brighter, brassier and louder – it was coming from the direction of the town of Auxonne. And I saw a large *conroi* of fresh troops – forty men, perhaps – approaching up the road from the farmland on this western side of the river. The leading knight, in full mail, wore a helm that completely covered his face in a cage of shining steel. Two goats's horns protruded demonically from the top of the steel. The large banner that flew above the leading horseman was green and white, an alternating pattern of cup-like shapes known as *vair*.

It was the Green Knight. Chevalier Raoul, Seigneur de Beaune-du-Bois. He and his forty men were coming to give victory to their lord.

For a moment, all the noise and clash and clamour of the battle stopped. My ears failed me. I could see the fight raging, the desperate men striking at each other, stabbing, battering, killing, dying, but I could hear nothing.

I saw the Green Knight's *conroi* approaching at pace, they were only twenty yards from the rearmost knots of struggling men in the road. Otto was still there. He was surrounded by a ring of six knights, all with blades drawn – a guard ordered to protect his person. They were cheering, their red mouths open, swords pumping the air, yet no sound at all emerged.

I saw the Green Knight lower his lance and, still without hearing a whisper, I watched him slam the long steel point deep into the back of one of my Marseilles men. I was immediately snatched back out of my silent dream state, snapping back into the real world – and I knew only one thing for certain: live or die, I *must* destroy the Green Knight, I had to cut down this man-beast with the inhuman metal mask, if it was the last thing I ever did. Raoul must die, and die now – for what he had done to me; for what he and his men had done to the two plain girls, and perhaps countless others; for what he might do to Jacqueline.

I let out a roar of rage and hefting my sword and shield, I kicked my tired horse directly towards the *chevalier*. I batted a man out of my path, not caring if I slew him; my horse shouldered another out of the road.

I was only ten yards from the Green Knight.

He saw me; he knew me. I imagined beneath the hideous mask he was smiling coldly. He saluted with his spear, and flew at me.

His first, clever, lightning-fast strike nearly skewered me. He feinted high, as if aiming for my head, and when I hunched under the line of the blow, he dropped the point to the level of my belly. It was only by great good fortune – perhaps Saint Michael's interference – that the spear-blade missed me and slid between my waist and my shield arm, scraping over my mail, and lodging in the wooden cantle of the saddle behind me.

The shock of the impact snapped his lance, and checked my horse's advance, the animal neighing loudly, tossing its head in anger.

I swung but mistimed my sword blow, and sliced through empty air, as the Green Knight cantered past me. I had to take a moment to sheath my sword, and pull the spear out from the back of my saddle. I turned my horse with my knees and before I knew it the *chevalier* was on me again, this time with a sword hammering down at my mailed shoulder. I caught the blow on my shield and hurled the shaft of broken lance clumsily at Raoul's head, the spinning wood dinging off his monstrous metal mask, but he was past me again and I knew I had not harmed him at all.

I was ready for his next pass, sword drawn again. I met his overhand strike with my raised shield and in return cracked my own blade over the top of his shield, the steel clanging against the back of his helmet. That was a good solid blow, and I saw him sagging a little in the saddle, but he turned his horse once again and came back at me. This time our swords met, a long scrape and grate of bright steel, sparks flying, and I shoved hard with all my strength against his full weight, forcing his body back.

Yet he was a strong man, no mistake, and very fast. He whipped his blade at my neck – a blow I just caught with my shield. We parted then, for a few panted breaths. I quickly glanced around, Robin was near me now, fighting two men one on either side of him, and I caught a glimpse of Little John further up the road, on foot, roaring and spitting and smiting his encircling foes with great bloody sweeps of his giant war-axe. But very few of our people were alive, their bodies lay thick in the mud and piled high on the verges of the road – and there were still scores of Otto's brutal knights circling, prowling, seeking out fresh prey.

One such fellow rode in fast and whipped his sword across at me laterally, and I blocked, and threw off the blade with the side of my now-battered shield. I heard the Green Knight cry out in Burgundian French, the words muffled by his mask: "Leave him, Heinrich, he's mine! I claim him, that English snake!"

Now the *chevalier* was striking at me again; two super-fast blows. I blocked, I parried, and spurred away. My sword arm was aching with tiredness now; my back muscles a mass of fire. I heard a peal of trumpets once again and thought only this: *Reinforcements. More of the bastards, is it? Well, I'll take this masked bastard with me, if it's the last thing I do.*

I surged towards the seigneur de Beaune-du-Bois with all the youthful strength and fury still at my command. I hammered the sides of my horse mercilessly, urging him towards my enemy, my blade pointed directly at him like a lance. I could see the man waiting, anticipating my attack – then he completely surprised me.

He struck early. He hacked down hard at the head of my horse, striking just below the ears of the poor beast, the sword sinking into its brown muscular neck. The poor animal screamed, rearing up, blood flying in great thick loops through the air. The Green Knight knocked my sword aside, sliced at me, and I had to duck under his scything blow.

But my horse was done for. Dying right under me. I could feel its legs wavering, crumbling and collapsing. I swung my blade desperately at Raoul, one last time, and missed by a mile. He circled away. My horse was foundering, sinking. I could see a wide oozing purple gash in its neck, blood flooding out and sheeting his neck and a glimpse of white bone through the steadily pulsing gore. The *chevalier* was ten yards away from me, and still securely on his horse. But he seemed distracted.

He appeared to be looking at something behind me.

There were more rippling, brassy notes and I heard the thunder of hooves, saw the shivering of the earth in the muddy puddles of the road, and I turned to look up the track and I saw a wave of chivalry pounding down the road towards me. Scores of knights charging together in perfect formation, five horses wide and many ranks deep. And in the centre of the front row, Stephen of Auxonne, leaning far forward, his long lance couched under his arm, his silly, chinless face milk-white with terror.

But he was, at last, leading Lord Eudes' knights into the fray.

Stephen saved us. He came to the battle late but he did arrive, and in the nick of time. I never discovered if his tardiness was incompetence or was a plot cooked up with the regent. I'm inclined to assign it to ineptitude.

He was son of a hundred lords, but he himself was no warrior. And he had struck me from the first as a man uncomfortable with subtle plots and low deceit. But he *did* come to our aid and that is what truly counted.

His ninety knights pounded down the wide road, shouting their war cries, screaming their insults, their lances couched... and they swept the battered, exhausted knights of the County before them like a vast broom.

I did not see Otto and his bodyguard flee the field, but I heard later that he took one quick look at the bright hued wall of charging Duchy troops, hurtling down the road towards him like a collapsing cliff, and he spurred his horse back to the bridge, into the town of Auxonne. I was told he rode right through the town, and didn't stop galloping till he reached his castle at Dole, ten miles to the southeast of Stephen's old patrimony.

I did not witness the Count of Burgundy's flight but I did see the Green Knight's departure – and to my intense frustration there was nothing I could do to stop him escaping. My poor wounded horse was dying under me and, through I tried to kick both my feet clear of the stirrups and dismount with as much grace as possible, my spurs became tangled with the horse's belly bands, and when the noble animal finally fell to earth, he landed on my left leg, pinning me to the muddy road.

I saw the *chevalier* turn his inhuman metal face to look over at me, pinned and helpless. I saw him heft his sword and I was convinced for an instant that he was coming over to finish me. Yet he did not. He glanced, instead, up the road at the oncoming horde of Duchy knights and did the only sensible thing. He turned and fled.

Trapped with the colossal weight of the dead horse on my left leg, I craned my neck round to see the Green Knight gallop away with a dozen of his grey-clad riders. They were heading north along the road on this side of the Saone, back to his forest-lapped home. To the Castle of Bones.

CHAPTER EIGHTEEN

"By Our Lady's bleeding bum-grapes," said a voice, "what are you trying to do to that poor animal, Alan. You must be truly desperate for love, if you're trying to get amorous with a dead one!"

I looked up from the mud of the road to see Little John looming over me like an ogre from some terrible nightmare. He was holding a blood-drenched battleaxe in one huge hand, his massive red face was equally well splashed with gore, and his mail hauberk was actually dripping.

"I know you've been unlucky in love, son, but there's no excuse for this sort of disgusting behaviour. The younger generation – such foul, depraved creatures – if they can't eat it, drink it or fuck it, they're just not interested. You aren't trying to eat that poor horse, are you, Alan?"

"If you've quite finished being hilarious, John, could you get me out from under this animal before my leg is squashed to jelly."

"Are you sure? I don't want to spoil your fun."

I glared at him.

Little John put down his axe and seizing hold of the saddle, and grunting a little with the effort, he lifted the entire limp corpse of the horse a full foot off the ground, and I unhooked my spur and scrambled out from underneath. I got to my feet, massaged my bruised left leg for a moment, straightened my clothes and tried to muster some dignity.

"I need another horse," I said.

"Already? I'm impressed," said John. "What it must be to be so young and full of sap! There are plenty of pretty ones to chose from."

He gestured towards the torn-up road, which was strewn with the bodies of the dead, County and Sherwood folk, and a few Duchy knights, too. There were indeed several horses, standing with drooping heads, some wounded, sword-cut or stuck with our arrows, some dying, some whole but confused by the carnage, nuzzling the bodies of their masters.

"Take your pick," said my big friend. "Promise I won't tell a soul."

"No," I grated, "I have to go after him – the Green Knight."

"Who is this you're going after now?"

"The *chevalier* – the knight with the steel visor and horns."

"That one. I saw you toying with him. He slew your horse?"

I nodded.

"That's the bastard who took your girl prisoner?"

I nodded again. A wave of tiredness hit me. I felt a strong desire to lie down and sleep for a week, and, as so often after a battle, to weep.

"You'd better go sort him out then, Alan, hadn't you. But speak to Robin first. He won't be happy if you decamp without a word."

"Where is he?"

"In the field yonder," said Little John. "Giving that chinless ninny a right proper scolding."

I found my lord beyond the fringe of the woods in the open farmland before the stone bridge over the Saone. He and Stephen of Auxonne were standing face to face, clearly arguing, and Robin was even jabbing a hard finger towards the younger man's chest.

"... all I am saying, Lord Auxonne, is that as a result of your delay nearly half of my men have been killed or wounded."

"I am heartily sorry for it, Locksley. The wounded shall be

tended by the monks of Saint Vivant, I swear it. The monks have a fine hospice in town, which I personally endowed, and the dead shall be buried with many masses sung for their souls, but first we must possess Auxonne."

Robin gave a long, sad sigh.

Count Stephen, though clearly nervous, was insistent: "We must retake my patrimony, my lord, immediately. You personally persuaded me to do homage to Lord Eudes and now I have lost my castle, my town and all my lands. You owe this to me, Locksley. You know you do!"

"Alan Dale," he said, as I drew near. "You're not hurt, I trust? Good. You did very well. The timing of *your* charge was perfect."

"I must go after the Green Knight," I blurted. "I cannot bear to leave Jacqueline at his mercy any longer. Let me go, lord."

Robin stared at me. I saw how tired he was; the lines of worry on his long face. His grey eyes were pale as a pigeon's breast.

"Go then," he said, "if you must. But take only two of my men."

"My lord," said Stephen, "surely you are not sending your fit men-at-arms away? We should attack Auxonne with our full strength."

"He has earned it. You, on the other hand..." Robin paused, and managed to keep the insult in his throat. "Now, regard the gates of your town, my lord. What do you see?"

The Count of Auxonne stared across the river at the low walls of his fiefdom. "What? They are plain gates. I see nothing out of the ordinary."

"The gates are open – see? – it is clear that the townspeople do not mean to resist our entrance," said Robin. "They are submitting to us..."

However, by that point, I had already made my bow and was backing away from the two of them, in an absolute fever to be gone.

I picked Hanno, of course, to accompany me; and Samuel, one of the few bowmen to escape any injury in the bloody battle. He was a steady, middle-aged Cheshire man and an excellent shot. I praised the surviving members of my *conroi*, told them to rest, sleep and report to Robin when they were ready for duty. I chose a good horse that had lost his rider, and made sure I had a lance, shield and suitable food and provisions.

The three of us were about to ride out, taking the road north along the western bank of the Saone, when Little John came trotting up on his huge grey mare. "Thought I'd come along with you," he said. "Robin won't need me. The town is wide open and the castle is already hauling up Count Chinless's flag on top of its keep. There won't be a decent fight to be had for days. So I thought I'd come with you, if you'll have me."

I was delighted. Despite his stupid jokes, there was something about Little John that made even the maddest, most reckless scheme seem possible. He was undaunted by enemy numbers; fearless in the face of Death. I wrapped his strength and courage around me like a warm cloak.

We had travelled no more than a mile north on the road, when we came across a pair of riders coming from the other direction. Two men on cart horses with by an unladen mule. One of them was Henrik the Tanner.

We all reined in and exchanged polite greetings. I saw that the other rider was Arlo, his sullen redheaded apprentice.

"Did you see the *chevalier* and his men on the road?" I asked.

"We passed them not an hour ago, galloping hard for the north," said Henrik. "I hailed them in a friendly manner but they just thundered past without a single word. The rude buggers."

"Heading for Beaune-du-Bois, did it look like?" I asked.

"Most likely. You're going after them?"

"I'm going to get Jacqueline out of there. If she lives."

"She's alive – or was this morning. I went to the castle to see if they had any raw hides for sale. I have bought a few deerskins, wolf pelts and some other furs and hides in the past from the *chevalier* – he sells me his furs in great bundles a couple of times a year. I paid him another visit this morning. But the gates were shut and the servants would not admit me."

"You chose to call on him?" I said, frowning. It seemed an odd time to trade, with war breaking out and, as far as Henrik knew, his lord dead.

Henrik looked searchingly at me. I could see he was fully aware of my suspicions. "May I speak frankly before your comrades?"

"I trust them with my life. Say what you will before them!"

"I know that Lord Eudes is alive – that all the rumours of his murder are false. I saw the very man myself, unharmed, peeking out of an open shutter on one of the upper floors of the palace. He saw me watching him and quickly ducked away. But he lives. I know this for certain. Then I remembered what you told me two days ago – that all would be well. So I knew something mysterious was going on."

I'd been indiscreet. Too late to worry about that now.

"So you decided you would go and purchase a few hides?"

"War will surely push up the price of leather – yes. But, in all truth, I decided that I'd go to the château de Beaune-du-Bois to see if I could find a way to rescue the girl, or just help her in some way."

"A change of heart, then," I said coldly. "You refused before when I asked for your help. You said your fighting days were over."

"I feared the Green Knight, Alan, and his grey riders. Indeed, I still fear them. But you have put me to shame. You, a mere stripling, a foreigner in this land, have showed me the true path of honour. And, well ... there is something that I have not told you about this business. Something I should have told you before. The girl Jacqueline is my kin. She is my dead wife's sister's daughter. I am not on good terms with Yvette, Jacqueline's old mother – she's a stupid, superstitious, stubborn creature, and she blames me for the death of my wife, her beautiful younger sister. She says it was God punishing us for the man-at-arms I killed in Swabia."

"So Gregoire the tavern keeper is your brother-in-law?"

"He is."

I could understand now why Gregoire had so quickly turned against me when I asked after the two apprentices that day.

"And you say you saw her, your niece, this morning?"

"I saw her walking on the castle walls, with a mailed man-at-arms in attendance. If you are going there, may I beg leave to accompany you, Alan. I have not forgotten my skills. And I have the falchion you kindly gave me – here." He showed me the thick blade sheathed at his left side.

"Why do you want to come with me?"

"I would help my niece and strike a blow in a noble cause."

I thought about this for a few moments. The Green Knight had at least a dozen fighting men alive, maybe more – I had seen this number ride off with him this morning when he was fleeing the battle in the woods. I had Hanno, Little John and old Samuel. Another man – and a trained man-at-arms, at that, albeit no longer young, could be useful. He spoke German, too.

In my head, a plan began to form.

"What about him?" I jerked my chin at Arlo, who was sitting on his horse looking a little anxious and petulant.

"I want to go home," Arlo muttered, looking down at the road. "I don't want to fight the *chevalier* and his *fee* riders. They'll steal my soul."

"He is my apprentice; he is mine to command," said Henrik. "He can come with us and hold the horses while we assault the castle."

I looked at Arlo, remembering all he had done. "I would not take a snivelling coward into battle," I said. "Send him home. Bring the mule."

We rode north, the five of us, leaving Arlo, his cheeks now as red as his thatch. The boy twisted in his saddle as he watched us ride away, ride off to save a fair damsel from the monstrous guardian of Castle of Bones.

We crossed the river at the ford, and held a council of war in the thick forest, north of the road about half a mile from the château de Beaune-du-Bois. The shadows were growing as the sun slowly sank in the west but it was June and the days were long. We still had a good hour or more, I reckoned, before it was full dark.

I was sure that we'd not been observed on the road – we had seen no one since Henrik joined us. Yet there might well have been hidden scouts posted in the dense foliage of the Forest of Chaux. On balance, I thought it unlikely. The Green Knight and his men had ridden out that morning to win a great victory; it would have been strange if they had anticipated being badly beaten and pursued back to their own castle, and had wisely positioned lookouts to watch out for pursuers in that remote eventuality.

I gathered my friends and said: "We must get to our positions before nightfall, then wait there, sleep if you can. I'm going in before dawn."

"Better tell us what you have in mind, youngster," said John.

We were crouching in a circle in a clearing in the woods, and I took a twig and drew a rough square in the dirt at our feet, marking the towers at each corner, then I drew rectangle inside the square near the top line.

"This is Logis de Seigneur," I said indicating the rectangle, "the steward's great hall. This Logis is where many of the men-at-arms sleep, and most of the male servants. The Green Knight has his solar at the end of the Logis, here." I stabbed the earth with the twig.

"There are also some guards who lodge in the gatehouse, but not very many – here – just a handful, three or four, I would guess."

"How many oppose us inside there?" asked Samuel. I looked at him closely but could detect no fear in him. It was a purely practical enquiry.

"I think fifteen, including the Green Knight," I said. "But perhaps sixteen, seventeen at most. They took a mauling in the battle in the woods. But I saw at least a dozen ride away with the *chevalier*. And he would probably have left only a small garrison behind at the castle."

"Uh-huh," said Samuel. I saw him thumb though his arrow bag, counting shafts. It looked like he had a full quiver, two dozen arrows.

"You won't be entering the castle at all, Sam," I said. "I want you to take up a position in the tree line here," and I sketched a line in the earth, "about fifty yards south of the castle, on the far side of the road to the river. I need you to get there and find a good spot without being seen by any sentries. Your task is to cover our retreat. When we come out, we'll be coming fast and likely pursued by angry Burgundians. I want you to slow them down a bit. If they come at you a-horse, retreat into the wood."

"I think you should tell us the whole plan, Alan," said Little John, and Hanno grunted his agreement.

I nodded. "It is this: I shall sneak into the castle late tonight, or very early tomorrow morning. I mean to scale the outer wall here – " I indicated the top right corner of the square " – I know where Jacqueline sleeps, in this tower here. And I will go to her and ask her politely if she wants to be rescued and, assuming she does, I will take her down from the tower and we will hide, until it is full morning, behind the stables, here." I stabbed the square again with the twig, near the right-hand side.

"What if she hits you with a chamber pot full of warm piss again?" said Hanno, grinning in the gloom. There were a few chuckles.

"It was a water jug," I said crossly. "And my back was turned."

"I'm more worried about horny young Alan trying to fuck the poor girl to death," said Little John. "You'll never guess what I caught..."

"Enough!" I snapped. "There will be time enough for jests later."

"But, Alan, seriously, what if she does not wish to go?" said Henrik.

"If she doesn't want to come with me, I will tie her up, gag her, leave her there and make my own escape, the same way I got in, and we can go home. But I don't think that will be the case. She must know the kind of man the *chevalier* is. I'm certain she'll choose to come with me."

There was also the matter of my faithful mount Ghost, whom I meant to reclaim, and my revenge on the Green Knight for the indignities he'd made me suffer, but I chose not to say anything then about that.

"At first light, or a little after it, Henrik, with Hanno and Little John, will present themselves at the front gate of the castle. Henrik they already know well enough, he has done business with them before. He will say he wishes to purchase some of the hides and furs they harvest from their hunting. He will offer to pay double, or something extra, in gold coin – would that work? We must be sure they do not turn you away again."

"I will say I wish to buy mink," said Henrik. "I know they have some fine pelts, which they offered me last time. I will say I have a rich furrier friend who will buy as many mink skins as I can sell him. They will admit me then. I know they will."

"The Green Knight needs money," I said. "He will smell a profit. All right. Little John and Hanno will pose as your servants, or guards – this is a wild region after all. You should disguise your faces with dirt, and pull your hoods well forward. They may have seen you in the fight in the woods but you won't have to fool them for long. I just need you three – on your horses, and with the mule – to get inside the castle gate."

"What then?"

"This is the hard part," I said. "The timing has to be exact."

Four pairs of eyes were watching me in the fading twilight. I felt a blush spreading up my cheeks. I was not used to ordering good men into battle. Asking them to risk their lives on my word.

"Just tell us, lad, tell us what you want us to do," said Little John.

"I need you to put down all the guards at the entrance to the castle and hold the gate until I can get Jacqueline out of there."

"That all?" said John. "I thought you were going to ask a

something difficult. It will be child's play. There are only a handful of 'em."

I felt a surge of affection for my friend. He was truly dauntless.

Hanno held up a hand. "Maybe it's best I come along with you, Alan. Over the wall. John and Henrik can hold the gate between them. No problem for them. Don't need me. For how you will climb up the wall?"

"No, you three must come in the front gate. Hold the gate. The fewer people creeping around a strange castle in the darkness the better. I *can* do this alone, Hanno. You taught me well. There is a rope there, I think, hanging outside the wall. Unless it has been discovered. And if it has, I shall use this." I tapped the hilt of the *misericorde* in my right boot.

I'd pound the steel spike into the outside of walls with a rock and use it as a foothold as Hanno had painstakingly taught me in Spain, that's if the hemp rope I'd left there had been removed.

Hanno shrugged. "All right. We take the gate; you come a-running."

"I will, believe me."

"Then what?" said Henrik. "They will be angry, furious, they will all come boiling after us – led by the Green Knight.

"We melt away into the forest. I've been in there twice now, and it is very thick. I'd wager that five well armed Sherwood men – two of them fine bowmen – could cause them a lot of problems if they come after us. Once a few have been skewered, they'll be cautious. I think they'll let us go. It's terrain for hunting beasts – or girls. Not dangerous armed men.

Samuel nodded at these words. "We gave the sheriff's men the slip, time and again, in the old days. I think we can evade a few of these here Burgundy buggers, even if we don't know the woods as well as they do."

CHAPTER NINETEEN

I stared at the rounded logs of the castle wall, faintly visible in the light from the stars and a mere fingernail of moon. I even brushed my right hand across its rough surface. Nothing. There was no sign at all of the rope I had left there, almost a week ago.

I had spent nearly two hours approaching the northern wall of the dark castle, crawling on my belly with infinite patience through the leaf trash, staying in the lowest hollows and hugging the shadows, once I was out of the trees and in the cleared space, and only moving when the high drifting clouds covered the fine slice of moon. It was now about an hour before dawn, I calculated, and Henrik had promised that he and the others would knock at the castle gates an hour after the sun came up.

I would have to do this the hard way. And I'd have to do it speedily. Soon the castle would begin to wake for the beginning of the new day.

I found a fist-sized rock at my feet in the filthy ditch that surrounded the fortress and pulled out the *misericorde* from its sheath in my right boot. The wall was twelve-foot high, and sheer, my plan was to knock the blade of the *misericorde* into the wall about three or four feet up its height, and wedging my eating knife in at knee-level, use the two blades, as step to allow me to make a leap for the top of the rampart, and then pull myself up with the strength of my arms. I had done this once or twice before and knew it could be done. Hanno had shown me how to do it in Spain, during a long period of loosely guarded imprisonment in that land.

A shadow passed over my head, and I could clearly hear the light footsteps of the sentry as he slowly patrolled the walls. There was only one man, and he walked a circuit of the castle ramparts in five hundred of my heartbeats. I had, in fact, timed him on my approach. I began to count.

At two hundred beats he would be on the far side of the castle and it should be safe enough to hammer the *misericorde* in without him hearing. I counted beats in my head and held the steel bar horizontally against the wood, with my left hand, and the heavy rock in my right.

I could feel something loose under the fingers of my hand.

The rope. Hallelujah! It was lying hidden in the crack where two round wall-logs met. I prised it out and gave it an experimental tug. It held. I tugged it a little harder. Then as hard as I could. The line was still secure. And I had counted a hundred beats in my head. Time to climb.

It was better than the step-method with the *misericorde*, but it was still no easy matter to climb up the slim rope. The various hurts I had taken over the past few days protested mightily, and my arm muscles seemed to creak with the effort required. But it could have been worse. I had removed my mail and abandoned my helmet and shield before embarking on this mission. Had I been wearing my full armour, I doubt I'd have had the power to haul myself up hand over hand. Yet I managed it and, a few moments later, I rolled over the top of the wall. I crouched in the dark of its lee, my eyes darting everywhere to locate an enemy.

This was the most dangerous time. The sentry, I saw, was on the far side of the walkway. He had paused by the gatehouse and was looking out over the forest to the south, the faint moon giving him a long, ghostly shadow. I wondered if he had seen something, one of my friends perhaps, who were supposed to be hidden in the tree line beyond the Dijon road.

There was nothing I could do if he had spotted them. In a

moment, he would either raise the alarm, or continue his tramp round the ramparts.

I had to move. Now.

Keeping a low as I could, I scuttled to the wooden staircase, and crept down it, my soft leather boots making little sound. God or Saint Michael was with me that night for the sentry did not move from his spot. He occupied himself by staring out at the dark ocean of forest, facing directly away from me, allowing me to proceed. He had raised no alarm, so I knew he hadn't seen my friends. But he wouldn't stay there all night.

I tucked myself away behind the bottom of stairway, in a dark corner, and contemplated my next step. A few yards to my left was the east tower, where I hoped Jacqueline was still lodged. The door had been unlocked, last time I had entered, but there had also been a man-at-arms sleeping in the ground floor room. I pondered what to do. I knew that Hanno and Little John would tell me to slay the guard in his sleep. One less enemy, they would say. A smaller risk of detection while I got Jacqueline out of there. But I knew could not do it. I could not kill an unsuspecting man in his sleep. Maybe I was too weak and lily-livered – Hanno would surely have called me that. But I knew I was no murderer.

I heard the sentry again, his boots scuffing on the walkway directly above me. The man paused, a dozen feet away, and I actually heard him yawning. I silently urged him to move. *Get going, fool.* Was it my imagination or was the sky becoming a lighter? *Move, you idiot, go away.*

Finally I heard his footsteps scuffing on the walkway of the northern wall, growing more and more faint. I slid towards the tower door, turned the handle, and pulled. The door didn't move an inch. It was locked tight.

I admit it – I panicked then. My brain seemed to freeze solid. I could not think what to do. If I could not get into the tower, I could not get Jacqueline out. This was a glaring, and possibly lethal flaw in my clever plan. What could I do now? What could I do except run back to the rope and make my escape as quickly as possible. I could imagine Little John's expression – and the hilarious comments he would make. The mocking laughter as he told Robin and the others that I had crept up to the walls of an enemy castle, climbed in without being observed and then been foiled by a simple locked door. And what of Jacqueline? What would her fate be? I believed knew the horrible answer to that question.

I tried the door again. It would not budge. It was definitely locked tight. I fumbled around in the pre-dawn darkness for the lock, and found it a few inches below the handle. I discovered something cold and hard sticking out from the lock. The key. *Thank God!* They had locked the door from the outside and left the key in the lock so the next visitor could have access. It meant, too, that someone was certainly a prisoner inside.

The key turned smoothly in the lock; the handle opened the door without effort, I stepped cautiously inside. There, lying on a pallet on the ground floor, her hands and feet tied with rope, was my girl Jacqueline.

She was awake; her eyes huge with terror.

I braced myself for screams. But none came. I looked closer and saw that her mouth was stuffed with rags, bound in place by a scrap of linen. Bound and gagged, inside a locked tower. Clearly, she was their prisoner.

Still I was cautious. I moved closer and whispered.

"It is me, Alan Dale. Don't be frightened. I'm here to help you."

Jacqueline stared harder at me. Her face was dirty, her hair matted and unbrushed. Yet she still looked perfectly beautiful to me.

"I'm here to help you, if you wish. Do you want my help?"
She nodded vigorously.
"If I ungag you, will you scream?"
Her head shook emphatically.
"If I untie you will you struggle and try to hit me again?"
This time she closed her eyes; then slowly shook her head.
"All right. Follow me, do as I say, stay close, keep silent, and

I will take you away from this awful place. Yes? Agreed?"

A little while later, we were inside the old storeroom behind the long stable block, at the back with the coils of rope, the huge sacks of flour and oats and old bits of horse tack, and I had Jacqueline hidden in a narrow space by the thin wooden wall behind a large stack of wooden apple boxes, covered by a large musty-smelling old horse blanket. It was a tight squeeze but I managed to crawl in beside her, and after giving one last look around the storeroom to see that we were undetected, I pulled the blanket over both our heads and breathed a sigh of relief.

We were unlikely to be found here, I reckoned, unless they searched the whole castle from top to bottom – and that would take a great deal of time. I was fairly sure we had not been seen while we left the east tower, and I had made sure that the door was locked again behind us.

Maybe they would check on her at dawn, to bring her breakfast, and her absence would be immediately noticed. It would appear a mystery. Locked door, no prisoner. Yet, on the other hand, maybe they would not look in on her for some hours yet. Either way, I believed we were safe for an hour. Time enough, with luck, for my friends to come a-knocking.

"Are you all right?" I said. I was squashed up close to the girl in that small space. She was clutching my right leg tightly with both her hands, as if it was a piece of floating timber, and she were adrift in a storm-lashed sea. I could feel her shivering against me in her thin linen shift; I was so close I could smell her breath. It was sweet. "Are you too cold?"

I put my left arm around her shoulders, and hugged her body to me. She snuggled in. "We may talk, I think, if we are quiet," I said.

She said nothing for a beat, then, "You have a plan, Alan?"

"My people are coming," I said. "When they get here we'll get my horse and we'll run. But you *must* do as I say, when they come."

She nodded, and curled even further into the crook of my

arm. I could feel the soft, delicate warmth of her skin against mine.

"I'm sorry I hit you with the water jug that night," she said. "I didn't know then what... I thought you were just trying to..."

"Don't distress yourself. I am entirely recovered now."

I could hear the stirring of the horses on the far side of the wooden wall we were pressed up against. I heard one animal whinny, and wondered if it was Ghost. I missed my friend. It would be good to swing on his back, pull Jacqueline up behind me and gallop out of the gates, to the astonishment of the castle men-at-arms. I'd like to see the *chevalier*'s face as I did, as I stole the loveliest girl in the world from under his nose.

I noticed that Jacqueline was stroking my thigh, almost as one might pet a cat or dog. The darkness had lifted, even under the blanket covering us, and I could see the raw marks on her wrists where they'd been bound.

"Why did they bind and gag you?" I whispered. "You were locked in and could not escape the tower – why tie you up as well?"

Before she could answer I grabbed her forearm and put a swift commanding finger to my own lips. There was now someone else in the storeroom with us. I heard a shuffling of shoes on the dusty, gritty floor, and someone humming tunelessly. There was a thump of a heavy sack, and the loud clatter of a kicked wooden bucket.

You fool! I thought. They will be feeding all the horses at this hour. And this is where the oats are kept! I put my hand on the cool hilt of the *misericorde*. I was no murderer, but if this cack-handed oaf of a groom did discover us, I *would* take him down before he could give us away.

I felt Jacqueline tense up beside me but she held her nerve like a soldier and did not move a single muscle. She remained taut and silent as a cat-threatened mouse. My brave girl! Eventually, the noises ceased outside the blanket, the humming faded: the storeroom was silent again.

I risked a peek out from under the horse blanket. No one.

But it was full day now and I began to relax. Soon my friends would be here. I'd be able to hear them when it all started; there was nothing to do but wait.

"It was a punishment," Jacqueline whispered. "That is why they bound me. I tried to run. The front gate was left open, and I saw my chance, and tried to get into the forest. To hide. But they caught me, I'd only got fifty yards beyond the road, when I tripped over a root and fell, and they dragged me back. I thought he would beat me but Raoul only laughed. It was worse than a beating. He is the very Devil, that man, a beast in human form. But you know this. You tried to save me from him."

"What did he say when he brought you back to the castle?"

"He laughed and said: 'You like to run, do you, my pretty one? Then we shall allow you to run. As fast as you like. Tomorrow. With a quarter of an hour head start, too. We shall see then how strong your legs are.'"

"You knew what he meant, then?"

"I knew. I knew he would hunt me like a beast, just like he hunted Minou and Pauline. And you . . . I did not know him then for the monster he is. I am so sorry, Alan. I did not know."

"It is all in the past," I said, my heart filling with wild, hot emotion. "Once we are free of this place, we never need speak of it again."

"I was such a fool," she said. "I thought he was a catch. I thought he was just the man for me. I met him and his awful henchmen in the deep woods on my way to my mother's house. Suddenly they were all around me, fierce men-at-arms on their mud-splashed horses. Laughing. Making jests. Wearing their long grey cloaks. And I looked up at the *chevalier* up there, high in the saddle, so strong, so confident. And he smiled at me . . .

"He said I was pretty; he called me beautiful. But I knew, I knew in my heart, even then, that I must have nothing to do with him. He was the Wolf. I was the girl with the red hood. Every girl in Burgundy knows that tale! And how it ends. Stay on the path, girl, or the Wolf will eat you.

"He got down from his horse, tall and noble, so handsome,

and took my hand and smiled again... He invited me to eat with him and his men. I was giddy, to be honest; I was flattered. I said yes though I knew he was the Wolf. Then he spoke of his loneliness, and his fine castle over the river. He said he would cherish me, love me, marry me in his chapel..."

"You came here with the Green Knight willingly?" I could not keep the surprise out of my voice.

"You do not know, Alan, what my life is. You travel the world, and fight the enemies of Christ. You live the life of a bold man of force and arms. I scrub plates and pans everyday until my hands are raw, I turn the hot roasting spit, I carry the food and pour the wine for all of Dijon, or so it seems. I run here and there, but never fast enough, and the old men leer and drool over my breasts and thighs, the apprentices pinch my behind till it turns black and blue, yet I can say nothing, lest lose my place...

"I'm at every man's command, all day, every day, I am their servant, a skivvy, and most men think me a whore. And when I go home to my mother, to rest for a day, I have those pigs to deal with, and always some fresh trouble of hers in Fontaine, a blocked well, a tumbled-down sty wall. Can you not see how I might be tempted by the good life of a fine lady in her own castle? A life of wealth and ease, with some skivvies of my own, and a brave and handsome *chevalier* to love and cherish me?"

I *could* see.

"Tell me of your home, in the county of Nottingham, did you say? Tell me about England. Is it always raining? Is the food really so very bad? I have heard people say that about your distant land."

I told her of the great beauty of Westbury, of the shady little paths through the woods, of the tall oaks and chuckling streams; of my fields, yellow as buttercups with the ripening crops in late summer, and lush and fecund in the spring. I told her about copses full of bluebells, like a carpet of purple under the trees, the scent of wild garlic perfuming the air...

Jacqueline kissed me then. And I was taken by surprise all over again. Her lips were warm and soft on mine. I felt the hot blood surge all the way through my body, from my tongue to my toes and back again.

"Raoul is *very* handsome, but you, Alan, you are a better man than him by far," she said and kissed me again. "Tell me you forgive me, Alan. Tell me. He's a lord of men, like you, and I'm just a village girl."

I had stopped listening to her and was responding to her kisses with growing passion, my heart thumping, my head dizzy, as if I'd had too much wine. We kissed deeply, passionately, and I realised in that moment that I truly did love her. That I had loved her since the moment we had first met. Then all ordinary thought ceased and we were united in our joy.

She climbed on top of me, awkwardly in that narrow space, pulling our clothing aside and we made love there and then in our cramped place of danger. And somehow, the peril that surrounded us, the imminent risk of death, made a fine, rich spicing for this most ancient of all human acts.

I heard her murmur hot in my ear: "You made a love song, Alan, my darling man; you composed a beautiful *canso* only for *me*..." Then she was riding me, legs astride, grinding down into me, and we moved together, writhing in exquisite unison. I do not recall for how long we were joined in this rocking bliss – time had no meaning – but, as she reached her ultimate climax, she arched her back, her body bunched tight around me, and called out my name.

Three times. Loudly. Very loudly. Far too loudly.

The blanket over us was suddenly ripped away and I found myself looking past Jacqueline's flushed face and open mouth into the eyes of a total stranger, a young man, in a full set of hunting leathers, who gaped at us as if he was seeing a holy vision.

He said something in German. I think he was asking who I was. Then he blushed, turned and fled. And I, still straddled and trapped under Jacqueline's half-naked body, my braies round my knees, was too slow to stop him running from the room and sounding the alarm to his comrades.

And I swear, by Almighty God, that my first thought on our sudden discovery was: *Little John will never let me hear the end of this!*

I got up as fast as I could. Which was not very fast at all. And found my sword and fastened my braies, retied my hose. I could hear yelling out in the courtyard outside and, my heart sinking into my boots, I picked up a wicker basket and stumbled to the door.

It was bright morning. I held the shallow basket in my left hand, as a kind of makeshift shield, and the naked sword in my right. And stopped in the yard-wide portal to see what was what. At least no one could easily get behind me then. The courtyard was rapidly filling with running, shouting soldiers. They seemed to be coming from everywhere, but particularly from the steps that led down from the Logis de Seigneur.

And who was that now, coming down those same stone steps but my mortal enemy and now my rival in love: the Seigneur himself.

The Green Knight caught sight of me, standing alone in the doorway of the storeroom, and he lifted a hand in friendly greeting and smiled.

CHAPTER TWENTY

I stood there, statue still. A loose semi-circle of men-at-arms formed in front of me, staying at a goodly distance, eyeing my naked sword. I could hear the sounds of men drawing weapons, and then the Green Knight was pushing his way through the throng. He had a long sword sheathed at his side, and a fine dagger, but no armour – he had been breaking his fast in the hall, I guessed, when they called him to arms. He came to the front of the mass of men – there must have been two dozen gathered before me.

He said: "So, Alan Dale, the English earl's wayward man, the forsworn *trouvère* and would-be rapist, the murderer of several of my people, has returned! And I find you skulking in my storerooms! What can you seek here, I wonder, snake. And who is that behind you? Ah, it is my guest, the fair Jacqueline. Who has become your whore, I am told."

I could feel the heat of Jacqueline's body at my shoulder.

"Tell your men to stand aside," I said. "We are leaving now."

"I don't think so," said the *chevalier*.

"Stand aside. We are free folk and shall leave your castle."

"Or what?" Raoul cocked his handsome head on one side. He scratched his neatly barbered beard. He looked disgustingly fresh and well rested. I was aware that I had not properly retied the cord on my right hose. The legging was even now sliding down my thigh. I felt half-naked. Embarrassed. And, though determined not to show it, terrified.

"What will you do if we do not meekly stand aside?" said the Green Knight. "Will you rush at us in a fury – at all of us here – with your cheap little sword and try to strike one or two down before we cut you and your whore into fresh meat for the hounds?"

"I'll kill more than a few of you," I said, jutting my chin. "And you will certainly be among the first to die. You monster. You coward."

"Insults – really?" said the *chevalier*. He was actually chuckling.

"I have a better offer," he said. "Step out from the doorway and drop your little sword. Surrender the girl and yourself to my mercy – and I shall let you run through the forest again. The terms of the hunt will be exactly the same as the last time. If you can put your right hand on the walls of Dole, snake, you shall be a free man."

"And what of Jacqueline?"

"Oh, I have plans for the whore. I shall take my pleasure on her, naturally. Then give her to my men for their sport. But you, Englishman, you may yet live out this day, if you yield to me now."

"No. But I will fight you, *chevalier*, one to one, you and I alone. A formal challenge from one fighting man to another. If I win, or if you yield to me, Jacqueline and I may both walk free. If I lose..."

"Do you take me for a fool? Why would I duel you? We are not equals in rank. And I have you in my power."

He gave me a long, cold, assessing look. Then said: "Just seize him! Bring him to me in the Logis when he has been subdued. Maybe I shall feed him directly to my hounds without giving them a good run. But bind the whore and put her in the tower. Take care not to mark her face."

The Green Knight turned his back and began to walk away.

I heard then the sound of loud knocking at the gate of the castle and the calling of familiar voices. And my heart gave a leap of hope.

The men-at-arms in front of me were all edging closer, bracing themselves for the fight. My sword twitched in my hand, a yard of razor-sharp steel; they watched the every movement of my blade like hawks.

The knocking at the gate grew louder. One of the guards, a man still on the walkway above the gate turned and shouted something in German across the courtyard to the Green Knight. I was only dimly aware of this; my focus was on the dozen men standing before me. I heard the *chevalier* shout in French: "Tell whoever it is to be gone. We are not accepting visitors just now! Inform them that we require nothing today."

The Burgundians jumped at me. All, it seemed, at the exact same time. One of them came in swinging a sword at my left-hand side. I blocked quickly with the wicker basket. Which received the blow well. The sword becoming wedged, stuck tight in the springy wooden frame. I simply twisted the basket's handle and disarmed the surprised man-at-arms. At the same time, a spear-point flickered at me from the right, and I had to fend off with my sword, batting away the shaft. Then I was punching my sword hilt into a shouting face, shouldering a fellow aside and I felt a strong hand grab at my leg and the fiery slice of a blade across my upper arm, cutting through my tunic, but not wounding me deeply.

There was a man on my left, a raised sword. Now swinging. He yelled something in German, a curse, the sword seemed to hang above my head, then something round and black swept past my right cheek – I felt its wind – and smashed into *his* face, knocking him flat on his back.

A heavy iron skillet. Its wielder was Jacqueline. She swung wildly at another man, two handed, and he was forced to jump away. I blocked a downward sword blow, and put my blade in someone's side. But I had now – somehow – come out of the shelter of the doorway, and there was a man behind me. Jacqueline smashed the fellow in the balls with the pan. She battered another man round the head, knocking him to the ground.

I tugged by bloody sword free of the dying man, slashed

wildly at a soldier in a mail shirt, making him stumble hurriedly back.

I yelled: "A Locksley! A Locksley!" And hurled myself into the press of men-at-arms, the forest of reaching arms that had formed around Jacqueline and her heavy swinging pan. I cut and hacked. My blade licked out, ripped through a grasping man's cheek. I sliced down with the backstroke, striking another fellow and sank my blade into a third man's thigh. Then someone barged into me hard – knocked me off my feet. I lay on the earth, the basket long gone, and swung at a pair of legs in range, and half-severing a man's foot. That made them all jump away at once.

I rolled, rolled, rolled again and scrambled painfully to my feet. I pulled the *misericorde* from my boot, crouched with a blade in both fists, and snatched a quick look around at the gate. *Help me, Saint Michael.*

I saw then – almost miraculously – the squat, shaven-headed form of Hanno fly up over the south wall and land with a crash on the walkway above the gate. He rose and dispatched a man with his hand axe, the blade taking his victim laterally in the throat, and whirled and killed another fellow with his sword; then Hanno was vaulting down twelve feet to the interior of the castle, landing as graceful as an acrobat by the gate.

I had no leisure time to watch him at his work. Two men-at-arms were rushing at me, one with a falchion, the other a shorter blade. The falchion swung at my head and I blocked it with my clanging sword; the other fellow sliced at my side and I had to swerve and twist sideways in an instant to avoid having my ribs crushed. He got the backswing of my sword hard in the back of his neck, and fell immediately to his knees. The second fellow got my dagger jabbed up deep into the meat of his forearm. More enemies were spilling from buildings around the courtyard. We had seriously underestimated their numbers. There were still half dozen men around me then, at least. I could not hope to stay alive for much longer.

A huge, bearded man at arms was grappling with Jacqueline on the ground ten paces away, rolling and struggling, and I saw her bite into his hairy face, her white teeth sinking in and drawing blood. He smothered her with his weight and bulk and delivered a crushing butt to her nose.

She went limp.

"Alan, get down now!" Hanno's voice behind me. I dropped to my knees and something spun over my head and smacked into the face of a man-at-arms, who was about to strike me dead with his falchion. Hanno was at my side then. I whipped my head sideways to grin at him and saw that the man-gate in the main portal was wide open and a huge, red-faced figure, wielding a double-headed axe seemed to be filling the space.

My heart soared with happiness, seeming to burst from my chest. If I had been cut down right then, I'd have died a happy man.

Little John charged into the château de Beaune-du-Bois like an elemental force of nature, a violent, unstoppable whirlwind, his great axe swinging like a pendulum, an inchoate bellow of mingled joy and rage volleying from his throat. Behind him, I saw Henrik, his falchion in his hand, and old Samuel, filing through the narrow slot behind Little John. Samuel with a strung bow in his hands and an arrow already nocked...

In that moment, in that instant, I knew we would triumph.

Little John immediately set upon a loose group of astonished-looking Burgundian men-at-arms in the centre of the courtyard, like a terrier in a pit full of rats, snapping and crunching the many fleeing rodents, killing with a vast and gory joyfulness, shaking the blood from his jaws in threads of jewel-like blood droplets. His great axe swung, the blood sprayed, another truncated body thumped to the sandy ground, the man screaming, coughing, dying. Samuel was an icy killing machine, picking shafts from his arrow bag, one after the other, nocking, loosing, and plucking yet another a fresh yard of ash from his side.

He was coldly impaling man after man. I saw him shoot down three men-at-arms in no more than five heartbeats – I swear it on my life!

Henrik seemed to have entered some sort of wild frenzy, his mouth, which was stuck in a rictus grin, was creamy with froth like some madman from another age. He hacked and sliced and slew the enemy with his brutal butcher's blade, heedless of the wounds that he took in turn. The falchion spraying life-blood with every swipe. Yet Henrik was not inviolate, despite his awful killing rage – I saw one Burgundian stab him in the back with a spear. And Henrik merely turned and stuck the man down with a massive blow that would have felled a full-grown ox.

Hanno too was killing with precision. He was here, there, everywhere, dropping men, staying close to me and warding my back.

And me? I fended off two men, in short order, wounding both but not finishing them. Then I searched wildly for the Green Knight in the mad, screaming, staggering, blood-splashed chaos about me.

Some of the Burgundians were surrendering, hurling blades away, falling to their knees in the sandy courtyard, raising hands in surrender.

I saw him then, his sword drawn this time. And he saw me.

The Green Knight came towards me, our eyes were fixed on each other, drawn like old lovers, untroubled by the other battling men.

He took up a high guard – his sword above his head, pointing towards me. I took the low one. Hanno's oft repeated instructions sounding in my ears. Then he flew at me. And, by God, he was fast.

Our clash on the muddy track on the woods, when we had both been mounted, had not prepared me in the slightest for his full speed and strength. His blade flashed down at my head and I only just got my own sword up in time to block – yet it was merely a feint, and now the point was driving lethally at my belly. I twisted madly and his steel sliced past my unguarded belly, an inch from my flesh, cutting the cloth of my tunic.

He was attacking again before I had even registered the shock of his blistering initial attack. A flurry of blows, from right and left and right again. I was parrying like a wildman, floundering, our blades screeching together when they connected. I was being battered down, pounded this way and that; almost bludgeoned into submission. I was tired, worn out; so much weaker than he. And he was so damned quick!

He wrong-footed me, fooled me with a feint and I found my belly wide open and saw him lunge, a killing blow that would have ripped through my lights, shredded my guts and ended me there and then. My life was saved only by one of his own men, who blundered into me and knocked me out of the path of his sword. I crashed shockingly to the ground. The blundering fellow, already bleeding, took the chevalier's sword though his chest, the blade punching right through his ribs, and it gave me the merest moment to recover, as the Green Knight, cursing in the foulest language, fought to free his stuck blade.

Raoul shouted: "This fellow is mine – I claim this back-stabbing snake. He challenged me. I accept. You will all leave him be."

Then the Green Knight looked properly around him.

I saw his eyes widen in surprise. I was still sprawled on the ground, clambering only slowly to my feet, aching, bruised and spent.

But even I took a half-instant to look about the courtyard.

The enemy were all dead or wounded, except for a number of men who were kneeling with their trembling hands in the air. We had won. We were victorious. That was clear. Then I saw poor Henrik lying on his back in a pool of glistening blood, his eyes tightly closed, and Jacqueline, his brave, beautiful niece, crouched over him, whispering something into his ear. Samuel was sitting on the ground, his legs splayed out wide, and he was cradling one bloody arm with the other. But Hanno and Little John were advancing on the Green Knight, stalking him like a pair of murderers creeping up on a helpless victim in some rubbish-strewn alley.

"No," I shouted, "I want him. He accepted my challenge."

Hanno stopped dead. He was spattered with filth from head to toe. His sword was slick with gore.

He pointed a red finger at me: "Do not mess this up, Alan," he said.

"If he puts you down, Alan, I'll take revenge," said Little John grinning through a mask of dried and drying blood. "But you'll be fine."

I was back on my feet by now, breath regained. I squared up to the *chevalier*. I had my sword in my right hand, my *misericorde* in my left. My enemy had a sword, of course, and I saw him now draw a slim, rather elegant dagger from a silver bejewelled sheath at his waist.

It looked like a child's toy.

"To the death, you treacherous snake," he said. Then he looked over at Little John and Hanno; both standing watching us from twenty paces. "And when I've dispatched this puppy, I'll deal with you curs."

I felt my rage bloom then. As the Green Knight and I circled each other, watched by my two good friends, I remembered all the foul deeds he had done. All the insults and hurts. How he had attacked and captured us on the road to Autun without good cause and, by his ambush, caused the death of poor Ricky. Then I thought about the cruel manhunts he and his men had enjoyed – the innocent folk put to death for his pleasure. Then how he chased *me* so humiliatingly through the woods like a hart, and pursued Pauline and Minou, too. And what he and his men had done to poor Minou – and how many others too?

How he would have done the same to Jacqueline.

The anger glowed like a red-hot coal in my belly and I knew, I *knew* that Saint Michael – or perhaps God Almighty – would guide my arm and help me end this miserable beast's time on Earth.

Judgment – and, surely, everlasting torment – awaited him in the hereafter. Suddenly all my fear dissolved, my tiredness too. God was with me. I felt light on my feet; strong as a bull, fast as a hunting falcon.

Sure of myself. Sure of my victory.

Then the chevalier struck... like a bolt of blue-white lightning.

There was no clever subterfuge, no feint nor strategy. The Green Knight leapt at me and lunged at my head, the point of his blade spearing at my face so fast I almost did not even see it. It was an astonishing feat of speed, the strike swift as an arrow leaving Samuel's bow, and once again it was pure luck that saved my life. I was wiping a bead of sweat from my forehead with the back of my left hand, the hand that grasped the *misericorde*, just as he struck. Sheer good fortune, for it meant that a foot of blackened steel was in the right place, at the right time to deflect the chevalier's thrust, with the merest flick of my left wrist.

The blade hissed past my left ear. And I reacted correctly. I ignored the yard of steel that had so nearly punched through my skull, and counterattacked with my own sword. My blade whirled and sliced down towards his left shoulder an instant after his missed strike. My steel looped down, and he was way off balance, and the chevalier was forced to block my heavy blow too hurriedly – and with his elegant little dagger.

My sharp yard-long blade, with the full strength of my young right arm behind it, crashed into his toy dagger's hilt and carried on, crunching into the flesh and bones of his left hand. He gave a little shriek of agony and surprise and the slim dagger tumbled to the ground. I saw a finger fall with it and fresh blood spurt from his ruined left hand. He stepped away, slashing at me like a lunatic with his sword to make me keep my distance. Sweeping again, and again, and stepping right back. Now looking down disbelievingly at his left hand, which was pissing a fountain of gore.

His pale face was now a horrible greenish colour. He let out a little low moan, then an animal-sounding whimper.

I heard Little John say: "That's the way, lad!"

And Hanno hissed: "Perfect."

Yet the fight was not over. Not by a long summer's day. The Green Knight gathered himself and attacked again; gliding smoothly towards me, one hand useless, yes, the other wielding a lethal blade and probing, probing to expose my underlying weakness.

He feinted and hacked and nearly caught me out. I blocked with the *misericorde*, and counter attacked with my sword: a hard killing lateral blow. But he slid under my blade – somehow stepping forward at the same time and lunging wickedly fast once more at my face.

I stepped back hurriedly, trod awkwardly on the round edge of an abandoned shield, stumbled, my legs tangling with each other, tripped and fell flat on my back like a flipped turtle, all the air being expelled from my lungs in one painful whoosh.

I tried to breath but found I could not, I saw, out of the corner of my eye, Hanno take a half-step forward, but too late: the Green Knight was standing over me, his left hand a clenched ball of blood, but the sword in his right lifted, and coming down like an axe at my undefended head. I saw Death himself reach out a bony hand for me in that flashing moment, in my imagination – I could *see* and *feel* the blade crunching into my skull, cleaving my brain in two, and knew the blackness that would follow. Yet the *chevalier*'s blade, my real enemy's real sword, moving in the real courtyard, in this real morning, seemed to travel through the air strangely slowly, like honey poured from a pot, as if time was hobbled.

I lashed out wildly with my right boot, a low sweep, and my shin connected with the side of his left ankle, and then he was rising up, up in the air, but still at a snail's pace. Then he was crashing down on the earth right beside me on his back too with a rattling thump and a puff of dust.

His sword glinted briefly in the sunshine and clattered away.

I rolled over, flipping my whole body, almost flopping, and swung my left arm in an arc through the air – and plunged the foot-long, slender, needle-pointed *misericorde* deep into the

ANGUS DONALD

Green Knight's foul black heart.

CHAPTER TWENTY-ONE

I felt the chevalier shudder and twitch under my blade – the iron spike that fixed him through the centre of his chest to the earth. But he was finished. I knew it even before the final wet huff of breath left his body.

Little John came over to where I was still lying, too weak with relief and exhaustion to rise. My big, red-faced friend peered down at me.

"This is the younger generation all over," he said, ruefully shaking his head. "God's great greasy gonads, they're too lazy even to stand up when they kill their enemies. If you could, Alan, I wager you'd prefer to fight all your battles lying down. Or from the comfort of a feather bed."

But that morning I did not mind his crass inanities all that much. Without his intervention in the courtyard, I'd be as dead as the *chevalier*.

John extended a hand and lifted me to my feet. I thanked him, thought for a moment and said: "How did you get Hanno on to the wall?"

"I threw him," said Little John. "Chucked him up there. He's only a little fellow; no heavier than big sack of turnips."

I saw Hanno scowl but I just grinned at them both, then took a look round the courtyard. There were bodies everywhere, and parts of bodies, and six live Burgundians kneeling, some wounded – all of them terrified.

Two of them, I recognised as the castle servants. One was the nervous little priest, who had wanted to give me the chance to confess my sins, before I was hounded through the forest by the master of the castle.

"What do we do with them?" I asked. "We can't take them prisoner. We couldn't guard them all the way back to Dijon."

"I deal with them," said Hanno, drawing his dagger.

"No!" I said. "Let them go!" I felt suddenly sickened by the violence of that day. There was a patch of blood and filth by my boot, and what looked like an eyeball, with a long, glutinous trailing string.

"All you Burgundian buggers," said Little John in English, but very loudly to aid the comprehension of those who did not understand our noble tongue. "You all bugger off!" He waved towards the open gate.

The captured men did not need to be told twice. They streamed out of the gate, some hobbling, some leaking blood. All eager to get away, far, far away. I saw a pair of them run directly into the forest on the other the road, and disappear into the trees.

Little John was tending to Samuel, who was now on his feet and managing to joke with the big man. I went over to Henrik who was lying on the sandy ground, his body was framed by a small lake of drying blood. Jacqueline was speaking softly to him in Burgundian French. She was squeezing his hand. I knelt down beside him. He was alive but only just. He opened his eyes a fraction and looked at me. He tried to smile but the pain was too strong; his features gave a spasm and went still.

"You fought well, comrade," I said. "You came to my rescue."

"To our rescue," said Jacqueline.

"Seems...I had not ... forgotten...my old rage," he said.

"Don't talk, friend," I said. "We'll get you back to Dijon, to the abbey, and Robin will see that the finest healers in the infirmary tend your wounds. You'll be on your feet in no time."

He shook his head but it was only a tiny shiver; his eyes were clenched with agony. "This is my ... last fight," he said.

I began to contradict him but he said, almost angrily, "No ... Be quiet, Alan. Listen ... to me. You are to ... bear witness. This is my ... dying wish. Are you ... listening?"

I said I was. "The tannery ... is to go to ... my ... niece. After my death. To ... Jacqueline. All my goods ... the hides ... the leather ... everything ... is for Jacqueline. I have not been ... a good uncle. But she should not serve ... lecherous drunks ... in a tavern, it's not ... right. You'll ... see to it ... Alan? Tell Arlo and Gerard ... of my wish."

He fell quiet and I saw that Jacqueline was weeping copiously. I loosened the tanner's tunic at the waist, peeled away the sodden cloth and trying not to hurt him with the movement. He had a huge gash in his belly pulsing out blood, as well as the deep spear wound in his back that I had seen him take. I felt a wave of black sadness crash over me and would have wept like a child myself but for the presence of my sweet lover.

I thought Henrik was gone but he opened his eyes a crack one last time. And this time he even managed a smile.

"I wanted ... to be a man-at-arms ... I wanted ... to have ... battles ... adventures ... the honour of a war ... this is ... what ..."

Then he died. And I did weep. The tears flowed like a river.

I freed all the horses and the few livestock animals we found in a pen by the kitchen, and chased them out of the gate, and I hugged Ghost's neck in my joy at seeing him again. Then, once we had searched the whole place and taken anything portable of any value, we put the Chateau de Beaune-du-Bois to the torch – with all the fresh corpses still inside it.

Little John was in a lather to get away; he was worried that Robin might be wondering where we had gone. The war Robin had engineered between the two Burgundies had begun and our lord would need our help.

Samuel had a painful sword cut on his right forearm, but while it was deep and bloody, I believed it would mend if the wound did not turn bad. The skilful monks in the infirmary would surely tend to it properly.

I helped Jacqueline up into Ghost's saddle on the rutted road outside the now-merrily burning castle, and I explained to her that we were obliged to seek out my lord and master, the Earl of Locksley, as soon as possible. It was well past noon and I hoped to be over the Saone and inside the borders of the Duchy before the shadows began to stretch.

"If you are an English lord, why do you have to run off to wait upon your master?" said Jacqueline, frowning down at me. "Surely your master is the king of England, and none other."

I stared at her. I had forgotten my silly little deceit.

"I confess, my love, that I am not a great lord of men, nor yet even a rich knight. I am a humble man-at-arms in the service of my own lord the Earl of Locksley. However, I do have a small manor of my own, in Nottinghamshire, which was granted to me by..."

"You are *not* a lord?"

"No, my love, I hope you can forgive me."

"You *said* you were – you lied to me. You deceived me!"

"Time to go, Alan," said John. He was mounted. Hanno and Samuel were a-horse too. The mule was laden with stores from the castle.

"One moment, John."

"We must go. Robin will be needing us."

"Why did you lie?" Jacqueline looked furious. I held Ghost tight by the collar; I feared she might ride off in her sudden rage.

"I must speak alone with Jacqueline. I'll be a few moments."

"Catch us up. We'll cross the river at the ford and be on the road to Dijon. You'll find us easily. But don't dawdle too long, lad."

I waited till Little John and the others were out of earshot, some fifty yards down the road – the last thing I wanted was for them to overhear this private conversation. I could imagine the endless jokes.

"Why did you lie?" Jacqueline repeated. "Was it a trick?"

"It was a simple misunderstanding when we first met at Gregoire's tavern," I said. I could feel my ears reddening. "I was well dressed and with a purse full of silver, and a good sword... And you first called me 'my lord' then. I just did not bother to correct you then. That is all."

"So you lied!"

"Not exactly a lie – a sin of omission, not one of commission."

"Clever words! I gave up my body to you. I gave you my heart!" She'd gone completely white; her eyes were dark pits of fury.

I almost said then: "And you seemed to like it a good deal! You almost brought the whole castle down on us with your reckless squawking!" But, at the last moment, I had the sense to hold my tongue.

"So you are a man-at-arms, a soldier – a servant, in truth."

I didn't like the way she said that. "As I have now admitted."

"And you have no wealth, no title at all?"

"Is that all you look for in a man? I saved you from a..."

She made a harrumphing noise, as if to say, "So what?"

I thought of mentioning the gold – what was left of it. And saying that at least some of that would be due to me. I thought of mentioning the joys of Westbury again. I chose not to. I was angry too. She spoke as if I was beneath her dignity, that my lack of a title made me worthless.

"Perhaps then you should not come with me to England," I said stiffly. "I do not think you would find life there to your taste."

"Go to *England*, with *you*? Ha! To a wretched realm of constant rain and revolting food, to live in a smelly hovel with a lying peasant; a poor boy who hoodwinks pretty girls with false tales of his wealth and fables about his noble rank. I would rather bed down with Mama's pigs!"

I saw Jacqueline then, perhaps for the first time, with eyes quite unclouded by my own lust. The distortions of my mind were all swept away in that very instant. She looked quite ordinary to me – not beautiful at all, even a little plain. I could not believe I'd ever thought I loved her.

I wanted to say hurtful things. I wanted to punish her somehow for tricking me. But, in the event, I managed to hold my tongue. "I shall take you to your tannery, then, my lady," I said icily, "and bid you farewell."

I mounted up on Ghost behind Jacqueline, trying my best not to touch her with my own body, although it was not at all easy. We set off at a brisk walk down the road towards the ford and the Duchy of Burgundy beyond.

We had not gone a thirty yards when the fringe of the forest to my left began to spew forth men-at-arms, mailed men with spears in blue and silver surcoats, dozens of them, scores. I could not draw my sword with Jacqueline in the saddle in front of me and I turned Ghost, hoping to make a run for it back the way we had come, past the burning castle, but I saw that there were yet more armed men approaching from that direction.

In a few moments, we were surrounded.

There was no point resisting them. There were perhaps a hundred mailed horsemen, knights and men-at-arms, all around me by then, jostling each other on their big destriers. Joking, laughing. I saw some of the younger men eyeing Jacqueline. I raised both my hands in surrender.

I looked at all the hard faces around me and saw two I instantly recognised. I found I was looking into pale eyes, fringed by a mop of red-gold hair – the face of the Count of Burgundy himself. Beside Otto sat the older and more stooped form of Amadeus of Montbéliard. A lord who, I recalled, was supposed to be secretly on our side, and even now attacking our mutual enemy, Count Otto, from the rear. This fellow was supposed to be besieging Besançon not here in the wild forest, smiling slyly at me.

Robin, it seemed, had made an error of judgment.

"Where is Lord Locksley," said Otto. "Where are the others?"

A rider spurred forward and I looked into a third face that I knew well. It was Arlo, the unruly tan-yard apprentice, now surprisingly well dressed, well mounted, and with an excellent sword hanging at his side.

"My lord, I only saw the big one, the blond giant, and two other fellows with this man on the river road," said Arlo. "I assumed the deceitful English earl would be joining them to take the castle," he said.

Spies, damned spies and double-damned traitors, I thought, remembering Otto's warning to Robin when we left his castle in Dole.

"I have agents in Dijon. Ruthless and capable men. They will be watching over you day and night."

I had plenty of leisure to work out what had happened. They escorted Jacqueline and me back to Dole and – at Arlo's suggestion – they allowed the girl to go free, even giving her an old mare to ride back to Dijon.

"I do not make war on women," Otto said grandly, dismissing her with a wave of his bejewelled hand. Jacqueline did not look back at me even once as she rode away. And I, sitting on Ghost's back in the castle courtyard in Dole, with my hands bound, surrounded by guards, watched her ride out of the gates with only a numb and empty feeling in my chest.

They put me in the same room that Robin and I had slept in on our first visit. They cut my bonds and fed me soup and bread. I slept a little. But mostly I sat at the small window, looking out and pondering my fate.

Hanging seemed most the likely punishment. I had attacked one of Otto's vassals – the Green Knight – and slain him, and burnt his hunting lodge to the ground. Maybe they would simply slit my throat and toss my body into the midden.

I did not foresee any future in which I was left unpunished by the vengeful Count of Burgundy. What surprised me was the long, painful delay before the sentence was carried out. They kept me in that locked room – well fed and watered, it must be said, and they even changed the chamber pot morning and night – for four full days.

None of the servants would answer any of my questions. I spent most of the time looking out of the barred window at the castle courtyard below, where there was always something going on. I saw riders coming and going, and men-at-arms being mustered into *conrois*. I saw the Prior Gui, with two other white-robed monks in attendance, arrive on horseback one afternoon, and watched them leave again next morning.

It was a buzzing hive out there. Evidently the war between the two Burgundies was still in full swing. A full *conroi* of armoured knights clattered out one morning and I watched them enviously, in their full panoply of bright surcoats, pennants on their lances, mounted on fine war horses. I watched them take the westward road towards the Duchy. Off on a raid, perhaps; off to attack some unfortunate town across the river.

I waited – and slept some more. I had been pushing my body very hard these past weeks and, even if I were to be horribly executed soon, I could not keep my eyes open when I lay back on that soft bed to rest my weary bones. Perhaps Little John was right, perhaps I would choose to fight all my battles from now from the comfort of a big feather bolster.

There was no chance of escape from my cell. I tried the door, and attempted to shake the bars on the window. No good. The servants who attended me, always came with a wary man-at-arms with a drawn sword, and I'd been disarmed when they took me captive.

I waited for my fate. I thought about spies. Arlo was undoubtedly an agent of Count Otto – that was clear. I also suspected that he might be an illegitimate relative, a first cousin, perhaps, trying to win his lordly cousin's favour – they shared exactly the same shade of red hair, after all.

Lord Montbéliard's treachery rankled more that Arlo's. Amadeus had clearly decided not to side with the Duchy of Burgundy after all, not to meekly fall in with Robin's plans, break from the Holy Roman Empire and accept his bribe of a position in Outremer for his nephew. Then I remembered what he had said to me in Dijon, when I delivered Robin's message. He'd asked what my generation felt about loyalty to one's lord.

I remembered my own answer almost exactly.

"For me it is the paramount virtue," I had said. "I esteem it greatly. I made an oath of loyalty to my lord and I shall never break it. I see it as a binding promise for a man's life."

Perhaps he'd taken my advice. He had described it as "illuminating". His overlord was Henry, the Holy Roman Emperor, Count Otto's elder brother. Perhaps he had chosen loyalty over treachery, virtue over deceit.

The old man himself, Amadeus of Montbéliard, with two young, strong men-at-arms, came for me on the morning of the fourth day of my captivity. And I steeled myself for imminent death on the gallows.

They escorted me, down the stairs to the great hall of the castle. As we descended, I said, "My lord, I see you've picked a dog for this fight."

He looked at me sideways, with just a hint of a smile.

"It took me a while to determine the true path of honour," he said. "But surely *you* do not mean to chide me for remaining true to my lord?"

I could not scold him for that. But he had betrayed *my* lord. So I said nastily: "What of your nephew Walter? No plums for him now."

He winked at me. "King Richard is not the only monarch with great powers of patronage in the Holy Land," he said. "The good emperor can reward my family as well, perhaps better, than a beleaguered Lionheart."

Those were the last words he spoke to me.

I found myself once again in the presence of Otto, Count of Burgundy, in the hall of Dole Castle. He was pacing up and down the centre of the room, this time, rather than seated in his X-shaped chair. I was unbound, my limbs were free, though I was unarmed and there were two score men-at-arms standing in their positions around the great hall.

Otto turned on me suddenly. He glared at me, his pale face flushed pink. His small eyes glittered like blue jewels. "I know that I have you and your tricksy master to blame for this whole bloody mess," he said.

"The Duchy is now fully mustered in arms, every man, I hear, and that faux-meek mountebank Eudes is threatening to sack my towns from Luxeuil in the north all the way down to Saint-Claude. I should strike you dead this instant. Or put you to the hot irons to see what you can tell . . .

"However, it seems that I cannot do that. I have received a private message from your Lord Locksley – an impudent missive – that said that if I harmed a single hair on your head, he would make it his sole business to ensure I did not live out this year. Assassins, he said. Bold as brass. He would set assassins on me. I'd never be able to sleep safely again, he said. He swore this on the Blessed Virgin. And on his own mother's life."

I reflected that Robin's mother was long in her grave. But I still appreciated his intervention. I felt it might just have preserved me from a horrible death. Otto was not finished: "Then Lord Locksley offered to ransom you – *you*, a mere man-at-arms – as if you were some great and puissant nobleman. Madness, I cannot understand his logic. But neither can I refuse him. So . . ."

Otto was clearly extremely angry. "So . . . " he said. "Get out of my sight, Alan Dale. Go now. Prior Gui will arrange the exchange. And you may tell the Earl of Locksley that if he – or any of his men – ever fall into my power again, then I shall make them beg me for a quick death!"

He turned his back on me and strode furiously away.

We made the exchange at the old Roman bridge over the River Saone. I rode Ghost slowly to the centre of the crumbling brick structure, with the wide, green Saone flowing beneath my horse's hooves. Prior Gui and one of his monks came with me also a-horse. And there we patiently waited.

On the far side I could see Robin, and Little John, both mounted and a mass of fifty or sixty men, with Hanno, too, among the crowd. There were carts and packhorses, and a few women and children running about between the legs of the beasts. It was the whole Sherwood contingent, my travelling family, all packed up and ready to set off somewhere new.

Robin came across the bridge to meet me. He was alone but leading a mule laded with several stout leather satchels. There was not much bulk to this cargo – but I could see that whatever they contained was heavy. As the mule came closer, I could see its stout legs trembling under the strain.

Robin stopped three paces away from me. He was looking into my face with great concern.

Prior Gui said: "That is all of it? As we agreed?"

"It is all there," said Robin, only glancing at the monk. "They did not harm you, Alan, did they? You're reasonably whole and hale?"

"Yes, lord. Unhurt. They even returned all my possessions."

"Well, then. Let us go. We've a long road to travel today."

He spurred his horse forward a few steps and passed over the mule's halter rope into the outstretched hand of Prior Gui. Then, without another word to the churchmen, he turned his horse and began to walk it back over the bridge. I rode along with him.

"How much of our gold did you give him?" I said.

"Oh, just . . . all of it," he said carelessly. "We still have silver in our coffers. But they demanded all the gold. I couldn't refuse them."

"My lord, I do not know what to say to you. I can never repay your kindness. You have saved me . . . and at such great sacrifice."

"You sound surprised that I would do this small thing for one of mine," said Robin, and he looked sideways at me, his eyes sparking with mischief. "I did the same for that rascal Reuben – or have you forgotten?"

"I *am* surprised, lord, I am in truth ... astonished," I said.

"I sometimes think, Alan Dale, that you do not understand me at all," said Robin with a sigh. "You assume that I think of nothing but money, day and night," he said. "Indeed, you very often nag me about it – and it is true I do love money. Gold, silver, jewels and what have you – they are all important to me. But what is more important, even than great wealth, is the kind of people I surround myself with. Look at Little John – how far would I have come without him at my side? And there is you – drunken, impetuous, well-meaning Alan Dale. You swore a mighty oath to me when we first met. I have not forgotten that. And I've a feeling that oath will prove far more valuable to me that a few bars of shiny metal."

Robin's words robbed me of speech. Indeed, such was the wild churn of emotion in my heart I had to fight hard not to weep like a baby.

We were approaching the far side of the bridge.

"I see ..." I gave a huge sniff, " ... I see that we're all here. Where are you taking us, lord? Are we abandoning the fighting in Burgundy?"

"Oh, I think we've more than done our part here," said Robin. "We have served King Richard's interests well. The Duchy and the County are now at loggerheads – with luck, at the beginning of a costly war. They will not combine against our king, I think. Not soon, anyway. Therefore our mission here is accomplished, and it is time for us to quit this land."

"Where will we go?" I said.

"West, to Anjou, of course," said Robin. "We'll begin the journey back to Richard's patrimony. Then home to England, never to stir again!"

And he turned to me and smiled.

AFTERWORD

When I had finished reading this manuscript, I telephoned Angus Donald to congratulate him on his sensitive editing of the original material.

I was also curious about several aspects of the history of this episode in my ancestor Alan Dale's life and I hoped that he might be able to provide information about some of the characters and places mentioned.

His answers to my queries were informative. He began by telling me that no trace no remains of the château de Beaune-du-Bois – the Castle of Bones – indeed, he said, so completely has this unhappy hunting lodge disappeared from the records after its fiery destruction at the hands of the Sherwood men that it might almost have been entirely imaginary.

Likewise, there is no mention in the annals of the time of the Earl of Locksley's visit to Dijon in the spring and summer of 1192. Yet, given that the earl was acting in a covert manner – undertaking a secret mission on behalf of his master King Richard – this is unsurprising. And Robin Hood had always proved a difficult character to pin down in at any exact time and place in history. This will-o'-the-wisp elusiveness is, Mr Donald always maintains, one of the main drivers for his enduring popularity.

Duke Hugh of Burgundy never returned to his homeland from the Third Crusade. He died in Outremer a few months after the events described in this novel, probably of disease. His eldest son Eudes, who was made regent of the duchy during his absence, succeeded to his throne and ruled for twenty-six years. He was a staunch ally of Philip of France in the long wars against Richard of England and fought at the Battle of Bouvines in Flanders in 1214. He was also a key player in the Albigensian Crusade against the heretical Cathars of southern France.

Across the River Saone, Count Otto of Burgundy, seemingly spent the rest of his life picking fights and feuding with almost all his closest neighbours. As well as the prolonged struggles with Eudes of Burgundy and Stephen of Auxonne, he soon fell out with his ally Amadeus of Montbéliard, and murdered him with his own bare hands three years after Robin Hood's visit to the region.

The final piece of historical information provided by Mr Donald during that long telephone call was the most intriguing, to my mind.

Otto, Count of Burgundy was assassinated himself in his capital Besançon by unknown agents in the year 1200. Despite the threats made by Robin Hood to protect his man Alan Dale, there is no evidence at all that the Earl of Locksley had a hand in this crime. But it would be a bold researcher who ruled this scenario out entirely.

Michael Westbury-Browne

Angus Donald *is also the author of the acclaimed Fire Born series of Viking adventures. The first novel,* **The Last Berserker,** *is available now*

Milton Keynes UK
Ingram Content Group UK Ltd.
UKHW021317301123
433559UK00027B/1601